This was [no other book in the]

no other [book in the]

when hated the

ending I wanted more

A I'd never read

this book before

CANDLELIGHT REGENCY SPECIAL

wow! whew! I went

on an emotional roller

coster with the heroine

I creamed for boy got Moe

for her + 10

Candlelight Regencies

LOVE'S TEMPEST

Elinor Larkin

A CANDLELIGHT REGENCY SPECIAL

Published by
Dell Publishing Co., Inc.
1 Dag Hammarskjold Plaza
New York, New York 10017

*To the West Country gypsy
who saw me through the storm,
with love*

Printed in the United States of America
First printing—May 1981

CHAPTER ONE

"I assure you, my dear. Love is an illusion. Only style is real."

Ursula Manning raised her eyes from her needlework and turned them with a look of mock indignation upon her brother, George.

"And you *do* have style," he added appreciatively from where he sat sprawled in the overstuffed parlour chair.

The early-morning sunlight through the leaded glass of the window was soft as the robin's-egg-blue color of Ursula's eyes. George knew that in different moods Ursula's softness could give way to an ever-darkening intensity. He had also learned in the course of twenty years of sibling companionship and dispute that his sister had a great reserve of stubbornness and willfulness behind her porcelain-delicate appearance.

"So marry for money," he continued in his unperturbed drawl. He flicked an imaginary speck from his fawn-coloured breeches. "You can always take lovers. Love, like the butterfly, is most beautiful when most ephemeral."

"If I thought you believed a word of what you were saying, I'd have to set you down proper, George." She laughed. Her even white teeth showed behind the pouty coral lips, which indicated a sensuality in contrast with her usually modest behavior. "But since you are merely funning—"

"Don't be a goosecap, my dearest," George cut her off. "You are altogether too intelligent to believe the poets and to ignore the factual evidence all around you . . . evidence as to how the world really gets on."

"As my elder brother, George, you should be protecting my virtue, not seeking to undermine it," she said severely, and then tried to hide her welling laughter with a shake of her tawny head.

"Ah, yes, poor motherless girl with no one to guide her. Ursula, darling, you know I have only your best interests at heart."

This reference to the mother she had never known silenced Ursula at once, and she bent her head again over her work to hide her agitation.

Most people who knew him found George insensitive and unfeeling, but Ursula had always known that her brother's callous attitude was but a camouflage, protection against the sense of loss that had threatened to overwhelm him when he'd been a six-year-old boy and his mother, Catherine Manning, had died giving birth to a daughter. Ursula had grown up longing for the love and tenderness she had never known, while her brother had rebelled in hurt resentment against all sentimentality.

As for their father, the Reverend Charles Manning had been a virtual stranger to his children. The life had gone out of him when his Catherine breathed her last, and he had spent most of his remaining years in the East, converting the heathen and ministering to the spiritual needs of Englishmen from Alexandria to Calcutta. He had left his children in the care of his sister and her husband. Uncle Alfred and Aunt Mary were a well-meaning and practical couple but had never had children of their own or the slightest idea of how to go about raising any. George had learned to hide his feelings beneath a veneer of cynical dandyism; Ursula had hidden hers behind silence and a world of daydreams. In spite of this basic difference, the bonds between brother and sister were strong, and both believed that the understanding between them was complete.

"I suspect you're simply jealous." Ursula picked up the conversation after recovering her composure. "You fear that if I marry for love, I shall exclude you from my confidence."

The colour heightened in George's cheeks as if he'd been stung by her words. But he leaped to his feet, and kissing his sister on the cheek, he placed his hands on her shoulders and asked earnestly, "Ursula, are you quite sure you're ready to marry?"

"Of course not," she replied frankly. "But I am twenty and shall be a perfect ape-leader soon if I don't."

"You'll still be a beauty at fifty," George assured her. "In fact, that is most likely when your beauty will show to greatest advantage. You've the head of a lioness, after all, and at age twenty, my dear, you're nothing but a cub." George completely believed his own words, but he was not unaware that his uncle and aunt had been considerably distressed by the unsuccessful outcome of Ursula's coming out back home in Hampshire two years earlier.

The Reverend Mr. Manning had come all the way from India for the occasion. Ursula had been just as beautiful and soft-spoken as anyone could have wished, and at least three young gentlemen of the district had promptly begun their ardent yet respectful courtships. But then the good reverend had returned to Calcutta and promptly died.

If the news of his demise was a shock to the family, the effect it had on Ursula was more shocking still. She broke down into uncontrollable weeping, and when she put on black and started to refuse invitations, it was clear that her mourning was sincere and not merely dutiful.

George had tried to understand. "How can you grieve so for a man you barely knew?" he'd asked.

"Because he was our father," Ursula had answered. "But also because I'd always hoped someday we *would* get to know him. Now it is forever too late."

Aunt Mary had her own worries about lost opportunities. "The young Warwick boy has off and joined a regiment, and we'll hear soon enough that your friend Sidney is setting up house in London. . . ."

Ursula did not trouble herself to answer. Privately she reflected that young Warwick had the dimmest wit imaginable. As for Sidney deRoche, nothing could induce her to contract matrimony with a gentleman who sported mulberry-coloured breeches. Reaching some sort of peace of mind over her father's death was vastly more important to her well-being, Ursula believed, than dancing quadrilles with silly and affected young squires.

In Aunt Mary's mind, retrospect transformed each absent suitor to a knight in shining armour, while to Ursula they were all eminently forgettable.

Still, Aunt Mary's worries were completely justified. The suitable young men of the district were being lured from home by the promise of wartime heroism or by stories of the fast life in London.

"It's up to you to encourage them to remain behind," she badgered her niece. "By the time you bestir yourself, it will indeed be forever too late."

The guardians held urgent consultations and at last agreed that their duty was clear. Despite the terrible expense, they would take Ursula to London and present her to the *ton* in the hopes of arranging a match. Otherwise, she was clearly destined to an unremitting spinsterhood.

That was how Ursula and her brother came to be discussing love in their new London residence on a

8

beautiful spring morning, and that was also why Ursula was particularly displeased by George's cynical tone on this occasion. For while she was pleased and excited to be entering a new and glittering world, she was distressed by the suspicion that her guardians were in too great a hurry to arrange for her future. She had hoped that George would take her part and protect her from being bullocked into a materially favourable but essentially loveless marriage. Unfortunately it seemed that George did not share her ideals.

"You shall have great fun, my dear," he said, "stalking your prey in the jungles of Mayfair. Be beautiful, merciless, and strong. Play with your meat like the sleek cat you are, and don't take any of the dashing rakes too seriously."

What terrible advice to give a blushing maiden, thought Ursula, regarding her brother with mixed affection and annoyance.

"I'm afraid I've neglected my study of natural history," she said at last with a languid sigh, "but I do believe the lioness is said to be faithful to her mate."

"So they say," agreed George with a smile. "But perhaps she is merely discreet."

Ursula cried out and threw a pillow at her brother's carefully combed locks. Though she laughed aloud, inwardly she was wondering if there was anyone who believed as she did, anywhere in the world.

"Still, I warrant you're no rake," she said sadly as he knelt and returned the cushion to her with a smiling plea for pardon. "That's the hope I cling to, George, that you're even such an impostor as the Fasting Woman of Tutbury."

"Give up your false hope, my darling," he returned. "That woman only pretended that no food had passed her lips for the space of a mere six years, while I claim that no noble sentiment has passed through my heart in all my life. And I shan't set my mark at the bottom of a confession neither, as your Fasting Woman has lately done."

"What a curious confession it would be!" exclaimed Ursula. "Just imagine! 'I, George Manning, do hereby confess that despite my protestations to the contrary, I have ever and always believed in the Power, Force, and abiding Strength of True Love, that which conquers all obstacles and sets free the heart in Joy.'"

"Perhaps you're right," George conceded at last, "for if I make such speeches as these, it's not to put you out of curl . . . it's that I don't wish to see you hurt Ursula, and if you set your heart on stories of romance I fear you will be."

"What? Are all members of your sex known to stoop so low as to misuse the love of a lady?"

"I shall not try to estimate the percentages, dear. I only mean that our guardians will see you soon married by hedge or by stile, and I don't collect that love enters into their calculations. I only wish to remind you that even should you fail to wed the man of your dreams, there's no reason for you to abandon hope of a happy life."

"Yes"—she sighed—"and when we visited those poor injured soldiers who were staying with the Cantwells, don't you remember how I told that poor dear young major he should soon grow accustomed to the loss of his leg? Oh, George, of course one can go on. One always does. But I shall not voluntarily see my own life . . . *dismembered*."

"Well, you may not have to wait long in suspense," said George, not taking his eyes off her, "judging by the amount of time Uncle Alfred has spent in his study with our mysterious visitor, and judging by the strange look on Aunt Mary's face when I passed her in the corridor not many minutes hence."

Ursula flushed and studied her brother's face to see if he was speaking in jest. His eyes flickered a moment beneath her inquiring gaze, but this seemed to be a response born of delicacy and not the flinch of the liar.

"But who is he? How would he have heard of me?" she asked almost breathlessly. Ursula had no desire to be given away to the first caller, but the man in question had made a deep impression on her. His light brown curls fell carelessly over an open face that revealed a great and natural enjoyment of life. His light brown eyes, almost golden in the light, had put her immediately at ease. She had been arranging irises in a bowl when he had stopped to exchange a few words, telling her the flowers remainded him of his West Country home. Struthers, the butler, had turned about impassively and waited for the two young people to finish speaking. He hadn't interrupted, but his presence had made both feel suddenly awkward, and the young man had quickly left her to follow Struthers down the corridor.

"Anyway," she added, "I asked Struthers later, and he said he came on urgent business. That would hardly have aught to do with me."

"Urgent business!" George laughed. "You know as well as I do that Uncle Alfred has no business at all, least of all any that could be termed urgent. Most likely Uncle Alfred has placed an advertisement in the papers announcing that you are for sale and that he will interview prospective buyers between the hours of ten and noon in his study. It's surely a more efficient way of disposing of you than to deck you out in satins and take you to Almack's."

"That is the outside of enough!" cried Ursula, hoping to bring the conversation at last to an end. "You know there has been no advertisement, and yet there's

11

no other way the man in question could have known of my existence."

"There you are wrong," insisted George. "The young man, in fact, is named Richard. He is just past thirty years of age. He is the Viscount of Uxbridge, and he knows everything there is to know about the fair sex. He's a bit of a connoisseur, you see, and with London ladies having so little innocence left, he makes it his business to learn of maidens fresh arrived from the provinces."

"And how do you know that?" demanded Ursula.

"I keep the company appropriate to a cynic and a dandy, my dear. It may even be possible that my own dissipation approaches the excesses enjoyed by His Lordship, but I shall not go into greater detail, for I do not wish to see you distressed on my wicked account. I do not know what story the viscount may even now be telling to our esteemed uncle, but Uncle Alfred is an honest man and will never see through his wiles until it's too late. So I wished to open your eyes to the gentleman's qualities and reputation in case you should find his engaging company thrust suddenly upon you. He is a wickedly shameless seducer, sister dear. And shamelessly successful at it, too. So enjoy him if you will, but protect your heart—if not other parts of you as well—by not believing a word he may tell you of love and marriage. I would not see a man of his nature treat you lightly as just another bit of muslin."

Having left this advice to his gentle sister, George stood and, after an exaggerated bow, was gone.

Perhaps it was only George's warning that rendered Ursula so terribly self-conscious. But she felt herself tremble when Aunt Mary asked her to join the company in the study. Ursula glanced quickly at her reflection in the glass and excused herself to dash upstairs

12

and throw a silk shawl over her shoulders. Let the visitor think her weak and subject to faintness and chills, she decided. She was determined not to let him see the high-waisted dress with tiny puff sleeves that proclaimed her to be no more than a chit of a schoolgirl. Her guardians had postponed the purchase of an adult wardrobe for Ursula again and again. She closed her eyes and counted slowly to ten, hoping the high colour would subside and leave her cheeks cool as marble. She held her head high and continued counting her steps as she descended again to the study.

The viscount rose gracefully to his feet when Ursula entered the study. Yes, he was decked out as a very pattern card of the fashionable Corinthian in his buffed and shining Hessians, tight around his strong, manly legs. His smallclothes were of the latest modish yellow, and his starched shirt points seemed to direct attention to his windswept hair. In short, he looked a dandy and a rake, and Ursula was inclined to give full credence to her brother's words. But there was nothing cynical or artificial about his smile. The man greeted her with a natural warmth unexpected in a stranger, which made her heart flutter with uncertainty and pleasure. At the same time she was not unaware of a certain curiosity in his regard, and abashed, she lowered her gaze from his liquid golden eyes.

The introductions were effected quickly by Uncle Alfred, who was so puffed up with contentment that his ample form strained against his waistcoat even more than usual and threatened to send his brass buttons shooting off from his tight blue coat.

"Well, Ursula," he said, so happy that any natural hesitation he might have felt was swept away, "we have good tidings, very good tidings indeed."

She looked at her uncle, scarcely daring to breathe.

Yes, it was clear that some business concerning her had just been transacted in the study without her participation. And yet he looked so very happy, his middle-aged face suddenly wiped clean of wrinkles and all signs of age, that Ursula knew that no matter how distasteful a plan he had conceived for her, Uncle Alfred still must have considered himself motivated by love and not by baser reasons. Frightened though she felt, Ursula knew she could not be angry at the jovial man who held her future in his hands.

Aunt Mary seemed to have some consciousness of the gravity of the scene. Her veined hands twitched like small, nervous birds.

"Do you remember having met with a Lord Charles Wickenham?" asked Uncle Alfred, his voice triumphant and his face beaming with pleasure.

"I don't think so," said Ursula in a whisper, now clearly perplexed.

"I go to join him in Bermuda," interjected the viscount, "with a royal commission. With my orders came an urgent letter to be delivered to your uncle."

"Surely you recall," prompted Aunt Mary, "the gentleman who accompanied your blessed father from India when he came home for your party."

Yes, she did remember him now, a very superior sort of person, who'd regarded her critically with his shortsighted red eyes. Lord Charles had been an old man with foul breath and the most toplofty manner. She remembered how he had lifted her chin and regarded her face. His fingers had been soft, but their grip was rough; she had felt he was judging her much as he would judge horseflesh. Only the greatest self-restraint kept Ursula from flinching. Then the old man had released her and drawn a bejeweled snuffbox from his pocket. Flicking it open with his left hand, he treated himself to a highly scented pinch.

"Perfect, almost perfect." He breathed appreciatively.

The Reverend Mr. Manning had beamed with joy but then turned to scold his daughter. "Where are your manners, girl?" he demanded. "Thank His Lordship for the honour he does you!"

Ursula curtsied, flushed, and blurted out, "Forgive me, Your Lordship. I hardly expected a compliment and thought you were directing such high praise to your snuff mixture."

This response served to mortify her poor father, but Lord Charles chuckled and scrutinized her with growing interest.

"Yes, it's an excellent mixture," replied the old man. "Fribourg and Treyer keep it for my particular use." Turning to the reverend, Lord Charles explained, "Dear friend, as I've told you before, the true gentleman is an unerring judge of horses, snuff, and women. Your daughter is wasted here in rural isolation. I truly hope you intend to present her in London."

Lord Charles had moved on to be presented to the assembled guests, and Ursula had followed his waddling gait with her eyes. He was certainly a terribly unpleasant personage, but at the same time he was ever so much grander than the people with whom it was Ursula's custom to associate. She could not help but be thrilled by his praise.

"Surely you remember him," repeated Aunt Mary, bringing Ursula's wandering thoughts back to Uncle Alfred's study and to the handsome and reputedly dissipated viscount.

"Yes, I do remember him," she replied, wondering what connection she could possibly have to that supercilious old man. The mention of Lord Charles cast a whole new countenance on matters. Obviously she had not been called to this family meeting to be thrust roughly into the arms of the viscount after all.

With this realization Ursula lost her sense of fear and nervous anticipation and felt free to regard Uxbridge quite openly. She found herself revising her analysis of his character in more favourable terms. She studied his attire again—the blue coat that fitted tightly across his broad shoulders, the stretched, draped, and dazzlingly white cravat. The viscount, she guessed, would never be guilty of such a lapse as to dress himself in mulberry smallclothes, but there was a subtlety about him, as though he were announcing to the world that clothing was hardly a matter with which an intelligent man should occupy his mind. The viscount, unlike George, would never make a crusade in the name of style.

When their eyes met, Ursula realized with a shock that the visitor had been studying her with equal curiosity.

"Lord Charles's letter concerned you, my dear," said Uncle Alfred, a little vexed by Ursula's inattention to the matter at hand.

"Yes, Uncle," she replied dutifully, and then smiled at him warmly in response to the happy look she saw on his face.

Only very good news could have cheered her uncle so, Ursula reasoned. Was it possible that Lord Charles was planning to leave her an inheritance or was offering to sponsor her London debut? She had heard of such things happening. Or perhaps, being off in Bermuda, the distinguished gentleman had only lately learned of the Reverend Mr. Manning's death and had hastened at once to the aid of the family.

"Being a good friend of your father's," continued Uncle Alfred, "and holding him in such high esteem,

Lord Charles is anxious to see to your future. He was most impressed with you at the time of your one meeting and most emphatically wishes you to have all the advantages of wealth and high social position. Well, what say you?" he prodded as Ursula remained silent and blushing.

"I'm most grateful," she managed to stammer. "And surprised. His offer certainly comes at a most opportune time."

"In all decency he couldn't have spoken sooner," said Uncle Alfred sternly, "with his wife an invalid, but still alive."

Ursula was seized with a horrid certainty. Surely she was wrong. Surely her uncle was not about to say the awful words she could sense forming in his throat. She darted a desperate glance at the viscount, as though this stranger could understand her better than either Uncle Alfred or Aunt Mary, as though he had the power and the desire to help her. She caught the pale surprise on his face, and then Aunt Mary spoke.

"He is immensely, immensely rich, Ursula. Beyond what people like ourselves can even imagine. And to think our little girl is to marry a man such as that."

Her throat grew so tight with misery and outrage that Ursula could hardly speak. At last she forced out a pathetic sound, little more than a gasp. It was the viscount who jumped to his feet and poured her a drink from Uncle Alfred's decanter. She felt his hand at her wrist while with the other hand he helped her to drink the strong, sweet sherry. Her pulse sped up wildly beneath his fingers. His lace cuffs brushed against her hand as he stepped back discreetly.

Aunt Mary and Uncle Alfred looked at each other helplessly.

"Aren't you happy?" asked her uncle at last in a hushed voice. In his concerned eyes Ursula recognized his terrible fear: that his niece was going to ruin the wonderful surprise that Providence had devised.

"No, Uncle, I am not happy," she replied simply. "If he is indeed as rich as you say, I shall surely never be comfortable and at ease in his company. And he's so very old, Uncle. Would you send me across the sea this way?" Her words began to rouse the sympathies of her listeners, and Uncle Alfred had even begun to reconsider his joyous response to the Wickenham proposal. But then Ursula made the mistake of trying to press her advantage. She spoke as soon as she sensed her uncle weakening in his resolve.

"Would you sell me, Uncle Alfred?" she asked.

And who could truthfully say whether it was real outrage or the uncomfortable pricking of a guilty conscience that made Ursula's uncle react so vehemently, almost violently, to her question?

"How dare you?" he asked quietly at first, but his voice rose steadily with his temper. "We took you in years ago, when you were newborn, and we did our best. I deprived my wife of her rightful due to provide for you and for your brother. Your father simply left you with us, do you understand, Ursula? He was dedicated to his mission and never thought to send any money toward your support. Not that he had any, of course. Mary and I, we were two happy people, accustomed to living alone in our quiet way, and you and your brother came and overturned our peaceful lives. Not that we don't love you . . ."

Aunt Mary was sobbing, her thin chest heaving convulsively.

"We never asked for your gratitude, girl," continued her uncle, "but to think you would accuse me of . . . what you said! When everything we have, we have

18

given everything for your future. Enough then. You shall marry Wickenham. And you shall spend his riches as you see fit. We shall not require any contribution from you. We don't ship you off to Bermuda to further our own ambitions, Ursula, but merely to secure your own future."

Ursula's mind raced frantically. She was stubborn and willful and proud, but this time she was not too proud to beg her uncle's pardon. She fell to her knees as gracefully as wheat bending beneath the wind. "Uncle Alfred," she said, fighting tears, "I love you, and I love Aunt Mary. Forgive me. I would never have spoken so if I hadn't been so shocked and distressed by the thought of . . ."

"On your feet, girl," he answered. Her uncle's voice wasn't rough but rather absent, distant. It seemed he had cut her out of his heart. There was no longer anger, but neither was there any bond between them that she could appeal to in her attempt to win him over to her side. "The viscount leaves for Bermuda in the morning, and you shall embark in his charge."

"Tomorrow!" she cried. It was unthinkable, impossible. That left her only the one night to make her plans, to find a way out. For a way out she would most assuredly find. No, they couldn't do this to her, not to Ursula Manning! George would help her. He'd have to, she thought. In spite of all the dreadful things he was wont to say, he couldn't possibly allow this to happen to her.

The room seemed to be spinning, but Ursula's senses fastened on the vision of Uxbridge, standing before her, coming closer. He didn't speak aloud, but she could see his lips moving. "I'm sorry," they seemed to say. He looked at her not so much with pity as with understanding. And abruptly the room stopped whirling. She felt strong and in control of herself once more.

19

She was still staring at the young viscount and shivered briefly when a spark seemed to jump from his eyes to her own.

"I'm sorry," the viscount said slowly to Uncle Alfred, "but though I had intended to embark tomorrow, there are business matters that will detain me here in London at least a week."

A reprieve! thought Ursula.

"Very well." Uncle Alfred sighed. "But we have made our decision, and I suppose that whether you leave tomorrow or in a sennight, it's all the same."

Uxbridge was not even listening to his host. "Shall I see you at Almack's on Wednesday?" he asked Ursula.

It was Aunt Mary who exclaimed, "Almack's! Why, we've just arrived in London and know no one."

The viscount smiled at this frank admission of provincialism. Bowing to Ursula, he merely said, "I shall have Madame de Lieven send you a voucher."

Ursula watched him leave the room, very much aware that her heart was beating with excessive rapidity. What was happening to her? She was threatened with marriage to a dreadful old man. But a dashing viscount was promising to introduce her into the loftiest realms of the *haut ton*. On the one hand, it seemed her happy life was over. On the other, it seemed life might only be about to begin.

CHAPTER TWO

"It was very kind of the viscount, I'm sure," said Aunt Mary in the carriage on Wednesday night, "but . . ." and she proceeded to repeat her reservations for what seemed to Ursula like the hundredth time. "After all, when a young lady of quality appears at Almack's, the natural supposition is that she is looking for a husband, and so, as you are already betrothed, it does seem somewhat inconvenient for you to—"

"I am not betrothed," interrupted Ursula calmly but firmly. Her face betrayed no agitation, but she could not restrain herself from tugging nervously at her white kid gloves.

"You're fidgeting like a child," complained Aunt Mary, taking one of her niece's hands in her own and ignoring the girl's declaration. "And Almack's! Really! If we had proceeded to present you, my dear, The Pantheon is quite as high as we should have aimed. I mean, we are all quite fine enough to hold our heads high in society, but dear me, in the *haut ton*? It seems to me, when one is not prepared to associate with such people, an invitation is hardly a favour."

There had been neither time nor money for Ursula to buy a new gown for the occasion, and so she had had to make do with the cream-coloured satin dress in which she had come out in Hampshire. She had added a gauze net embroidered with pastel sprays of flowers for what she hoped would be a note of sophistication. The neckline was still impossibly high, but even had she bought an entirely new wardrobe, Ursula was certain that Aunt Mary would never have allowed her out of the house in the state of undress so favoured by people of fashion.

"For your sake, Ursula, I hope they will be kind and that you won't be laughed at . . ."

Ursula silenced this unceasing uncomplimentary stream with the only weapon in her arsenal. "If you think it best, Aunt Mary, I shall pull the check string and ask Corrie to take us back home." For all of Aunt Mary's complaining, Ursula knew that her aunt was delighted beyond all measure at the chance to enter Almack's and penetrate society's most exclusive temple.

"No, no!" cried Aunt Mary, and then, recovering herself, added lamely, "It would be too rude after the viscount's trouble on our behalf. I do wish he had not arranged this invitation, but as he has done so, I do not see we are left any choice."

One always has a choice, thought Ursula silently. For she had quite made up her mind that she was not, under any circumstances, going to be shipped off to marry her aged suitor. But a choice implied alternatives. If she didn't go to Bermuda, whatever would she do instead?

At last they arrived, and Corrie handed the ladies down from the carriage. Aunt Mary, overcome with excitement, opened the strings of her reticule to be certain she had remembered her smelling salts, while Ursula breathed deeply to steady her own nerves. Although she would not allow it to her aunt, she was also uneasy at the thought of what reception she would receive. Her usual self-confidence had quite given way, and as the two ladies entered Almack's, Ursula was debating to herself whether it would be preferable to be the focus of cold, critical eyes or to be ignored altogether.

"I understand there's a cardroom," whispered Aunt

Mary, "and we shall retreat there directly if no one asks you to stand up. . . . It's bad enough you have no fortune, but to have been born blonde as well"—that lady sighed—"it's just too much to overcome."

"Do you think they play for very high stakes?" asked Ursula in an innocent voice, leading Aunt Mary to wonder whether the cardroom would be such a very good idea after all.

Inside, the orchestra was playing a set of country dances. Ursula scanned the crowd, hoping to see a familiar face.

"How dreadful," exclaimed her aunt, "to know no one here!"

"I'm looking for Madame de Lieven," answered Ursula coolly. "I must thank her for the voucher."

"Do you think you'll recognize her?"

"Of course," replied Ursula with great self-assurance, although she was asking herself the same question. She had studied a picture of that unattractive but commanding face and committed its features to memory, yet she knew the lady might make quite a different impression in flesh and blood.

"Oh, look." Aunt Mary fluttered helplessly, trying to determine how to direct her niece's attention to the opposite side of the room without making an impolite gesture. "There's Uxbridge—oh, several feet to the right of the velvet-backed sofa. Do you see?"

Ursula's eyes picked him out at once, and she was surprised by his appearance. The easy, natural smile on his face was quite gone, and in its place was an expression of unrelieved boredom that gave way only when a dowager approached and the viscount looked her way long enough to scowl at the lady's fat and florid daughter. His lips moved briefly, and then the viscount turned away.

"He certainly snubbed them cruelly," ventured Aunt

Mary. "I wonder who they are. Dreadful people, no doubt, to merit such treatment."

"Probably no more dreadful than we are," corrected Ursula cheerfully. "If I am to believe you, that is exactly the sort of treatment we are about to receive."

In that instant Uxbridge looked toward the door, and his face softened at the sight of Ursula. With a broad smile he hurried across the room, causing several mammas to whisper to one another behind their small ivory fans.

His Lordship paid his courteous but swift respects to Aunt Mary and then whisked Ursula off to the dance floor.

"I would rather have a waltz," he told her, smiling, when the vigorous country-dance was over.

Ursula was somewhat taken aback. The waltz, in which the partners held one another, was notorious for the romantic opportunities it afforded gentlemen of a libertine persuasion. The viscount laughed at the flush that spread over her face.

"Because we have to talk, my dear Miss Manning," he explained, "and these country-dances leave me too out of breath. Come, let's sit a moment and let me bring you some lemonade. Or would you prefer orgeat?"

He gave her his arm and led her to the sofa by which she had first spotted him. "What I should most like, Your Lordship," she answered shyly, "is to be presented to the countess so that I may thank her."

"She's not here tonight," he said. "I'm sure Madame de Lieven finds these evenings at Almack's quite as tedious as I do. She enjoys the power and the social politics, that's all."

"Why are you subjecting yourself, then, to so much tedium?" asked Ursula.

"A little ennui is good for the soul. Now, was that lemonade you wished?"

"Yes, lemonade."

As she waited for him to return, Ursula felt many eyes upon her. To her dismay the dowager who was mother to the florid daughter approached the sofa with a determined step and sat down beside Ursula.

"I am Lady Stanhope," she said in an inappropriately girlish voice, "and so very pleased to meet you. I don't believe we've been introduced."

"No, we haven't," agreed Ursula. "My name is Ursula Manning, and I've been in London less than a fortnight."

"Yet you already have some noteworthy admirers," was the rejoinder. "Where did you first become acquainted with Richard?"

Ursula was spared answering by the viscount's return. His face clouded momentarily at the sight of Lady Stanhope, but he recovered in an instant, handed Ursula her refreshment, and addressed the dowager in intimate terms.

"My dear, I do not wish to alarm you, but my concern for Elizabeth makes me speak."

The dowager's eyebrows shot up in surprise. "Yes?" she asked cautiously.

"I saw her on the terrace moments ago engaged in a tête-à-tête with Sir William Littlefield. While I don't suggest there is any impropriety, I happen to know that Sir William is lately come to ruin and in desperate need of an heiress to marry."

"Sir William Littlefield? I don't think I know the man," answered Lady Stanhope, trying to control her alarm.

"You wouldn't," said Uxbridge smoothly. "A gazetted fortune hunter. I can't imagine why they let him in here. A terrible lapse."

Lady Stanhope made her excuses, nodded to Ursula, squeezed the viscount's hand, and hastened off to save Elizabeth from her looming fate. Uxbridge watched her go.

"You seem to know everyone," said Ursula, to break the silence.

"I do," he replied. "And those I do not know, I invent. There is no such person as Sir William, but I needed to speak with you alone."

Ursula laughed, but beneath her amusement she was disturbed by the facility with which Uxbridge dispensed with the truth.

"I hope what you have to say is urgent enough to justify perpetrating a deception on a poor dowager," she said.

The viscount merely chuckled at these delicate scruples. "Telling a minor falsehood to Lady Stanhope hardly signifies. Her real problem is her infinite capacity for *self*-deception. She has quite convinced herself—without any encouragement from me—that I'm going to marry her horrid little Elizabeth. But she will no doubt return, so let me speak my mind. I wanted you to know, Miss Manning, that I did not know the contents of Wickenham's letter when I delivered it to your uncle." He paused.

"I didn't think you knew it," she rejoined. "I'll allow I've heard many stories about you, but no one yet accuses you of reading correspondence meant for another."

The corners of his mouth turned up in a smile, almost in spite of himself. "No, you're not a simpering miss, are you?" he asked.

Ursula flushed, realizing she had been altogether too outspoken. "You seemed embarrassed, sir, to broach such personal matters with me. I thought a forward tongue might put you at your ease and conceal the fact that I'm scarcely out of the schoolroom. I'm sorry that I . . ."

"No," he insisted. "An apology would spoil it. I was about to say I believe you have been bullocked most shamefully, but now I see you are not the sort to let herself be misused."

"You are quite right in guessing I shall not let myself be married to that man," she said, surprised by her own certainty.

He regarded her closely. "Of course, I don't mean to criticize your family. I am convinced they believe they are acting in your best interests—"

"That, of course," she said, "is understood."

"Exactly. But I am not happy to see anyone," he went on, "no matter how well intentioned, ride roughshod over a maiden's sentiments. As I think you are shrewd enough to have guessed, I have no business detaining me in London. But I have no desire to escort a prisoner to the New World."

"Very well. We are agreed. For I am not embarking on any such voyage."

The viscount searched her face again and then slammed his fist in exasperation on his knee. "Miss Manning, I respect your spirit, but if you are to avoid this wretched misalliance, you will need help. I am here, ready and willing to offer that assistance, and you stubbornly sit there and pretend you do not need it."

Ursula's inclination was to trust everyone she met, but George had most particularly warned her against the Viscount of Uxbridge. Yet she certainly did need some help, and while George might scrupulously warn her against others, he offered no help himself. Yes, he loved her, but he tended to think marriage to Wickenham was a wondrous opportunity.

"Most likely he'll not live out the year," George

had said, "and I am unable to think of a better thing to be than a young, beautiful, and scandalously rich widow."

So she could not count on George.

She hesitated, looking into the viscount's eyes. She was frightened by the way he had so easily seen through her bravado, but at the same time she felt quite disarmed.

"What do you suggest?" she asked in a voice that emerged surprisingly meek in tone.

He smiled at her capitulation. "My dear, let's talk frankly. Am I correct in assuming that you have absolutely no fortune? Not even so much as a couple of hundred a year?"

She nodded.

"And that your relations are most anxious to see you settled before another year passes?"

She nodded again. It was easier to give her acquiescence in a gesture than to speak aloud of such personal matters.

"But we may both accept that neither your aunt nor your uncle would object to your being happy, as long as you are properly provided for?"

"Of course."

"Well then, it's simple," he said. "We shall give them hope that a satisfactory match can be made for you here in London. By the time they realize—if they ever do—that they have been fooled by a carefully staged drama, you will no doubt have made the acquaintance of a young man who does, in fact, nurture a passionate regard for you."

"What? Do you propose to pay court to me yourself, sir?" she asked, laughing.

"Certainly not!" he replied immediately, rather too quickly, thought Ursula. "No," he said, softening his vehement negation with an explanation, "I have lately had some unfortunate entanglements that have left me with an unsavoury reputation. Should our names become linked, your name would suffer, Miss Manning, and the young man who might someday make you happy might very well be deterred. But I have many friends, suitable, respectable, and rich, and I shall see to it that at least some of them begin to show you the most marked attentions."

"You know we have only a few days left," she pointed out. "And Uncle Alfred has already sent a letter to Lord Charles accepting the proposal."

"Trust me," said the viscount, taking Ursula's hand.

A thrill tingled from her fingertips up to her elbow. "But what is your interest in the matter?" she asked, fighting her desire to do as he asked.

The look in his eyes turned guarded. "I'd rather been looking forward to my sea crossing," he said stiffly, "and don't fancy spending it as a young lady's chaperon. It's not in my nature to be a maiden aunt."

This answer delighted Ursula. "Then you don't claim to be motivated by some unaccountable generosity to me!" she cried. "Very well, I shall trust you, my lord, since I realize our interests do indeed coincide most conveniently. I judge it unlikely that you should choose to betray yourself."

Uxbridge shook his head, and his eyes danced with amusement. "We've been alone together long enough. Now I see a friend of mine. Come, I shall present you."

"Who is it?" she asked. "Sir William Littlefield?"

"If I'd known you were so sharp-tongued, I should never have offered my services," he returned. "No, I wouldn't try to foist an imaginary baronet off on you," he continued as he led her across the room. "I refer to Stanley Carstairs, sixth Earl of Staunton. You see him, the gentleman dancing with the tall brunette, his cravat tied in what looks to be a poor imitation of the Gordian knot. Now, Miss Manning, as soon as the music stops, I'll see that he's yours. Temporarily, of course."

CHAPTER THREE

Ursula woke late to a bedroom splashed with sunlight. She smiled and stretched happily. It was the first day all week that she had opened her eyes without being besieged by the blue devils.

She looked back over her night at Almack's and smiled even at the memory of the daggered looks she had received from angry mammas and jealous daughters. Ursula had been a sensation, sought after by all the most eligible young men. Of course, she knew none of them was actually in love with her, but how could she help but be moved? It was so excessively amiable of them all to aid her in her distress. There were so many good, kind people in London!

Her good humour was short-lived, however, for Uncle Alfred was waiting for her in the parlour, seated behind a monstrous brazilwood desk, the legs of which were carved in the Egyptian style to represent lions. The London house was actually the property of a friend of Ursula's uncle, a retired army major who had chosen to commemorate the Egyptian campaign in the furnishings of his home. As Ursula tried to meet her uncle's frosty stare, her attention was distracted by the carved sphinx heads, crocodiles, and lotus leaves that grew out of every piece of furniture, adorned the mantelpiece, and rendered fantastic the cornices of the ceiling.

She waited with some trepidation for him to speak. She knew her uncle always sought a desk to sit behind when treating a matter of grave import. There was every indication that the conversation about to take place would not be a pleasant one.

"While you have been sleeping," Uncle Alfred began ominously as his face grew red above his tight collar, "we, or rather I should say *you,* have been the recipient of several tokens of estimation. One dozen roses from a Sir Arthur Pease. A spring nosegay from a Lord Stanley Carstairs." Here Uncle Alfred refreshed his memory by reference to a small stack of cards before him on the desk. "Hyacinths from Algernon Lovelace. What? No title? He must be the only one."

"His father is Earl of Merton, and the title is hereditary," said Ursula with quiet amusement. "Algernon is, of course, the eldest son."

Uncle Alfred stacked the cards together and used them to beat out a nervous tattoo against the desk top. "Ursula, this is outrageous. I do not mean to accuse you of impropriety. I am certain you did nothing to fan so much ardour from so many sources unless, of course, your ingenuous nature caused you to behave a little too freely and encourage false expectations."

"Dear Uncle," she replied, "when a young lady makes her first appearance at Almack's, this is exactly the reception she hopes for. What can be the harm in my success? Rather, can we not rejoice together? What good fortune! I shall be able to choose a husband from among the best of English families and no longer need travel across the ocean and be separated from you."

His weak blue eyes softened a moment, and to Ursula's surprise Uncle Alfred heaved a sigh. "Ursula," he said gently, "I'll allow that I haven't moved in the most exalted circles and that I know very little about the ways of the *ton.* But I fancy I understand a little more than a sweet country miss with no experience at all. Believe me, my child—for I do think of you as my own child, you know that, don't you?—I would rather have avoided this conversation, for I do not wish to cause you any pain. But you are young, and your head—probably from those dreadful novels you read—is filled with romantic faddle."

"If you had been at Almack's with us last night," interrupted Ursula, "you would have seen there's no romantic faddle to it at all. It's really quite fusty and boring. Still, it was pleasant to dance and converse with well-bred people. We really did live in some isolation in Hampshire. Please don't blame me for finding city life so very agreeable."

"You force me to be too blunt," said her uncle with another sigh. "Have you asked yourself why so many young men with names and fortunes should take so great an interest in you?"

"First, I can hardly call their interest so very great," she said promptly. If only he knew the real reason! she thought to herself. "And second, Uncle Alfred, if they already have names and fortunes, I suppose they are free to turn their affections in any direction."

Uncle Alfred unbuttoned two more buttons of his coat. The interview was not going easily for him.

"There is only one possible explanation," he concluded in a gloomy voice, "and that is that through no fault of your own you are generally considered to be ruined."

"To be what?" she exclaimed, rising from her chair.

"You see, I didn't want to tell you," he muttered apologetically. "Your aunt heard many interesting stories last night concerning the Viscount of Uxbridge. It seems society has been relieved in the past year that he has turned his amorous attentions to married ladies because there were episodes in which he compromised young girls and then refused to make good by marriage. If only we had known this earlier, we should never have permitted him to secure that voucher on your behalf. Unfortunately, as it stands, he appears to be in some way your sponsor. Apparently conclusions have been drawn, my dear. So you see, it is more imperative than ever that your marriage to Lord Charles take place as soon as possible. All these attentions you are receiving can mean only one thing: Here in London, your virtue is considered easy and your chance of marriage is gone. I know how you feel about Lord Charles, but consider, Ursula, is he not a better alternative than for you to remain here and be degraded into the role of a Fashionable Impure?"

"I am not impure!" she exclaimed, genuinely angry.

"Ursula, that hardly signifies. London is ruled by the *ton,* and if the *ton* says you are impure, you are. If the *ton* says you are Greek, you will find your dancing partners will compliment you on your charming accent and will strain to understand your curious English. If the *ton* says—"

"Uncle, this is lunacy!" she cried.

"I have only your best interests at heart," he reiterated, but Ursula did not wait to hear more. She rushed from the parlour and collided with Struthers, who handed her a salver on which rested no fewer than five gilt-edged invitations.

Tears welled up in Ursula's eyes, which were china blue in the morning light. She crumpled the cards in a tiny fist, and the hard, sharp edges of the stiff paper cut into her palm. These invitations were supposed to have been her salvation, but her guardians had already made up their minds. They were ready to interpret anything and everything the wrong way. The viscount had asked her to trust him, and so she had done, but his plan had clearly gone awry.

"Ursula!"

She turned to see George, grinning as mischievously as a child. His chin was jutting outward, whether to draw attention to his intricate cravat or because the starched fabric was irritating his neck Ursula dared not guess. In his good humour George failed to see the tears in his sister's eyes. "It is excessively wonderful to live in London!" he exclaimed, and then in a lower voice added, "Do you think the viscount might, if I asked him, put me up for Watier's and the Four-in-Hand Driving Club?"

"The viscount is very obliging," she said in a trembling voice, "but his kindness does not always yield the desired result." Then, unable to control herself any longer, she burst into loud sobs.

George showed his true nature by taking her into his comforting arms without giving a thought to the havoc this wreaked on his carefully ordered cravat. "We can speak more privately upstairs," he whispered as he led her away gently.

They took seats in Ursula's sitting room.

"They could at least have let me have my flowers up here," sobbed Ursula. The retired major had not been acquainted with many members of the fair sex, and so he had not shown the most felicitous taste in the arrangements he made for the comforts of ladies. This room was overpowered with its heavy dark wood. To Ursula the very decor of her quarters was indicative of the oppression under which she suffered.

George listened attentively to his sister's report of the night at Almack's and of the conclusions their guardians had drawn. When she had finished, he sat still a moment, his brows knotted in an attitude of concentration that was so unusual for him Ursula almost had to laugh. His words, however, did not inspire mirth.

"You shall have to go to Bermuda," he said when he spoke at last. Anticipating her disappointed fury, he grasped her hand and continued speaking before she could react. "You may be quite right that no one can force you to marry. But here we are, without a hundred pounds between us. We both know only too well that while we live in Uncle Alfred's house, he controls us as closely as he controls the purse-strings. Embark for Bermuda as they wish, but once the ship leaves England behind, take your freedom."

Ursula looked at him in wonder. "I thought you were the pragmatist, George. Whatever am I supposed to do, alone in the world without money or protection?"

"You won't be alone," he replied slowly. "I intend to accompany you."

"What?"

"I shall discuss it with Uxbridge. Perhaps I can prevail upon him to make me his secretary or find me other work. At any event there are many opportunities in the Americas."

"A moment ago you were consumed with the desire to join the Four-in-Hand . . ." she protested.

"Darling, when have I ever made a sacrifice?" he asked quietly. "When have I ever thought of anyone but myself? If I propose to do so now, surely you will not wish to dissuade me."

Ursula was too overwhelmed with surprise and love to speak.

"And it will be a grand adventure," George added somewhat lamely as his fantasies of London life began to recede before the force of his new and unexpected commitment. "Together, and free of the supervision of relatives who lack imagination, why, we shall set the whole island of Bermuda agog."

It was a seductive idea, but, "You cannot make so important a decision in such haste," urged his sister.

"I have been thinking about it since this whole nasty bumblebath began," he replied. "It seems the viscount has been very gracious to you, but I was never at ease in my mind to think you would pass a long ocean voyage in his company."

Ursula flushed. "Really, George. You give me as little credit for good sense as Uncle Alfred does."

"I give you much credit, Ursula, for being young, beautiful, and trusting. You won't deny that Uxbridge has already managed to win a portion of your trust."

"He has earned it," she replied hesitantly.

"That remains to be seen. But consider the convenient circumstances that throw you, a maiden in distress, upon his protection for weeks aboard a ship in the middle of nowhere with a desperate fate awaiting you at the end of the voyage. Don't you think the stage is set perfectly for an easy seduction?"

"You weren't so concerned with my virtue a few days ago," she pointed out, "when you urged me to stalk my prey in Mayfair."

"But you weren't to be thrown to society all alone, my dear," he argued. "That is why I intend to go with you. I shall be the perfect chaperon. You'll need only raise an eyebrow to cause me to disappear. I shall be discreet and not reproach you should you wish to be somewhat wicked. But should you find yourself getting in too deep, I'll be there to defend you. The viscount is a very attractive man, Ursula. I can see that, and it's no sorry reflection on your character if you've conceived a *tendre* for him. It will merely be up to me to see that this connection remains within bounds."

"George," she whispered, squeezing his broad hand, "I haven't conceived a *tendre* for the viscount or for anyone. But now, after I see what you are willing to do for me"—and the tears began to pour from her luminous eyes as she spoke—"I assure you that the man who does wish to win my heart will have to display more than a few easy gestures of kind concern. It will be no simple task for anyone to measure up to the love that *you* have shown me."

This gentle scene was interrupted by a knock at the door. It was Struthers, who solemnly announced that the Viscount of Uxbridge was downstairs, wishing to see Miss Manning.

"You should join us, George," suggested Ursula. "The three of us have matters to discuss."

"Only let me withdraw long enough to tie a fresh cravat, and I shall be at your disposal."

Ursula wondered if George had not completely reconciled himself to the arrangements they had just agreed on. Would he have been so anxious to impress the viscount with his elegance were he not still dreaming of a membership to Watier's? But all she said was: "Very well, but I beseech you to make haste and choose a knot that is easy to tie. We had best transact our business with our caller before Aunt Mary learns he is in the house—or I may be forbidden to see him."

"My valet and I shall make heroic efforts," replied George.

Brother and sister exchanged a fond look, and Ursula hurried downstairs to greet the caller.

She found Uxbridge examining a seven-branch candelabrum with arms worked in the shape of the inevitable lotuses and palmettos. He turned when she entered, and his eyes went directly to her face and stayed there.

"I collect our conspiracy proceeds apace," he said, smiling. "I encountered two gentlemen on the steps relinquishing flowers to the hands of your butler, and I assure you, I am not intimate with either one of them. So it seems you've made some conquests of your own."

In spite of her distress over the events of the morning, Ursula could not help but be gratified to fancy that she had inspired at least *some* unstaged and unsolicited admiration.

"Has your esteemed uncle had the time yet to cancel the cabin that's being held for you aboard the *Fortitude?*" Uxbridge asked.

"No," she replied with equal directness, fighting to keep her voice calm. "It seems I shall have to keep the cabin after all and, in fact, will require additional accommodations."

He raised his eyebrows in question.

"I am going to Bermuda, and my brother, George, will accompany me." She wanted to wilt under his cold gaze. "What? Are you disappointed in me?" she asked.

"Yes. And surprised. Why are you surrendering?" he asked.

"I am *not* surrendering," she answered in some heat. "I am running away from home." And she proceeded to tell him of the interview with her uncle.

"Damn!" he swore. "So it's my blemished reputation that's put it all to wrong!"

"You've been only too kind," Ursula hastened to assure him, hardly noting his profanity in her anxiety to let him know she did not blame him for the failure of the plan.

"I never cared about it before, but damn it all!" His face coloured dark with emotion, and he had to pace the drawing room for a few moments to discharge his angry energy. "And do you know the cause of this reputation, Miss Manning? Seven years ago the family of a certain young lady contrived to leave me alone with her for a few moments, then raised the alarm and insisted I marry her. There was absolutely no reason to do so, you understand, but I was young and inexperienced enough so that I might have married her out of consideration for her position, except that it was only too clear that she was no innocent pawn but had been privy to the scheme."

"You really do not have to tell me this," said Ursula softly.

"But I will," he replied. "So I became known as a shameless seducer of innocent maidens. A convenient reputation, let me assure you, as it has kept the husband hunters at a distance. Except for our friend Lady Stanhope, few mammas let their daughters wander unguarded anywhere in my immediate vicinity. And the fact is, I have precious little interest in ladies of quality and virtue, so it's all suited me quite well. But in the end you have been made to suffer, and, Miss Manning, I can hardly find the words to express my regret."

How kind he was! His explanation reflected favourably upon him, yet George's repeated warnings had taken root to some extent in Ursula's mind. She could not help but consider that the ease with which Uxbridge had gained her confidence only proved his skill at insinuating himself into an untried heart. While she hesitated, silent before his apology, George broke the tension by joining them at last and quickly turning the conversation to practical questions.

Now it was the viscount's turn to hesitate as a cloud passed over his face and conflicting emotions clearly warred within him.

"You put me in a most distasteful position," he said at last. "Though I shall endeavour to assist you in some way, please appreciate my position. I go to work under the authority of Lord Charles and can hardly play an active role in helping his bride escape him—much as my sympathies may reside with the lady." He paused. "I suggest you continue to try to soften your guardians' hearts, Miss Manning. But if you—both of you—must set sail with me next week, that is how it shall be." He turned to George. "I hardly believe it will be within my power to secure you a position in Bermuda, but there is a world of opportunity across the sea. If you truly intend to see this adventure through, certainly you will be able to make some sort of life for yourselves."

"My resolution is taken," said George with a bow.

"And though it must be done in secret, I shall be willing to help you financially," concluded Uxbridge.

"We could not accept your generosity," interrupted Ursula.

In return he cast an amused yet cold smile upon her. "This is not the first time I have told you that your pride must bow before your necessity," he said. "You may consider it a loan if you choose." He stood as if to take his leave. Then, to soften the blow of his critical remark, he added, "May you find a true shelter at the journey's end."

"That hardly seems likely," she responded, and immediately regretted her caustic tone.

Uxbridge stood poised a moment, uncertain whether to leave once and for all or to speak. At last he turned to Ursula and spoke in a soft, earnest tone she had not previously heard from him.

"Bermuda has surprised the luckless in the past," he told her quietly. "Did you know, Bermuda is the place that Shakespeare called 'the blessed isle'? *The Tempest,* you see, was based on a true incident . . ."

"Ah, *The Tempest,*" she replied with a bitter laugh. "Now I am thoroughly convinced of my misfortune, for if it's to Prospero's island that we're bound, there remains no doubt but that I've been betrothed to the monster Caliban."

"I don't know Lord Charles," admitted the viscount, "but I can hardly believe him to be quite so impossible a companion. . . . But do listen. Bermuda was long known as the Devil's Island, until one day in 1609. A ship of colonists—men, women, and children—en route to Jamestown in Virginia was caught in the most terrible, tormented storm ever seen at sea, a veritable battle of the elements. For five days they quite gave up all hope of survival as the ship was flung about by heaven and sea." He drew a deep breath. "Then the captain spied a dread and rocky coast— Devil's Island. The assembled company could do nothing but pray for their souls as their vessel was flung forward toward the rocks. The ship was carried high upon the back of a wave, and—it must have seemed to them a miracle—this monster wave overswept the jagged reefs and deposited the ship in a clear, calm pool between two great rocks. All disembarked safely in a sweet land of clear skies and fresh meadows and fragrant woods." He paused a moment. "And that, Miss Manning, is the island of Bermuda—an unexpected haven for those who've been tossed and tormented in this wicked world. I am convinced that I shall find there what I seek. And I trust that you, too, in spite of all indications to the contrary, will there meet with safe harbour."

With these words he nodded to George, bowed to Ursula, urged them to let him see himself out, and was gone.

Ursula sat confused in the gold and black japanned chair and marveled at the viscount's words. She did not wish to meet her brother's inquiring eyes. All she could think of was Uxbridge. Who was he? What was he? Could she trust him? It was too late to ask that last question, she told herself, for she trusted him already. But was her instinctive confidence a grave mistake?

42

That a seducer should speak to her of the colour of her eyes or freshness of her complexion was only to be expected. But how was she to understand the motivation of this man who spoke to her in soft, intense tones of a safe harbour?

She could not deny that he exercised a strong physical attraction over her. She was only too aware that she experienced a glowing sense of well-being whenever he spoke to her. And much as she hated the thought of embarking for Bermuda, she had to admit that she thrilled to think they would be traveling together.

Then, reflecting upon his words, she set a new interpretation upon them. The viscount threatened to bring to life the sort of stormy feelings that would shatter the calm of her existence. And so, she reasoned, if Bermuda was the haven toward which she was bound, it was clearly the Viscount of Uxbridge who represented the tempest, the torments of the wicked world. Each time their eyes met, she had felt ready to plunge into a whirlpool.

She could picture his liquid eyes before her.

I must not succumb, she thought miserably. If I am to reach my safe harbour, I must not succumb.

CHAPTER FOUR

Ursula did not abandon her efforts to cause her uncle Alfred to change his mind, but her wiles and pleading had little effect. Passage to Bermuda was booked for the first day in June, and her guardians persisted in their intention of seeing her sail.

And so, early one morning, George helped her into the carriage, gave her hand a squeeze, and then helped Aunt Mary up beside her before he joined them. Uncle Alfred chose to sit outside on the box with Corrie. It was most unusual for Uncle Alfred, not being much of a whip and privately decrying horses and such persons as managed them well as dirty and stupid, to put himself in such proximity to the coachman. However, he rightly suspected that his popularity with his family was not at its zenith. He was unwilling to abide the arguments, tears, and quiet, reproachful looks that might be directed his way in the interior of the vehicle. So, much as he would have preferred to spend the short trip dozing inside against the plump squabs with a couple of buttons to his waistcoat undone, he chose Corrie's company as the lesser of evils.

Ursula shut her eyes as the carriage broke into a not-very-smart trot. She did not wish to see the London house vanish from view. There was too much finality, she thought, to this departure.

"Look, she's already seasick." She heard George's voice. "This ain't such a splendid idea. . . ."

Aunt Mary said solicitously, "It's just the headache, dear? Isn't it just?"

"Yes, just the headache," Ursula agreed.

44

When she opened her eyes, which showed violet for a moment before adjusting to the light, the unfamiliar surroundings which were revealed excited her interest to the point of banishing her own concerns from mind. If Almack's had been an alien milieu to Ursula, the Dutch East India Company wharf was stranger still.

"You don't suppose *they* are going to sail a ship today, do you?" she asked at the sight of three red-eyed sailors who stumbled along together in a state of inebriated comradeship.

"Sit back in your seat," whispered Aunt Mary. "These are not the sorts of persons one wants a well-bred girl to quiz."

Ursula did indeed wish to quiz them. However, she decided to indulge her aunt's sense of propriety in this last instance. Soon enough, she reflected, she would answer to no authority save her own.

The morning had come up not only on sailors full of blue ruin but on old men in rags, who pushed carts heaped high with unrecognizable but vaguely objectionable cargo, and on urchins, whose milling rowdiness obstructed the passage of simple wheelbarrows and fine carriages alike.

Aunt Mary fumbled for her smelling salts. Their pungent scent was much to be preferred over the odor of rotting garbage that characterized the vicinity.

The wharf made a fascinating scene, but certainly not an auspicious one. This vision of how rude and rough the world could be was surely calculated to make Uncle Alfred reconsider the wisdom of ever allowing his female ward out of his sight. But the gentleman's mind was made up. Uncle Alfred had enjoyed so few opportunities in his life to make decisions that he was, it seemed, unaware that a decision once taken need not be irrevocable.

Corrie reined in the team, and Uncle Alfred leaped down with surprising agility, rather like a barrel that had suddenly sprouted legs and was all impatient to try them. He opened the carriage door in haste.

"Hold up your hem," instructed Aunt Mary with distaste as Ursula descended to the filthy street. "Not so high, dear. Think of your ankles!"

Several screaming urchins ran to assist Corrie in unloading the baggage, and their proximity caused Aunt Mary to reach once more for her smelling salts.

Ursula hardly noticed the children. The *Fortitude,* at anchor before her, claimed her whole attention. She felt small and insignificant faced with a three-deck vessel almost fifty meters long. The sailors climbing high in the rigging were reduced to the size of toys.

Aunt Mary was also powerfully affected by the appearance of the vessel. For in such turbulent days even merchant ships were armed as heavily as any man-o'-war in the King's Navy. The sight of so much artillery was too much for her, and the good woman promptly broke into tears. She saw nothing wrong with forcing her charge to marry a rich old man, but she was horrified to realize all at once that Ursula would be exposed to danger. For the first time in her married life an excess of emotion caused her to challenge a decision her husband had reached through his powers of ratiocination, which she had always acknowledged as vastly superior to her own.

"He shall have her," she cried, "but let him come to England for her. What kind of family are we to send our own dear girl over the sea in time of war?"

Aunt Mary's tongue was so unused to voicing objections to her mate, it seemed, that in the course of a lifetime together Uncle Alfred's ears had quite lost the capacity to hear any. So, in all fairness, his failure to make any reply to his wife's words should be attributed not to discourtesy, but rather to this unfortunate deterioration in his aural sense.

"I see at least fifty guns, and they look to be nine-pounders," drawled George, hiding his own agitation behind a casual tone of voice. "So just let Frenchie try to come out to play."

He looked his uncle over closely to see if this evocation of a possible naval engagement had had any effect. But the only person impressed by his speech was Ursula, who had not suspected her foppish brother had any expertise in distinguishing one weapon from another.

"A very seaworthy vessel," pronounced Uncle Alfred.

"But what of the broadsides?" cried Aunt Mary, still deeply distressed. She was not entirely certain what a "broadside" was, but she knew that when a man started talking about French broadsides or, just as bad, American ones, he was usually leading up to the thoroughly nasty report that some proud English ship had been sunk, and the crew and passengers either taken prisoner or left to cold, grim death.

No one bothered to answer Aunt Mary, her husband owing to the previously mentioned disability and her young wards from the knowledge that her fears were most expeditiously dispelled when ignored.

"We'd best get aboard," said Ursula, fighting for calm.

But minutes passed, and the four figures stood uncertainly on the dock while a yellow haze rose off the river and sea gulls scavenged in the trash and wheeled and plunged against the sky.

This state of suspended animation might have continued indefinitely had a sleek black phaeton not appeared with the Viscount of Uxbridge seated on its high perch. He jumped to the pavement with a leap

47

that made the many capes of his coat whirl about him with vigorous grace. As he approached with energetic step and confident mien, both brother and sister were struck by the great eagerness his countenance displayed.

"Here comes our moneyed rakehell," whispered Ursula to George. "If all the stories about him are as true as you think them to be, I shouldn't have thought he would be so eager to quit London in midseason."

"Perhaps he flees some scandal . . . in the form of a vengeful woman," teased George in return.

"You are irredeemable," she complained before they cut their private conversation short and greeted the viscount with friendly courtesy.

"I hate farewells," Uxbridge exclaimed. "And when they are prolonged, they cannot escape the opprobrium of being excessively painful or, worse, excessively maudlin. So say what must be said and let us get aboard."

Ursula was happy enough to end the stalemate on the dock, and so she kissed her guardians with as much sincere affection as she could muster up under the circumstances. Aunt Mary wept openly, and even Uncle Alfred found it necessary to flick away a few tears from the corners of his eyes.

"You're going to be happy, girl," he said in a broken voice. It was hard to tell whether he was commanding her or beseeching her. "I know you're frightened. Everyone is frightened when it comes to marriage, my dear, but it will come right, you'll see. You're going to thank me for this some day, even if you don't see the wisdom in it now."

This discourse, which was blatantly sentimental by Uncle Alfred's standards, was interrupted by the unexpected arrival of another personage: a veiled lady dressed in lilac satin, who threw herself at the feet of the viscount. Uxbridge coloured with rage.

George put a reassuring hand on Ursula's arm and drew her close to him as the woman spoke through her sobs. "You don't really mean to go, Richard?" she cried. "You can't . . ."

It seemed George's random shot about a "vengeful woman" had hit a mark. Ursula tugged at his arm, wishing to go aboard without further delay. Her own sense of privacy was offended by this public display involving others.

"Don't go!" the woman cried again to Uxbridge. "But if you must, keep your eyes on the shore as your ship weighs anchor, and you will see me cast this worthless body into the water that bears you away!"

The veiled lady's entreaties made as little impression on Uxbridge as Ursula's had made on Uncle Alfred. However, her emotional fever seemed to communicate itself to others on the pier as though it were a contagious disease. Aunt Mary broke down completely. "We can't let them go!" she shrieked, and clutched at her husband with as much desperation as the stranger showed vis-à-vis Uxbridge. Ursula clutched at George. At the same time Uncle Alfred was assailed by still another party: an urchin who had finally found the courage to impress upon him the fact that the gratuity rewarded for unloading the baggage had been insufficient. And a female fruit vendor, dressed in black and swathed in an unseasonably heavy shawl, demonstrated her outrage at the injuries men were wont to inflict upon the gentler sex, as typified by the viscount's callous behavior, by pelting him with samples from her stock of rotten apples.

In short, the scene became so unpleasant as to overshadow the difficulties inherent in taking the final steps to the ship. Ursula and George embraced their guardians one last time, but before they could follow the route their trunks had already taken up the broad wooden gangplank, they were vouchsafed the opportunity to witness still another strange scene.

A carriage pulled up, lined with pale blue satin and bearing two well-dressed and smiling young women.

"By Jupiter," whispered George, "if it's not early in the morning for Harriette Wilson and Julia Johnstone to be up and about!"

Ursula studied the occupants of the carriage with frank curiosity. So these were the Fashionable Impures whose ranks she had been in supposed danger of swelling.

"Richard!" cried a musical voice. "I so feared we'd be too late." Completely ignoring the veiled lady, who was still kneeling and clutching at the viscount's legs, the cyprian leaned out of the carriage and handed Uxbridge a bottle.

"Champagne, darling," she said. "Bon voyage!"

George watched in awe. "Uxbridge must be a great favourite," he told his sister, who simply gasped in return.

"I've seen quite enough," she declared, and turned her steps resolutely toward the ship.

George followed, but not without a somewhat reluctant glance behind him. "That's not the sort of scene one ordinarily wants his sister to witness," he commented once they had gained the deck. "But in your case, considering your inclination to be so favourably disposed to a certain individual, I should say it was instructive."

Ursula's displeasure increased when Uxbridge joined them ten minutes later. Turning back to the shore, he casually remarked, "So much for a lover's suicide.

Rather than casting herself to a watery grave, you can now observe the lady climbing into a hackney cab and returning home to her husband." He shrugged. "I gave her the champagne as a parting gift."

Ursula's eyes flashed with anger. Hadn't the scene been bad enough? Why did he have to make it even worse? Instead of being silent or regretful, the viscount had the heartless audacity to be amused.

Odious, she thought.

But rather than throw dark looks at Uxbridge, she turned a bright smile upon the sailor who had been charged with showing her to her cabin. She followed him belowdecks without a word to the viscount, who had, at least in her eyes, quite fallen from grace.

Ursula's cabin was small box with a neat, narrow bed. If not a delightful habitation, it was at least no less charming than her dreadful chamber in London. In fact, she rather admired the trim economy of line and did not mind the lack of feminine refinements. It was refreshing not to have her eyes assailed with carved crocodiles at every turn.

The deckhand showed her the storage drawers beneath the bunk. " 'Tis a pleasure to 'ave ye aboard, miss," he said politely enough, but without being able to hide the frank appreciation in his eyes.

Men, she thought. I suppose they're all the same, but some at least are more honest about their fancies. Uxbridge was more than odious, she decided. He was devious as well.

George was the exception, she told herself as her brother appeared and stooped to enter through the low doorway.

"Hurry," he urged her. "We cast off in minutes. Do let's watch from the deck."

She joined him, more grateful than ever for his presence. Whatever would she have done without him, a lone female surrounded by men and traveling to a distant, still unknown fate?

On deck Ursula's heart rose in her mouth as the *Fortitude* lurched and began to move amid the shouts of sailors, the creaking of sails and ropes, the slamming of wood. At moments she felt it was not the ship that was moving, but rather the whole city of London with its rooftops, spires, and bridges that creaked and groaned and cut itself loose from the Thames and retreated slowly against the sky.

Uxbridge joined them shortly, smiled at Ursula, and whispered, "Courage, Miss Manning," as though nothing had happened. She returned neither the smile nor the salutation. His friendliness rankled, but in the next instant her spirits rose at a most welcome sight. A young lady accompanied by an older gentleman had suddenly appeared, laughing, on the sun deck. Happy though Ursula was to see a feminine companion, she felt herself somewhat diminished by the girl's attire.

"Her dress must be silk!" she exclaimed. "It's much too fine and light to be muslin." Over her cream dress the girl wore an elegant green pelisse of soft, twilled levantine. "And her bonnet!"

"I hardly expected to see such an independent creature as you envious of another lady's wardrobe," said Uxbridge drily.

"I'm not envious," Ursula defended herself, forgetting her resolution not to speak to him. "It's just I feel such a child in my old frocks."

He touched her arm lightly, and she pulled away from him at once. "Fashions are hopelessly behind the times in Bermuda," he assured her, pretending to be unaware of her reaction to his touch. "I'll wager a monkey that the finest ladies in St. Georges will be copying your schoolroom frocks before you've been in town a fortnight."

"You make a safe wager, sir," she replied, "knowing I haven't got the fifty pounds to match your stake." She'd intended her words to be cold, and yet she could not deny that she enjoyed bantering with him. Part of her wanted to take her brother's arm and leave the awful viscount standing dumb and solitary as a mast. But curiosity made her relent. "Do you know who she is?" she asked.

"No," he replied. "And why do you ask me? Has someone told you I know every female in London?" Before Ursula could answer, he added, "But we are about to learn who she is. They are headed this way, and much to the delight of your brother if I do not misread his countenance."

A sudden gust of wind blew the bonnet so admired by Ursula from the stranger's head. The young woman reached to catch it by the fluttering ties and stumbled, misjudging the roll of the ship. The older gentleman hastened to help her to her feet. His face was strained with concern, but the girl righted herself easily and laughed gaily like a child at her mishap. Then she sauntered forward and stood before Ursula, letting the bonnet swing lightly from her gloved hand.

"Miss Manning?" she asked. "I'm so glad to meet you. I'm Amelia Crandall, and this is my father." She indicated the gentleman, who was pressing his steps to catch up with her.

"How do you know me?" asked Ursula.

"Papa and I will be sitting at the captain's table for meals, you know," replied the girl, "and I made it my business to learn the names of our companions." Then, turning to the viscount, she said, "Are we to be presented, or must I guess whether you are Mr.

53

Manning or the Viscount of Uxbridge? Oh, it's not much of a guessing game," she said upon noticing George for the first time, "for it takes no special power to mark the resemblance between this gentleman and Miss Manning, and I'm no genius to conclude that Mr. and Miss Manning are brother and sister rather than father and daughter."

George opened his mouth, delighted at the chance to engage this dark-haired, dark-eyed vision in conversation, but before he spoke, the elderly Mr. Crandall had joined the company.

"Josiah Crandall of Halifax," he introduced himself, "at your service and begging you to forgive my daughter's North American manners."

Crandall was a slight and quiet man who wore neither his own hair nor his own teeth, but he seemed not at all to mind his own homeliness because Nature had more than repaid her neglect by her generosity to his daughter. His pride in Amelia was matched only by his fear lest she commit some faux pas that would outrage the delicate English sensibility.

"We're on our way home now," Amelia explained to Ursula, taking her as a new friend and confidante without any preliminaries. "Papa did so hope I'd acquire some London polish and good manners, and of course, I failed dismally. But I came off quite well, I think. My only expectations revolved around acquiring a new wardrobe, and I did. Papa, of course, says that all the silk in the world won't turn a barnyard pig into a damsel, but really, considering I've a father who speaks to me so frankly, how should I have grown up simpering and delicate?" She glanced affectionately at her father as she spoke. Crandall did not notice. He was well out of earshot and engaged in deep conversation with the viscount.

George hovered by Ursula's side, too courteous to

insinuate himself abruptly into the conversation between the girls, but plainly unhappy to be left to his own devices.

"The captain says your destination is Bermuda," continued Amelia.

Ursula realized with a shock that she couldn't really say for sure. "Ultimately, yes," she agreed, "though we may choose . . . our itinerary is somewhat open."

"Then I shall make a valiant effort not to be rag-mannered," said Amelia, "in the hopes that you'll like us well enough to stop in Halifax. For I don't know how you feel about the sea, but much as I love it, four weeks afloat from London to home is more than sufficient."

At this point Ursula's attention was drawn to her brother's face, which seemed to be undergoing the most unaccountable spasmodic twitchings. She almost laughed aloud when she realized George must be signaling her by "raising an eyebrow" to indicate his desire that she desert the scene and leave it his sole responsibility to entertain the girl from Halifax. Ursula was willing to cooperate. She was afraid Amelia would ask more questions for which she had no ready answers. And so, citing the brisk ocean breeze, she excused herself on the grounds that she must go below and fetch her spencer.

"I do hope that's not just a story," commented Amelia, "and that you truly do intend to return. It will be just my luck if you prove to be one of those English girls with such a horror of the sun and wind. I know freckles are hideous, but keeping belowdecks is more hideous still. So go get your spencer, but I hope you understand that I expect you to expose yourself to the elements with me."

On her way through the passageways Ursula crossed

paths again with the bold-eyed sailor. Though she did indeed require some help in climbing down the ladder to the lower deck, she could not help but feel that he was only too eager to lift her down and that he held her longer than was strictly necessary.

She hoped that George would not become so smitten with Amelia as to neglect his fraternal duties, for it was becoming very clear that aboard the *Fortitude* it would be impossible to avoid inconvenient meetings.

A chill passed over her and made her shiver. Apprehension, she wondered, or anticipation? No, I'm not going to like this, she thought, confined here day after day in such proximity to an admiring deckhand and a dissolute viscount.

Don't think about it. Don't think about it, she repeated to herself.

But she could not keep from reflecting on all that might happen aboard the ship before they reached port.

CHAPTER FIVE

The captain's table was laid more elaborately than any Ursula had ever seen at a formal dinner party. Soup was ladled out from a silver gilt tureen which boasted a handle in the form of a winged dragon. The roast beef was served on fine bone china, and the accompanying oyster sauce was passed around in a small mazarine blue china pot. Besides plates and soup bowls, the diners made use of artichoke cups, little butter tubs, asparagus trays, side dishes, custard cups. The chicken came in its own tureen, the apricot tarts were served up on individual plates, and everyone received a dish of peaches along with a smaller dish to receive the pits.

"I allus hope fer calm weather the firs' night out," commented the captain, enjoying the surprise in the eyes of his guests. "Can't serve proper like when the ship's rockin' to an' fro wi' the waves. An' o' course, fine provisions don' keep on a long voyage like this un, so ye won' be feedin' like this ev'ry night." This was a theme he frequently repeated to Ursula, who was unable to summon up much appetite. She had begun to be uncomfortably conscious of the rolling of the ship. This strange sensation joined forces with her nervous excitement and robbed the feast of its appeal.

The captain was especially pleased to be transporting a nobleman of such exalted rank as viscount, and he nodded his head deferentially in that gentleman's direction at the end of every utterance. " 'Spect yer sorry to leave London behind, Yer Lordship," he ventured, at last daring to address the viscount directly.

"No, actually I'm not sorry at all," corrected Uxbridge. "The most exciting event of the spring was the visit of that savage Cossack warrior, and it requires something more than that to afford me satisfaction."

"What? Did you actually see him?" exclaimed Amelia in something very like a schoolgirl squeal.

"Yes, I did and, as you see, have lived to tell of it." Uxbridge laughed as his tone grew easier and lighter. "I am grateful that the Cossacks are our allies," he added, "but I'd much prefer them to be killing the French on the steppes, or wherever, than for us to have to entertain them in English drawing rooms. Fancy, when I was introduced to the man, he simply glowered at me and never for a moment put aside his spear, which measured almost twice his height."

Amelia's dark eyes were alight with interest. "Is it really true," she demanded, "that the Cossack commander has offered his daughter to any of his soldiers who brings him Napoleon's head?"

"That's what *on dit*," answered the viscount, "and faced with the brave Zemlanowkin—and his spear—I was not about to question the veracity of the report."

"Oh, the Cossacks may be brave"—Amelia sighed—"but Boney won't be easily taken. I fear the poor commander will have as little luck in disposing of his daughter as my poor papa has had with me."

Ursula marveled at the girl's ability to laugh at her own circumstances with such honest amusement.

"But I'm sure, sir," Amelia continued, teasing, "that London held more attractions for you than you allow. Bermuda *must* seem a terribly small stage by comparison."

The viscount paused a moment and regarded the assembled company over the rim of his wineglass. "Small places are often of great interest," he said at last. After another sip of wine he went on. "In fact, your father's reports of Halifax were most intriguing. I rather fancy the idea of dispatching George here to look after my British North American interests."

"Dash it all," interrupted Crandall. "You interrogated me for hours and never let on you've got investments of your own."

"I haven't"—Uxbridge smiled—"but I've made up my mind to acquire some, with George as my representative." At these last words the viscount did not look toward George as one might have expected. Instead, both he and George turned to study Ursula's face.

She tried to hide her surprise. So it had been decided, and so quickly. Uxbridge was going to establish them in Halifax. She was chagrined to think of relying on his charity, for the business position he was creating for George could not really be considered anything else. However, as he had pointed out to her on more than one occasion, what alternative did she have?

"How marvelous!" cried Amelia, lifting her glass. "We must have a toast!"

George hastened to touch his own goblet to hers, and Ursula could see that Uxbridge had not needed much power of persuasion to convince George that this arrangement was the best that could be hoped for.

The viscount raised his eyebrows slowly and smiled at George. "I observe you toast with the young lady. Does that mean you have accepted my proposition?"

"With the greatest pleasure, Your Lordship," George said in a rush, and only then addressed his sister. "Your heart wasn't really fixed on Bermuda, was it, Ursula?" he asked hopefully.

A fine choice of words, she reflected wryly. "No, Bermuda has no claim at all on my heart," she answered, and with this assurance George smiled freely and raised his glass once more in Amelia's direction.

So it's all been settled, thought Ursula. She was somewhat relieved now that the uncertainty was over, but she could not help but resent the way in which the odious, devious viscount had simply presented his idea at the table and turned it into a *fait accompli* before she had a chance to say a word.

When the meal at last ended, Ursula would have repaired directly to her cabin, but Uxbridge caught her eye and spoke softly. "May I have a few words with you?"

She rose and examined the brocade hangings which did much to disguise the nautical nature of the dining saloon. The viscount did not speak again until the rest of the company had withdrawn.

"I hope the arrangements are satisfactory," he said at last.

She meant to berate him for not consulting her but, instead, found herself thanking him profusely. "I only regret," she concluded, "that you have felt compelled to act in our behalf. We have no claim on your generosity."

"I think George will prove very useful to me," he insisted. "I've never understood gentlemen who disdain business. I shall enjoy seeing my wealth put to some use besides my own amusement. So you see, Miss Manning, I consider that I shall be gaining something."

"I hope that George proves equal to the task."

"And I hope that you will be happy there. Consider: Josiah Crandall is the principal shareholder in this vessel. With him as a connection, I'm certain that George will prosper. And you and Amelia look likely to be bosom-bows by the time the ship docks, so you

60

will not be starting your life in a place devoid of friendship."

"Indeed," she replied softly, "my flight from home is turning out better than I could have expected."

"You understand, of course, why Bermuda was out of the question."

"I had no real desire to go to Bermuda," she said.

"You may well develop such a desire," he warned her lightly, "once you've become acquainted with the climate in Halifax." Then he continued in a more serious vein. "I think you do understand, but I'll say it anyway. You have seen me, I am sorry to say, in circumstances that do not show my character in the best light, so I do not wish to leave my actions open to speculation. Working with Lord Charles, I shall be starting my life afresh. I don't know what he may have heard of me, but I wish to enjoy his confidence, which I should surely forfeit if he were to learn I was a party to the scheme which wrecked his wedding plans. I hope you don't feel I am simply trying to dispose of you, but Bermuda is a small place. You would not be able to refuse Lord Charles and then live there without everyone knowing the circumstances. And neither should we be able to hide the friendship we began in London."

Ursula looked at him in surprise at the word "friendship."

"Yes, friendship, Miss Manning. I have the desire to be your friend and to help you, but my other paramount interest is the work for which I am bound and the trust I hope to gain. Putting George to work for me in Halifax is the only compromise I see."

"You have been more than good, Your Lordship," she said with sincere conviction.

"Whether I am good at all remains to be seen," was

his almost bitter response. "I hope you are right, Miss Manning."

An awkward pause followed this strange avowal.

Ursula sought a way to put an end to the interview and settled at last upon a conventional "Thank you." Uxbridge remained at the table and poured himself another glass of port, while she retired below to muse over the conversation and hope that the tossing of the ship would not keep her long awake.

Sleep, when it came, however, was unsettled and disturbing. She dreamed of a dense and heavy fog weighing down upon her until the air turned noxious, and then even the noxious air was no longer there to be breathed. She struggled awake, choking.

She soon realized that she need not consider her nightmare a supernatural ill omen because the air belowdecks was indeed heavy, hot, and stale. The viscount had advised Uncle Alfred to book Ursula's berth on the lowest deck, being the only area that had any real protection in case of enemy fire. As usual, other people's concern for her best interests seemed to counter her own concept of comfort and contentment. Ursula would gladly, she thought, face death rather than spend the night in the bowels of the vessel.

"I can't bear it any longer!" she cried at last, half stifled. She jumped out of her berth and pulled out the storage drawer below the bed. She found her wrapper and stumbled forth. Ursula was still not accustomed to the rocking of the ship. She was not fully awake, and the flickering shadows of the lanterns made it hard to judge exactly where the deck could be found underfoot. Ursula hugged the walls and pushed herself along like one drugged or drunk.

The fresh air hit her like a welcome splash of cool

water on a sultry day, and she broke into her first spontaneous smile in many hours. Standing on the bow with her hair flying free, Ursula briefly fancied herself a figurehead and tried to stand absolutely still so as not to spoil the effect. Then, distressed at her own playful vanity, she sat down in the curve of a U-shaped iron fixture as though it were a garden swing. She recalled she'd seen the crew's hammocks stored in the row of prongs during the day.

She looked around for a place to take shelter and hide in case anyone approached, and even while she abandoned herself to reverie, she tried to stay alert for any footfall.

But the sailors, except for those on watch, were asleep in their quarters. She envied them their ability to adjust so easily to life afloat, but at the same time she was glad she was looking with fresh eyes at a new world. She'd never seen so clear and bright a night sky. She lost herself in contemplation of the swirling nebulae and throbbing stars. There—that one star above, it certainly did throb rather than twinkle, in an almost violent expansion and contraction in the black sky. Like a heart, she thought. Did the sailors see this beauty? she wondered. Or were the stars mere navigational aids? Did they search the midnight sky, and were they moved by its infinite mystery? Or was the sight so common that they soon gave it no further notice?

"Miss Manning?" A voice broke into her reverie. She turned and saw the viscount standing behind her. She noticed in a vague sort of way that she did not start in surprise at the unexpected interruption. And she realized that though he had not expected to see her in such a place at such a time, neither was he terribly surprised.

"One would think we'd made an assignation," he

said quietly, "when I perceive we are simply kindred souls whose footsteps will quite on their own seek the same destination."

In spite of his use of the word "assignation," she heard no suggestion of impropriety in his voice. As she faced him, Ursula was surprised to find she was glad to see him. Somehow she felt he was the person with whom she most wanted to share the beauty of the night.

They were silent a moment; then he moved quietly to the rail, as if afraid he was embarrassing her. But once alone, looking down at the water, he turned back to face her. "Come, Ursula, you must see this," he said.

She noted the use, for the first time, of her given name and somewhat unsteadily moved forward to join him. The ocean was as infinite as the sky, spreading like rippled cast iron in all directions. The starlight and moonlight illuminated the white froth on the low black waves, and the occasional bright reflections of the heavenly bodies added magic to the regular, hypnotic rhythm of the water.

Ursula could have stood in silence beside this man forever, for as long as the sky and sea stretched through time. She was acutely conscious of his warm, breathing body and of her own trembling. She had the oddest sensation: Every time they both looked at the same star, or when at the same instant they turned their heads to the moon, a thrill ran through her body as surely as if they had actually touched.

"Will you not call me Richard?" he asked, and for a moment it seemed as though the dark curtain of the night had been viciously torn, so frightened was Ursula of the implications of her growing intimacy with the man.

"I think I understand why you are going to Bermuda," she said quickly, trying to initiate a conversation. The silence between them was too charged with emotion, too unsettling. "But I still should have thought that London would be the perfect haven for a gentleman."

"The perfect haunt for a rake would be putting it more accurately," he correctly her lightly. But then his tone turned more serious. "I'm not ashamed, really, of my youthful excesses and shall not try to deny them. Life in London offered me all imaginable delights, and yet suddenly I felt so useless, Ursula. Aside from the time I spent in the Navy in '09, my life has had no meaning. In London all my desires could be satisfied almost at the instant in which they made themselves felt, but suddenly the one greatest desire of my life was to be useful in some serious way. I changed, Ursula, but my former companions thought it some sort of jest that would be short-lived. My reputation was such that I found I could not be entrusted with any of the serious matters to which I would gladly have set my mind. I feel quite sure that my will is strong enough to turn me from London temptations, but as things stand, London offers me nothing of worth with which to replace those temptations. Bermuda has few attractions for a London gentleman, and so it was not overdifficult to secure a commission for that island. I shall prove myself there, Ursula, and return to London when I may return as a new man."

She turned toward him and saw the intensity of his will pass swiftly over his brown-gold eyes as the moon sailed through the clouds overhead.

"I respect such resolution," she said, moved by his confidence. "But what crisis provoked such a change in direction?" Unconcerned as to whether her questioning might prove to be indiscreet, she persisted. "Surely one does not give up his old life without the promptings caused by some unexpected event . . ."

"You are right," he said, almost in surprise. Then, "Promise you will not laugh at me, Ursula," he said, half in jest but with a degree of earnest pleading that could not be disguised.

"I promise," she said, intrigued.

"It was a meeting with Sir Henry Halford that did it for me," he said, "though I hesitate to speak of such matters before a lady."

Ursula looked at him uncertainly, reluctant to press him if the subject matter was really one inappropriate for her ears.

"Sir Henry, as you may know, was the physician who opened the coffin that . . . Well, you do know, don't you, that when the Duchess of Brunswick was buried at Windsor, a coffin was found which was believed to contain the body of Charles I?"

"Yes," she said. "I had heard of it."

"It was Sir Henry who was called upon to examine the remains and, along with Prinny, to determine if the body was truly that of the late sovereign. Shall I continue?" he asked hesitantly.

"Please," she said, though her voice trembled a bit at the thought of the awful subject.

"Sir Henry was quite amazed and shaken by the matter. For as you know, the king was beheaded almost two hundred years ago. Yet within the coffin— and the wooden coffin itself was badly decayed—within he found a body wrapped in cere cloth. And within the cloth—Ursula, the king's face was quite recognizable, just as it appears in portraits. There could be no doubt. Sir Henry was confused at first because the head was quite firmly set upon the shoulders, as though the beheading had never taken place. But as he handled the head, it came quite off and even tumbled to the floor."

Ursula gasped with shock and disbelief, and the viscount placed an arm around her to steady her. "Shall I go on?" She nodded in assent.

"The head had been replaced on the body with cement," he said, "and over the years the cement had not preserved its strength. The cement didn't last, but the king's long, oval face and his pointed beard— these things were unchanged." He looked at her searchingly and continued. "It is hard to sort out the different emotions that passed through me upon hearing the story, but all of them pointed out to me the necessity of changing my way of life." He paused again. "I had never before really thought of death. In its indignity, that is. How does death for a young man come? In a romantic and illegal duel, perhaps, or a hero's death at war. I had never feared my end before. But when I heard of the king's head falling to the floor, something within me rebelled. I was angry at death, and that anger, making me put a greater value on my life, made me see for the first time that the pursuit of pleasure cannot be all we are intended to do with our limited days. I did not turn Puritan. Pleasure draws me as strongly as ever, and I shall not expend my energy in holding back. It's just that I now know there must be more. I thought about the king's beard, Ursula. That struck me so forcefully. . . . One hundred sixty-five years is not eternity, but to think that a man's beard had endured that long after death. If so insignificant an aspect of a man shall endure, what of his reputation, his acts, his works? I came to look upon my accidental meeting with Sir Henry as a warning. I hope you will not find my reasoning morbid. I tend to see my previous habits now in a morbid light—as the wanton waste of my time on earth."

Something in the way he was looking at her made Ursula abruptly aware that she was dressed in her nightclothes and had foolishly allowed herself to be put into a very compromising position.

"Call me Richard," he said suddenly.

As if hypnotized, she obeyed. "Richard . . ." she began, and then words of protest rose to her lips.

"Ursula, listen to me!" he cried, seizing her by the shoulders. "Our meeting has strengthened my resolve. Only three months ago I could not have dreamed of sharing the company of a young lady of quality. Only three months ago I never dreamed that a proper young lady could hold any interest or attraction for a rake like myself. And if it weren't for circumstances, for the fact that we shall soon be separated and that for us there can be nothing . . . if it weren't for all the obstacles between us, I doubt I should be so forward as to speak so freely. But, Ursula, you have shown me what is possible, and so I'm grateful to you. Someday, I pray, I shall find one like you and make her mine!"

A sob escaped from Ursula's coral lips. Had he no idea how he was tormenting her? He must have realized. She looked at him with anger. He had to be aware of her frightening attraction to him, and he responded by playing with her sentiments, tantalizing her with visions of what might have been.

No, she thought, he doesn't mean it at all. What can such a man know about love?

No, he wouldn't talk to me this way if we were free, she thought. It is only because he knows he cannot have me that he tends to think he might have wanted to . . .

"Let me go, Richard, please . . ." she managed to say.

"In a moment," he replied hoarsely, and very slowly, very gently, and oh-so-slowly so that her heart beat crazily and then stood absolutely still, he took his hands off her shoulders, and keeping her frozen where she stood by the powerful look in his eyes, he raised his hands to touch her cheeks lightly and tilted her face up to his. His lips were hot against her mouth and lingered there till it seemed each was living only by the other's breath.

"It will be dawn soon," were his first words when the kiss ended and she stood tingling and leaning slightly against him still. His fingers folded lightly a moment over her hand. "And much as I would love to watch the sunrise with you, it's best we not be seen together like this."

He was gone before she had recovered herself enough to cry, "How dare you?" or to slap him or to do or say any of the other things she had been brought up to believe appropriate under the circumstances. He was gone. And so there was nothing left for her to do but look once more upon the throbbing star she had earlier picked out in the sky. Now it was nothing but a pinpoint of distant light. How could it have seemed so violently bright before? Now it was as nothing, dwarfed and diminished, in comparison to the spasms of joy and of grief that tore her heart.

CHAPTER SIX

After several hours of restless tossing in her berth Ursula dressed and emerged again from her cabin. She fought against thoughts of Richard. How would he act when they met? Whatever would she say to him?

She soon spied her brother, not usually an early riser, strolling the deck in the company of Amelia. The girl from Halifax looked fresh as the morning. As for George, she noted that his eyes, usually veiled and languid, were filled with energy and pleasure. The animated voice that reached her ears, carried on the morning breeze, was filled with good cheer. Whatever had become of that cynical, lazy drawl?

Perhaps a man *can* change, she thought. But no, what am I thinking? she asked herself angrily. Her emotional dilemma seemed hopeless of resolution. For if Richard's words were sincere, then she was in danger of falling into an impossible love, one that could never be fulfilled. Surely it was better to go on believing that he was a liar and a scoundrel and that his kiss had been an insult and not an act of love.

But Ursula wanted to believe him in spite of herself.

At breakfast it was now George who toyed with his food, while Ursula had regained her appetite in spite of her nervous excitement. She was almost embarrassed at the eagerness with which she went to work on slice after slice of cold tongue and piece after piece of buttered toast. George broke out of his reverie from time to time and poured her more tea with a great deal of solicitude and an amused smile. Richard, who sat across from her, also regarded her with fond amusement. Pretending to be unaware of all these signs of affection, Ursula continued to eat and drink. She had passed the day before almost in a fast. Now she needed to satisfy her hunger and also to keep her mouth full so as to free her from conversation. She didn't trust herself to speak.

After the meal, much to her relief, Richard set off by himself, and Amelia made her excuses and returned to her cabin.

"It seems I have you to myself at last," said Ursula, taking her brother's arm. "I find myself in need of some disinterested but loving advice."

"Then you have addressed yourself to the right person," he replied promptly, and gave her plump arm a squeeze. He scanned her face quickly with a serious expression, and Ursula marveled once more over the change that had come over him.

"I believe I have," she said. "I do not wish to pry into your personal matters, but particularly at this moment I collect you are the best authority on the matter I have in mind—"

He raised his eyebrows quizzically. "You intrigue me, my dear. But then I always did love a woman of mystery."

"But I collect your tastes have changed," she said, and then continued hurriedly before he could protest. "George, do you believe a man can change—I mean profoundly change—his attitude toward life and particularly toward the role a woman plays in his life . . . ?"

She almost shrank back in surprise when George lifted her face, much as Richard had done, and studied the expression in her eyes intently. "That rakehell has been trifling with you," he pronounced in a voice that was cold and angry. "Darling Ursula, I should not give you a trimming should I think you were merely amusing yourself with the viscount. But I fancied you for better sense than some ignorant chit of a schoolgirl. What has passed between you? Hold nothing back, sister."

Ursula adjusted her long cambric sleeves and avoided his eyes while she felt her cheeks burning. "What has passed between us? George, how can you be so ragmannered as to talk to me as if I were some sort of light-skirt? What do you imagine has passed between us? How far do you think I would go to forget propriety and my own position?"

"What I think is that our friend the viscount has been making love to you with sweet words and practiced sighs."

Still finding it hard to lift her eyes, Ursula recounted in full the incident of the night before, only looking up to face her brother hesitantly when she had finished.

He shook his head and laughed bitterly. "Well, my advice is simple. Hold him to his words, my dear. Encourage him to find that other like you of whom he spoke. And pending her appearance, let him learn to keep his lips from yours."

She blushed so violently at these words that George studied her again with interest.

"Unless, of course," he said softly, "you are hungry for romance now. Just remember, it is safer to take lovers *after* marriage. But stroll the deck, my dear, with your knight in shining armour. Let him tell you how beautiful you are in the moonlight—"

"Since I shan't now play the lioness in Mayfair," she interrupted, "you suggest I make the most of that role aboard this ship."

"Yes," he said. "He is playing a game with you, Ursula. If you think it is more than that, you'll be dearly hurt. So, if you do not wish to give up his company, you must make up your mind to take it as a game. Of course, in every game there is a loser, and with his experience the odds are very much in the viscount's favour. But I can tell you from what I've learned at the gaming tables, my dear, a man may lose a few guineas at Brooks's, and that's good sport. But if he's not careful, he may throw away his life."

"I shall mind my losses then," she said, then added thoughtfully, "But really, George, do you find it so very inconceivable that his words were sincere?"

"Would you add to his titles then, sister?" he asked. "Viscount of Uxbridge, S.S.?"

"S.S.?"

"Sinner Saved." He laughed, but then, turning serious, George took her hands in his. "Ursula, consider carefully. I am sure you are thinking how simple it would be to act as though Lord Charles's offer never existed and to begin a life with our friend the viscount. But if any of the man's words were sincere, I'll warrant they were the words he spoke about wishing to find a new meaning in his life, to be useful. Because those are feelings I've sometimes had myself and can well understand." This confession took Ursula by surprise, but George continued before she could comment. "He needs to prove his worth by accepting this commission in Bermuda. If he really sees this appointment as his great chance, do you truly think he would risk falling out of favor with Lord Charles and ruining it all for a bit of muslin? For that's all you are to him."

"Yes," she agreed quietly, "that is very much the way he explained it himself." She followed this capitulation to reality by looking up instinctively at the sky, as if expecting last night's moon to be there, bearing witness to the beauty and truth of what had happened. Instead, she saw the white, scudding clouds being blown off toward the horizon, while darker clouds loomed overhead, pushing the blue patches of sky farther and farther away. The sun was hidden, and the morning breeze turned to a cold, brisk wind that filled the sails.

"There's going to be a storm," she said, choking back tears. "I think I'd best go below." She turned but then looked back at her brother. "Thank you," she whispered as the tears began to well up in her eyes, which had turned a deep violet, darkening even as suddenly as did the sky.

The storm soon broke, and Ursula, wretchedly sick in the cabin, forgot her other problems.

It will be impossible to sleep tonight, she thought, even if the weather turns calm. She shuddered to wonder how long the terrible stench of sickness would endure belowdecks. The ventilation of the vessel would not, she thought, manage to dispel so much noxious air quickly.

She refused an offer of dinner served below as it was impossible so much as to think of food without gagging. But by suppertime the *Fortitude* was all but becalmed on tranquil seas.

Like the other passengers, Ursula was eager to appear for the evening meal and had the same thought as the others: to dress gaily and richly in order to celebrate their safe passage through the first rough seas. She had little to choose from in the way of gowns and had to settle for another old-fashioned sprig muslin, but she decked herself out in her mother's sapphires and tried to do her hair in Grecian curls. It would have been difficult to arrange without assistance even under the best of circumstances, but Ursula had a real battle on her hands. Armed only with hairpins and combs, she struggled against the rolling of the ship and the strong unruliness of her hair, which believed its own natural and lazy waves were preferable to any imposed by artifice.

The company assembled in the dining saloon, and Ursula could not suppress her admiration at the sight of Richard in his formal attire. He had dressed as for a private party among the most discriminating company, from the striped silk stockings up to black pantaloons, white waistcoat, and perfectly cutaway blue coat.

The diners at first took the same pose of superficial frivolity that had characterized their previous meal-time meetings. But over boiled cod and roast fowl the conversation took a sudden turn for the serious when the captain learned of the viscount's mission in Bermuda.

"So ye'll be assistin' that rotten land rat, will ye?" he asked, leaving behind the veneer of fine manners with which he had overlaid his speech until that moment. "Ye'll forgive me the rough talk of a sea dog, I trust, but that gentleman . . . those of us wot makes voyages Bermuda way calls him not Lord Charles but Lord Constipation. Seein' as how His Royal Majesty did give'm his seat five months ago, and he's yet to *do* anything."

Amelia could not help but break into laughter at this crude but quaint construction, while Ursula felt herself grow cold and pale. She had known full well she did not—could not—love Lord Charles. It was still a shock to hear such unflattering terms used to describe the man her guardians would have had her marry.

"Do go on," said Richard calmly with a meaning-ful glance at Ursula. "Your word will doubtless help me understand my duty."

"Well, it's the privateers, Yer Lordship, sur, as wot's been the bother and the trouble, d'ye see? I don't wish to alarm any of ye, but it's been a dangerous trade,

75

plying Bermuda waters. See, the king commissions these Bermuda sloops there to engage in acts of piracy. There be no nicer word for it. The idea being this piracy is to be directed against the Frenchies and the Yankees. But our friends in Bermuda get theirselves carried away more with greed than with patriotism, if ye'll accept my word, sur. They wouldn't dare attack a fifty-four-gun ship like this one be, but plenty of English shippin' be attacked by the privateers. And then there's the coastal folks, puttin' false lights on the rocks to lure ships onto the reefs. Ship run aground, the good Bermudians come swarmin' aboard for plunder while another ship is left to sink. Let 'em do it to the enemy, I says, but wot of us? And it was this Lord Charles who was to put an end to the marauding like, and instead, he sets himself up on his hill and abandons hisself to luxury."

Perhaps the situation is not as bad as it began to seem, thought Ursula at the word "luxury." Perhaps what we are hearing is simply the understandable hostility of a hardworking sailor for a rich and titled gentleman.

But the captain had not finished speaking. "Luxury, I tell ye. I been a seaman all me life. And I warn't born cap'n. I've swabbed the decks meself, ye see, and I'm grateful for me lot, to be where I be today. But I reckon I know well enough wot sort o' life the sailor leads ashore. I been in me fights and tasted me rum and sampled me share of women in port, beggin' yer pardon, ladies," he added in an aside. "So ye needn't think I be some Methody churchman or such wot tells ye this. But I be ashamed to tell ye all that Lord Constipation do fer his pleasures. There be not a woman or young boy either, beggin' yer pardon, ladies, that can be let near him without his havin' his way. ... Yea, he be a bad one, one wot drove his poor dear wife to her death, and a kind lady she was, I tell ye, though she looked many years more than her age when his excesses drove her six feet under."

"I think we have had enough," said Richard abruptly.

"No," said Ursula. "This is most interesting. Pray continue."

But the captain adamantly refused to add any further intelligence. "I've said more'n is fittin' fer ladies' ears a'ready," he insisted.

"An ugly tale," was Crandall's opinion, but he raised his goblet to the viscount. "You'll soon set matters to rights I trust."

"I trust," repeated Richard without enthusiasm.

Ursula was brushing out her curls before the small glass that was built right into the wall of her cabin.

"Ursula? May I see you?"

It was Richard at the door. When she released the bolt, he entered the room and closed the door behind him.

"We can talk outside," she suggested in a shaken voice.

"Don't be prim," he replied, overriding her objection. "I don't want any interruption." He looked about for a place to sit and, seeing only the bed, remained standing. He held his hands clasped behind him in an attitude that would have looked pompous in another individual.

"I wanted to talk to you alone," he said, stating the obvious. "I've been pacing about on the deck since dinner, trying to decide what I must do. My mind is made up."

She watched him hesitantly from the other side of the room.

"Oh, do sit down, will you?" he demanded. "I'm

77

nervous enough without your making me more so."

"The Viscount of Uxbridge? Nervous?" she asked in genuine surprise.

"Yes. So please sit down. I'm not going to jump on you, Ursula."

He speaks a little too freely to me, she told herself. And yet she had to admit she much preferred talking to Uxbridge, with whom she could be quite frank, compared to all the other young men she had known. Engaging in conversation with gentlemen had always seemed like reciting lines from a play. With Uxbridge, even when she distrusted him, she felt she could be herself, Ursula Manning, and need not play the role convention demanded. She silently settled herself upon the bunk.

"I've been in a turmoil since we met," he stated baldly. "I needn't tell you that you are beautiful. You are, of course, but I've known many beautiful women. A pretty face, an exquisite form . . . it takes more than that to turn my head. But I was convinced, Ursula, that ladies of quality were all alike. I told myself a lady of quality has manners rather than feelings. A lady of quality is carefully taught so that she can react in any situation without ever needing to make recourse to her brain. A lady of quality may know how to scheme, but never how to think. When I met you, I saw I was wrong."

"Richard, please don't go on," she said weakly.

"Oh, but I must. You know my reputation, Ursula. You know what I've been. And I hope you believe my desire to change is sincere. So imagine my consternation. No sooner had I vowed to dedicate myself to new values—to responsibility, to service—than I met the person for whose sake I longed to throw my new responsibilities away."

Ursula stared at the floor, shaking her head, and so

she did not see him approach and sit beside her. She looked into his eyes with alarm when he took her hand.

"I love you, Ursula," he said. "But I put my duty to Lord Charles ahead of that love. I thought I should have to be loyal to him and turn away from all the happiness I was sure we could find together."

She dared not believe her ears. Surely she was dreaming or being deceived. How could she accept such a declaration? Should she begin to think for a moment that any of this was truly happening, reality would surely soon deal her a blow from which she would not easily recover.

"You heard tonight what sort of man Lord Charles is. How can I choose him over you? What kind of obligation can bind me to such a monster?" he demanded.

"If he is really so bad, you are needed in Bermuda, Richard," she urged.

"But not as his assistant, Ursula. Do you really think I should be able to accomplish anything working under his authority? No, I am sorry for the people who must rely on him; but for myself I rejoice to learn what manner of man he is. Otherwise, I should never have dared. I shouldn't have known the right course to take. No, I am not needed in Bermuda, to join the old man in his drinking and wenching. I am needed by you. And you by me," he insisted. "I shall prove my worth in Halifax, or if not, we shall back to England. But together. I love you, Ursula!" He dropped gracefully to his knees, never letting go of her trembling hand. "Marry me and be my wife," he whispered.

"Richard . . ." She shook her head in confusion, and he rose again from his knees and called another weapon into service for his cause.

"Ursula," he said in a voice that was almost a moan, "its' not safe for us to be alone together here."

His lips sought hers and then moved to her throat. His hands upon her shoulders pinned her down and caressed her gently at the same time. "Say yes, my darling, and then I shall go."

I don't want him to go, she realized, as she was flooded with sweet sensations. Now she withheld her consent, not out of doubt, but rather to prolong the breathless pleasure of their kisses. But though she did not speak, her impassioned response told him clearly that Ursula was his.

"Yes," he said, triumphant, and stood to leave.

She reached out to him, and their hands twined together briefly before she looked into his eyes and whispered, "Yes," drowning in love and in disbelief.

CHAPTER SEVEN

Josiah Crandall had never seen anything like it. He was part owner of the *Fortitude* and had plumed himself on its guns and military capability. Suddenly the ship had been transformed from an almost-bellicose vessel into something very like the Assembly Rooms he had visited at Bath. But at the subscription dances there his daughter had been singularly unimpressed by the gallant young Englishmen and had amused him—but also distressed him—by her caustic remarks. On board the *Fortitude,* however, Amelia had not held herself quite so aloof but rather had apparently allowed herself to be swept away with a romantic passion for a young man with no money or family to recommend himself. And she had become a bosom-bow of her admirer's sister, a beautiful young Englishwoman who was disporting herself just as openly with a viscount.

Actually "disporting" was too strong a word. Crandall was old-fashioned, but he always believed in being fair. It wasn't that the young people did anything improper, he had to admit to himself. It was simply that the obvious delight they took in each other's company was downright erotic to his practical eyes. He felt uncomfortable and unsure of himself in the midst of such radiant and blooming love.

And when he allowed himself to consider how much more he would have welcomed the situation had Amelia fallen instead for the wealthy viscount, his fairness forced him to concede that Ursula could not very well fall in love with her brother, and things were most equitably left as they were.

As the days passed, he existed on the periphery of a

81

world of long strolls on deck, intense conversations, and hours spent watching the sun rise and the sun set. Every sky was new and perfect; every sigh was the first a lover ever breathed. He thought back to the days when he and Amelia's mother had first met. "How beautiful she was!" he found himself exclaiming aloud. The lady had been dead many years, but suddenly those long-gone days no longer seemed so very lost and distant.

Eventually the merchant was drawn into the magic circle of enchantment. In his fancy, which was released from the bonds of practicality by the witnessing of so much joy, Crandall often smelled the perfume of roses rising over the stale air of the hold. Impossible! he told himself, and breathed deeply, enjoying the fragrance, though he knew it was only in his mind. And at last he was so carried away with enthusiastic approval for the young lovers that he withdrew his violin from its case and carried it to the galleries in the stern. To Josiah Crandall the purpose of music had always been discipline. He was a man who had been urged to practice his instrument from an early age by parents who were more interested in developing perseverance and precision in their son than in awakening an artistic bent or a love of beauty. But now Crandall learned to put his skill to a better use as he played minuets and gavottes for the lovers to dance to. Throwing all parental sense of propriety to the winds, he even attempted to provide a waltz, but he was not familiar with the piece and soon put it aside. In any case, he thought in agitation, it was not right for him to drive his daughter quite literally into the arms of a man they scarcely knew.

The merchant's perplexity surfaced most at mealtimes.

"Halifax is my home," he would say in puzzlement,

"and I've spent most of my life there. Fine little town, but not the sort of place they write romantic ballads about, if you get my drift."

George solemnly replied, "Mr. Crandall, I'm a man of no distinction. Halifax is a land of opportunity, and I intend to carve myself a name and a place."

"There are many places where a fortune can be made more easily than in Halifax," the merchant pointed out quite reasonably, and was flustered beyond all measure when the young man looked him straight in the eye and replied, "If I am to make a success, I would it should be done before the eyes of those whose good opinion I most cherish."

"And you, sir," he said to Uxbridge, "you'll find Halifax little more than a primitive backwater."

The Viscount of Uxbridge heard the words, but his only reply was a smile.

These young people act fast, thought Crandall to himself. He did not know that Richard and Ursula had good reason for staying away from Bermuda, and so he silently wondered how an English lord could be so irresponsible as to throw over a commission awaiting him in order to run off and be married. Perhaps it's all for the best that he had no eyes for Amelia, he concluded, for he seems a man of passing fancies and sudden enthusiasms, hardly as firm and steady a partner as I would wish to see her joined with for life.

The lovers took advantage of the fair weather and the utter lack of society, entertainment, or responsibilities aboard the ship. They had nothing to do but fall back on each other's company, and they did so with pleasure.

"I think this is the only haven I shall ever seek!" exclaimed Ursula, held tight in Richard's arms. "Oh, do look at that sunset!" she added, glorying in the sight of the sky, in which a soft mother of-pearl glow was slowly deepening to an almost unnaturally bright pink.

In his dealings with women Richard had never known anything like the feeling inspired in him by this girl he would soon wed. For while he ached to possess her warm and supple body, to join with her in total union, the self-restraint imposed upon him was quite without pain as long as he was with her. As long as he could look into her eyes, touch her hand, and hear her soft voice, as long as she could lay her head so trustingly on his shoulder and he could run his fingers through her hair, his happiness was complete. It was only when he was lying alone in his narrow berth that he longed for her violently, to hear her breathing close beside him, to teach her love, and to hold her trembling and warm all night.

As for Ursula, her words that she sought no other harbour reflected the dread with which she faced their actual arrival. The days of love on board the *Fortitude* seemed to fly by in the space of minutes and yet seemed to fill an eternity. She was happier than she'd ever imagined possible, but still, she feared the journey's end, because deep inside, Ursula could not believe her good fortune could be true. Although she spoke brightly and with optimism about life in Halifax, she could not shake off an insinuating doubt that the future there would never come to pass. Something would go amiss; she was certain that something was wrong. And so each time she surrendered her warm lips to Richard's, she kissed him as though this kiss, the memory of this kiss, would have to sustain her for the rest of her life. So fearful was she of trouble ahead that had Richard chosen to press his advantage, she surely would have yielded to his importunities.

Ah, but port was still far off! And until then she had a world encompassed within two strong arms.

She had the fullness of love, and she had kisses more dizzying than the captain's headiest wines.

One night at supper the captain's claret mounted too quickly to Josiah Crandall's usually abstemious head.

"I suppose it's all very well for you gentlemen of noble blood," said the man, more with curiosity than with malice, "but a man like myself, I wasn't brought up to change course so lightly. 'Tis strange to see the flower of noble English youth put love so high above duty, yet I suppose it's for the best. After all, should you always put duty ahead of love, how would our future peers come to be born?" He belched.

Richard politely ignored the belch but was not able to keep the man's words from reaching his heart.

" 'Tis not to be your critic, please understand, Your Lordship." Drink had loosened Crandall's tongue. "But the administration of the kingdom depends on you. And those like you, of course. We cannot expect the King, even if he weren't mad as a coot, to oversee what passes in all the far-flung regions of the world, from India to the West Indies. So what I am asking, Your Lordship, is in what way you reconcile your decision to jump ship, as it were, with your duty?"

"I'm not one of your responsible nobles, dear friend," replied Richard, hiding his feelings and trying to make light of the matter since he did not wish to reveal the complete state of affairs that had prompted his decision. "I am a London rake and a dandy. I won my commission to Bermuda at the gaming tables. Any man who would appoint me to do an honest administrator's work was taking a gamble he must have known he was doomed to lose."

Josiah Crandall sputtered to hear such frank speech, not guessing it was sheer dissimulation, and he poured himself another glass.

Ursula's eyes clouded, and she shivered with a premonition. Why would Richard demean himself this way?

As he set the bottle back upon the table, Crandall's hand shook, and he upset his glass. Amelia quickly put the glass upright, though not quickly enough to prevent a spill, and gave everyone a look that beseeched indulgence for her father.

"No harm done," the captain laughed, but considering the number of shares in the enterprise owned by Mr. Crandall, that good seaman would have said the same thing even if great harm *had* been done.

George gave Amelia's hand a reassuring squeeze, and Ursula looked toward her own suitor. He reached a hand toward her, and she saw that the spilled claret had been soaked up by his shirt cuffs. She knew it was only wine, but rational thinking was of no help in her agitated state of mind. She fought against an ever-growing feeling of despair, her eyes fixed on the cuffs where the stains on the Dresden lace were red and thick like blood.

Later that night, as she took her customary stroll along the deck with Richard, Ursula could not keep from shivering with apprehension.

"I'm frightened," she told him, trying to explain. "And I can't even say of what. I don't know, just as I cannot tell you all the reasons why I love you. How does one explain it? The feeling exists, and that's all that can be said."

The light in her eyes had turned opaque, Richard noticed, as in the sea before a storm. Was some turbulent scene about to trouble the understanding he enjoyed with his beloved? Had the magic gone already? The sun disappears from view at times, he reminded himself, but always reappears. Was it possible that the pure, clear days of their happiness were really reaching an end?

Richard was troubled, too. Crandall's jug-stung

words had spoken too directly to his own conflicting feelings, and he had hoped to regain his high spirits in Ursula's company. So why had she chosen this particular night to be so distant and agitated? He put his arms around her, as he had done so many times, but she stiffened.

"Forgive me, darling," she said. "I suppose I need some solitude. I need to be alone and to think." She tried to make light of her distress. "It's all your own fault, you see, for choosing a woman with a brain. So let me descend to my cabin for a while. My spirits are just in such terrible disrepair."

"Then let me comfort you," he urged, but she kissed him gently and left him alone on the deck.

Richard seemed a changed man as he stalked the decks. Days passed in the sunlight had flecked his brown hair with gold, and he had seldom been seen without a smile on his face. But now, under the bleak and starless night, his was a dark figure that paced to and fro, and the expression that disfigured his handsome face could only be described as a brooding scowl. It was not only Ursula's unaccountable behavior that had destroyed his mood; Josiah Crandall's criticism had cut him to the quick.

Such was his humor as he approached the forepart of the deck where he had first opened his heart and kissed the woman he loved. This night, instead of finding Ursula clad only in her wrapper and gazing at the stars, he came across a group of sailors hidden behind a barrier of tightly rolled hammocks and passing around a bottle of Jamaica rum.

"Have you a bottle to spare?" he enquired, surprising the men. "I've a guinea if you do."

"Nay, sur," replied one of their number who seemed somewhat in better control of his tongue than the rest. "We dinna ask yer money, but come 'n' join us in a sip if ee've a mind." So saying he took the bottle from the drooping hand of one of his companions and passed it up to the melancholy viscount.

Richard took the bottle without a word and drank deeply. Then, squatting down among the men, he passed it on and spoke. "Thank you," he said, "from the bottom of my heart."

"That be all right," replied his host, "long as 'tis not the bottom o' the bottle." Laughing at his own humour, the sailor spat noisily on the deck.

Soon another bottle was making the rounds, and then another. The sweet and fiery liquor was potent, but to Richard's dismay it did not serve to ease his mind or put distressful thoughts from him. "You're a quiet lot," he observed. "I thought you'd be taking your pleasure with song and laughter."

"Nay, sur," said the sailor, who had taken the role of spokesman for the group. "When we be ashore, that be one thing, d'ye see? Thar, whar thar be women and places of distraction to delight a man, we can be festive enough, sur. But here aboard, when one must take his drink on the sly, like, and with no pleasure or comfort in sight, the rum—'tis no matter how good nor how strong—put a man in mind of his family and put him in a sad state o' mind."

"What? Are you all married then?" asked Richard.

"Aye, sur, all but he," came the reply, and the sailor pointed to a comrade who looked no more than fifteen years old and badly marked by the small-pox. "And he be thinkin' most likely on his mother. Ye look surprised, sur, to hear we be husbands," ventured the sailor.

Richard laughed, perhaps more freely than he intended what with the strong drink's having an especially powerful effect on him owing to his lowered spirits. "I should think you are a hardy lot, that any one of you might risk his freedom for the sake of a good brawl. Yet I'm surprised you all voluntarily made yourself prisoners bound by chains of muslin."

"Come, sur, it's to break the chain of muslin that many of us put to sea."

Richard laughed along with the men. "Ah, women!" he exclaimed. In his more profligate days he had often had recourse to low company, and now, surrounded by sailors far beneath him in class, he automatically reverted to the kind of talk that had previously been his staple conversation when the subject of the fair sex came up. It was not that he meant to be dishonest or that he felt disrespect for his companions. Rather, he was buoyed up by their comradeship and easily fell in with their way of talk. And so he talked on, recounting adventures from days past with ladies of easy virtue.

Unbeknownst to him Ursula had appeared on deck, drawn to this very location by her memories of their chance meeting almost a fortnight previous. She had bitterly repented of her irrational coolness and had left her cabin in search of Richard, eager to make everything aright as quickly as possible. Now she stood unnoticed behind the very barrier erected by the sea dogs to ensure their own privacy. Her eyebrows drew together in incomprehension as she listened to her lover's speech.

"Wot, sur?" enquired a deckhand. "Then will ye ne'er take a wife?"

"I'll take a wife any time of day or night"—Richard laughed—"and willingly, long as she be someone else's wife and not my own."

Ursula's hand flew to her throat. She remained unobserved; her cry of shocked anguish was drowned out by the sounds of general merriment.

"But speaking true, sur," interrupted the sailor, taking great liberties of speech in his firm belief that nothing equalizes men so effectively as a shared bottle of Jamaica, "that can hardly be yer attitude to the lady with the violet eyes."

"And who says I'm to marry her?" replied Richard, gaining some consciousness of his surroundings and unwilling to discuss Ursula with this crew. "After what I've learned of women, should I be such a fool?" Rum might make equals of a gang of drunken sailors and a viscount in his cups, but there was no reason to bring Ursula's name into the conversation. He quickly resumed his account of exploits among the Fashionable Impures of London.

The sailors, who had bitterly criticized and mocked their own dearly loved families—for such was the custom among their sort of men and all knew to pay such talk no mind—all understood that Richard's dismissing remark about marriage, brutal as it seemed, was actually rooted in delicacy, in an unwillingness to sully his real feelings by too much common exposure.

"Aye, we well understan' yer thinkin', sur," said a rough, voice. "But does she?"

He pointed a work-hardened finger. The merry crew all turned to see Ursula standing like a ghost.

"What are you doing here?" demanded Richard as he struggled to his feet.

"Don't mind 'im, miss," she heard. " 'e's jug-stung an' don't know 'is mind."

"You can dress 'en like a prince, but a man's a man," came additional commentary from the crew.

"We're going below," said Richard.

"That's right," cried a voice, offering an unsolicited opinion. "Stow 'er below fer private use, and devil take the rest o' us."

Richard swung around in a fury but then decided the only course of action was to get Ursula away from the drunken men immediately. He grabbed her shoulders and tried to lift her in his arms, quite forgetting that he looked no more reputable than his companions.

Ursula shrank from him in horror, and when he let go of her, she drew herself up in a proud shell that hid the devastation within.

"I'm not the woman you thought me," she said coldly.

"Ursula!" He realized at once that she had misconstrued his attempt to carry her away. "I was not going to . . ." he began, but she cut him off.

"To do what? To take advantage of me? You have already taken advantage of my credulity," she declared. "You claimed to respect my intelligence. But if I had a brain in my poor skull, I never should have believed a word you said."

Was this possible? she thought. Could it be that so much happiness could turn to gall so quickly?

She turned and fled. Richard followed, but while the rolling of the ship impeded their speed, he suffered an additional disadvantage owing to the quantity of rum he had lately consumed. Ursula reached the safety of her cabin without being overtaken.

"Let me in!" Richard cried drunkenly, knocking at her door.

Ursula sat on her bunk and held her pillow to her, soaking it with tears, until there was silence outside her door once more. Richard had either gone away or fallen unconscious with drink. Everything was over. Exhausted and in despair, she fell into the void of sleep.

CHAPTER EIGHT

In the morning Ursula did not appear for breakfast. When Richard hastened downstairs to her cabin, she would not see him. And when George was granted admittance, he found his sister sitting stiffly in her berth with an icy and determined look on her beautiful face.

"I have decided to go to Bermuda after all," she informed him brusquely. She plunged ahead with her story before she should dissolve into tears with too much left unsaid. "You were right all along, George," she conceded.

Yes, George had been right about everything. Love was an illusion, a heartless trap set for the gullible. The trap was hidden behind the unnerving sensations of fresh-awakened passion and baited with nothing but empty promises.

"Richard was playing a dangerous game with me."

She shuddered, wondering what her fate would have been if she had not found out in time.

"Are you quite sure?" he demanded. "I allow I was suspicious at first, but in the last week he has had me convinced. . . ."

"He made it clear last night," she said with finality. "Richard had no intention of marrying me, although I have no idea what he did intend to do—abandon me in Halifax, or press me to join him in some . . . some irregular arrangement."

"Very well. So you're not going to marry Uxbridge," said George, still confused. "But that doesn't mean you must give yourself to Wickenham."

"Why not?" she asked. "I thought you told me love was an illusion."

"That may be or no," he replied, "but disgust and loathing are no illusion. Dearest sister, if you bind yourself to a man you loathe, you will end by loathing yourself and your very life. Yes, I'll warrant there is many a good marriage that has made man and wife perfectly happy and yet was not founded on love. But the case of Wickenham is another extreme altogether."

"I know that," she said softly, touching his hand. "And if Wickenham is what he is said to be, I shall not marry him. But I'd just as well go there and see for myself. I cannot think of any place else to go."

"But you do have a place to go," insisted George. "Dash it, you can still disembark at Halifax with me."

"No," she said. "George, don't you see? You cannot trust Uxbridge. He says now he has a position for you and will help you get settled. But you cannot believe what he tells you. If you go to Halifax alone, George, you stand a chance. You'll make your way, I'm sure of it. Perhaps Mr. Crandall will help . . ."

"And if that's so, why shouldn't I earn your way as well?"

"I'm thinking of you, George," she said. "Of you and Amelia. Your position in her father's eyes will hardly be enhanced by my presence. Consider the viscount's reputation, not to mention the privacy he and I have enjoyed."

"Ursula!" he exclaimed. "You didn't . . . ?" And hitting his forehead, "How could I have been so negligent?" he cried.

"No, no, of course not," she hastened to assure him. "But our circumstances will leave little doubt in scandalmongering minds. If I go to Halifax with you, I shall be looked on as a foolish, pitiful, fallen woman." She paused shyly. "I am happy for you, George, and I refuse, categorically, to do anything that might ruin your chances with Amelia."

93

"If you persist in this nonsense, that's exactly what you will end by doing," he exploded. "You don't think for a moment that I shall let you go off to Bermuda on your own. If Richard is the scoundrel you now claim him to be, you are not going to travel alone with him. And I will do everything in my power to keep you from throwing yourself away on Wickenham. Understand me, sister. Amelia leaves the ship at Halifax, but if you will not disembark as well, I shall have to say good-bye to her and continue south with you."

"There is no reason to make all three of us miserable," she argued.

"Ursula, Ursula!" he cried in exasperation. "There's no use your arguing with me any more than there's any use my arguing with you. Either you leave the ship with me at Halifax, or I shall leave with you at St. George's. Remember, you shall bear the burden of all our ruined lives, and not just your own, if you persist in this folly."

With these words George rose and walked out without a backward glance. He did not abandon hope, however, of inducing his sister to change her stubborn decision but dispatched an emissary, who was shortly knocking on the door.

When Ursula admitted Amelia into the cabin, she noted at once that her friend's demeanour was subdued, though she had not lost her unabashed candour.

"Ursula!" she cried. "I cannot conceive what maggot you have taken into your head!"

Ursula smiled wryly. She felt herself living on another plane of existence altogether, one in which her own painful problems could not reach or vex her. "Your father would not approve to hear you use cant terms like that with such facility," she commented with detached amusement.

"I can see why we are friends." Amelia sighed. "You are quite as impossible and intolerable as I am."

"Amelia," said Ursula with a sudden access of sympathy for the other girl, "believe me, I don't wish George to follow me to Bermuda. I shall do everything in my power to see that he leaves the ship with you."

Amelia laughed so heartily at this declaration that Ursula was given pause, wondering if they all were not in the throes of lunacy.

"Really, Ursula," she said at last, catching her breath, "women are simply never, never, never satisfied. I do mean *never*. I assure you, we create our own predicaments. Take my example if you will. Your brother is pretty, and your brother is charming, but I shouldn't love him for that." At these words she caught herself and blushed. "Well, I've just about said it, but it was no secret, so why blush? Yes, I love George . . . because he is the sort of man who is capable of setting his own happiness to one side and selflessly following his pigheaded sister to Bermuda."

"Please be careful," cautioned Ursula. "My brother is a chattering coxcomb! If you love him for his selflessness, you may be sorely disillusioned."

"Oh, how can you speak that way! I imagine you are so in the habit of loving your brother that you have quite forgotten how to *appreciate* him. But just consider what I am doing to myself," Amelia complained, "working at cross-purposes all in the solitude of my poor, befuddled mind. You see, if George follows me and abandons you to your fate, I shall directly cease to love him. And should he accompany you to Bermuda, my passion will flare anew, but at the same time I lose him. You are most wicked to arrange things this way."

"What else am I to do?" asked Ursula. "Pray don't blame your poor, befuddled mind on me."

"Why, it's clear. George has told me everything, and I don't see why you are making such a hobble of it. You're not in the briars at all, really, you're not. Come with us, Ursula. You are welcome to stay in my family's house until you can see a way out of your predicament. There's ample room, and I should love to have you with me. And Halifax is a growing town. We'll find a place for you there soon enough. Though if you prefer to stay on with me and later with me and George . . . why, I've said quite enough!"

"Has your father consented to the match?" asked Ursula.

"Why, no, but in time . . ."

"In time he will like the idea even less should he find himself in the position of billeting two portionless wanderers without family or connections. . . . No, Amelia. Once I'm settled in Bermuda, George will find his way back to you. At least, so I fervently hope. But I honestly fear that should my brother and I accept your offer of hospitality, your father's limited enthusiasm for a wedding will diminish day by day."

"My father is quite right about me, I see," said Amelia, standing and sighing. "My solitary future becomes evident. Not only does my dearly beloved suitor think nothing of leaving me, but even his sister rejects me. Ursula, have you no weak spot in your heart that I can touch to prevail upon you?"

"The Viscount of Uxbridge found the weak spots easily enough," replied Ursula with some bitterness. "But I have since rooted them out. So abandon hope, dear friend," she added with mock melodrama. "My mind is firm and my resolution taken."

"Insufferable!" exclaimed Amelia.

The two girls looked into each other's faces a moment, and both pairs of eyes mirrored identical affection, frustration, and despair.

If she says another word, I shall give in, thought Ursula. But Amelia sighed again and marched out, allowing the cabin door to slam indecorously behind her. Ursula's moment of regret was short-lived. Of course, I seek a means of escape, she concluded, but my better judgment tells me I must on to Bermuda. And that is what I shall do.

She rose and went to the door, locking it again, and just in time. For a minute later Richard was knocking and beseeching that she let him explain.

She did not open to him. Although she had assured Amelia there were no soft spots left in her heart, Ursula knew better, and she feared the persuasive force of Richard's words.

It's not that he's such an accomplished liar, she told herself. The danger is that I so badly *want* to believe him.

"There is nothing to be said," she insisted, and then ignored him as best she could until he gave up his attempts to communicate through the heavy wooden door.

And so overnight everything aboard the ship changed. The *Fortitude* was no longer a fairyboat floating down an enchanted river in a world of love. The young people were all at cross-purposes and in dissension, but all shared in common the feeling of being cast into the doldrums and beset by blue devils.

Josiah Crandall, on the other hand, was delighted to hear his traveling companions were not abandoning passage to Bermuda after all. His daughter's romance had been much too sudden for his liking. And unaware of the reasons for the changed plans, he clapped Richard on the back jovially as they met at the captain's table for dinner.

"Im really awfully glad, Your Lordship," he said. "I believed all along there had to be a way of recon-

97

ciling love and duty. No reason to shirk your responsibilities just because you want to tie the nuptial knot, after all."

Richard nodded his head graciously. Except for a momentary flicker of his left eyelid his countenance gave Crandall no cause to suspect that anything might be amiss.

With the change in spirits of the passengers the winds also seemed to change. First they died down altogether and left the ship at a near standstill, and then they turned wild and blustery as if with anger and frustration. And like much of the frustration that was experienced among the ship's passengers, the rage of the winds was as directionless as it was turbulent. By nightfall the crew was as physically exhausted as the passengers were spirit-weary.

Ursula retired for the night with a volume borrowed from the captain's library: *A Plaine Description of the Barmudas*. She hoped to glean some information about her future home, but her mind was not on the pages. She had retained only the fact that there were hundreds of islands in the chain when a sudden draught extinguished her lamp. The ship rocked violently.

I shall have to tie myself into bed to keep from being thrown, she thought in wonderment. It was almost inconceivable that so large a vessel as the *Fortitude* could be thrown about in so extreme a fashion. The ship pitched again, and Ursula was thrown to the floor.

She huddled against the cabin wall, bracing herself against its steadiness. Suddenly there was a deafening crash. The *Fortitude* lurched again and sent the girl spilling across her small, cramped quarters. To her surprise Ursula was more intrigued than frightened. She hugged herself and then clapped her hands over her ears as thunder pealed again amid flashes of light. What will happen if lightning strikes the mast? she wondered.

I can't be alone now, she thought. I just can't bear it. On her knees, hugging the planks of the cabin floor, she began to make her way out. She unlocked her door, but at that moment the ship seemed to roll on its side. Ursula kept herself from falling backwards by clutching the handle of the door, but in this position, fighting gravity, she could not push the door open. Just as abruptly the ship listed to the other side, and Ursula went flying out of her cabin.

"What are you doing?" cried a voice. In another moment Ursula had gone tumbling again, into a collision with the person she least wanted to encounter. "Where are you going?" he demanded as they were thrown together on the floor. She was only too aware of the bruising crush as his body was flung against hers. "Get back to your cabin," Richard ordered her. "We're under fire."

He loomed above her, and Ursula could not tell if this was the result of the pitching of the ship or whether he was purposely trying to shield her from harm.

"Where are you going?" she managed to ask.

"Above decks to help in whatever way I can."

And then she was thrown back into her cabin. Had Richard shoved her so roughly or was it only due to their uncertain balance that she had been deposited in a stunned heap on the cabin floor?

I hope George stays below, she thought fervently. What does he know of fighting? As she desperately prayed for her brother's safety, she added a few prayers for the viscount as well, though she told herself that her concern was only a matter of proper charity.

When the shelling ended, it was like slipping into a pleasant dream following the rigors and heart-stopping terror of a nightmare. Never had the sea seemed so calm, nor the *Fortitude* more like a well-loved home.

The captain and Josiah Crandall earnestly discussed the terrors of the night over hot rum toddies, which had replaced the accustomed chocolate on this particular morn. Crandall was proud of the guns that had enabled the *Fortitude* to put up strong resistance and prevent capture. The captain, on the other hand, decried the military appurtenances of the vessel. "In the stormy`night," he maintained, "the Yankees took us for a man-o'-war. If we'd looked more like the merchantman we be, I reckon they ne'er would've raked our sides with fire."

The engagement had not lasted long. The turbulence of the weather had discouraged a true fight, and only because the two ships had passed so close in the storm was some sort of warlike exchange rendered inevitable. The *Fortitude* had sustained little damage. Although one yard had been almost totally destroyed, the reserve mizzen spar was easily put into service to replace it.

Because of the energy—both physical and emotional—that had been expended during the night, the passengers were almost drained of feeling by the time the vessel reached Halifax the next day.

To the surprise of everyone, not least himself, Josiah Crandall invited the Mannings, and Richard as well, to sup and spend the night at his house in order to enjoy some time ashore before embarking again the following day.

"Please don't go to such trouble on our behalf," protested George not too forcefully.

"No trouble," insisted Crandall. "I shall be busy all day watching the cargo unloaded, and so it will be entirely up to Amelia to entertain you. I have no objections if she voices none."

Predictably enough, Amelia did not.

Ursula had been about to make a feeble excuse but was forestalled by Richard's decision to remain aboard the ship and by Amelia's direct positive action. Like a dark-haired whirlwind, Amelia flew down the ladders to Ursula's cabin and packed a bandbox full of overnight articles.

"Here's a change of clothes," she announced, handing Ursula her box, "so prepare to walk the plank, me beauty." Then in a lower voice, she urged, "Oh, do cooperate, you wretched creature! The storm and cannon fire last night were so awful, they quite prevented me and George from having a proper farewell. So do be good, and give us another chance."

They docked in Halifax in a light fog. It was mizzling out, a cold, damp, penetrating precipitation that obscured much of the view.

"I told you I'd love to have you stay," said Amelia brightly, apologizing for the weather in her own way, "but I never ventured to suggest you would like it here."

She and Ursula walked arm in arm through the rain, with George hovering behind them, trying to figure out whether to try to shield them from the elements with his cloak. They huddled together in the waiting carriage, laughing at and bemoaning their wet clothing and bedraggled curls, while the Crandalls' luggage was retrieved from the *Fortitude* and loaded on top of the coach.

"Will you treat us to a tour of the city?" asked George.

"Gracious, no!" Amelia replied. "If you wish to see the sights, you may walk. Ursula and I plan to hasten home and towel ourselves dry and get comfortable with nice hot bricks at our feet."

"Hot bricks?" objected George. "At the end of June?"

"Don't be an addlepate," chided Amelia. "The pertinent factor is not the calendar, but the temperature."

101

"If this conversation goes on much longer," interrupted Ursula, "you will both be only too happy to say good-bye to one another."

"Not I!" replied Amelia stoutly. "I cannot be so sharp-tongued with my father or any other man and consequently shall miss your brother excessively."

"And you, George," persisted Ursula, "will you miss such a hornet?"

"Amelia's no hornet, but rather a bee," he corrected, "and I'll gladly brave her sting to get at the honey."

This last sally succeeded both in silencing Amelia and in making her blush—no mean feat—and left Ursula satisfied that though her brother and her friend might make an eccentric couple, they were indeed splendidly suited.

Amelia was as good as her word. As soon as they reached the large wooden mansion, Ursula was able to change into dry clothes and was then installed before a cheery fireplace with the promised brick warming her toes. The parlour was dark and not particularly well furnished, but it boasted a large bow window which looked out over a most romantic scene: the grey and moiling water and a stand of spruce trees on the headland.

At a signal from Amelia, George withdrew and left the ladies alone so that his beloved might make yet another attempt upon his sister's irrational thought processes.

"I shall write to my sisters tomorrow," said Amelia innocently. "They're both married, you know, and living in York. Now that I'm home, I do hope they'll come and visit, though I fear it's unlikely. After all the society I've enjoyed in the last several months, it will be so awfully dreary to be here alone again. . . ."

But that was as far as subtlety could take her, and Amelia soon abandoned indirection for the blunt approach.

"Really, you see we have ample room here. Papa is always busy, and I am de facto mistress of the house, so if I invite you to stay, you needn't have any scruples about accepting."

Ursula stared into the fire, at the flickering tongues of orange and gold.

"Honestly, what do you think to accomplish? You say no one can force you to marry against your will, but be practical a moment. You go to Bermuda knowing no one but Lord Charles and Richard, and I'll lay you fifty-to-one odds that you end by marrying the one or the other. So if you want neither . . . or is it possible you still do want Uxbridge in spite of all your brave words?"

"Amelia, you know that's out of the question!" Ursula protested. Her friend seemed convinced by her ready vehemence, and Ursula wished she herself could be so certain of her own sentiments.

"Well then, if you want neither, your best course is to stay here. I know we're not very grand here, but—"

"It's not that," said Ursula quickly, hurt to think her friend could suspect her of being a snob. "Perhaps I'm just tired of running away. My passage was booked to Bermuda. Wickenham is waiting for me there. I'm tired of thinking and worrying and fighting right now. Once I get to St. George's and have a chance to look around, I'll know better what to do. After all, what effective strategy can I conceive until I've assessed my situation? So don't think I don't appreciate your concern, but something tells me to go to Bermuda. Amelia, I don't know why, at least not completely. But in spite of my disillusion over Richard, something he told me still seems true. I still think of that island as a safe haven. I can't stop thinking that there is something for me there."

Amelia threw up her hands in surrender. "I'm afraid I have no sort of rational argument that can combat such romantic drivel. But I'd do anything . . ."

At this Ursula's eyes lit up. "Would you have any old books or periodicals you don't mind parting with?"

"What?"

"It will be a sennight or more to Bermuda. I intend to take all my meals in my cabin and hardly set foot outside so I'd give anything for a few good novels that will keep me happily occupied and out of the way of an individual I'd rather not encounter."

"Very well," Amelia conceded. "I would have rather done you a different sort of favour. But I have everything Mrs. Kitty Cuthbertson ever wrote, and you can have every volume, except for *Santo Sebastiano,* which I still adore. And you're welcome to my copy of *The Dairyman's Daughter,* which I find so instructional and improving in nature as to be positively odious. But I collect at this point you would find the prissiest courtesy book less odious than the Viscount of Uxbridge. I disapprove wholeheartedly of your choice, dear Ursula, but my library is at your disposal."

Josiah Crandall arrived home in time to join his daughter and his guests for a supper of roasted lobster and potatoes with parsley. After the meal the company moved to the drawing room, where Crandall supervised the evening from an armchair while going over his account books. Amelia set up the backgammon table and challenged her lover to a match, while Ursula watched for a while without much interest. At last she excused herself, expressed her thanks to Mr. Crandall, and spoke to Amelia and George in a lowered voice.

"I'm leaving you alone now, so you may promise each other the moon or else trade insults to your hearts' delight." As she left, she could not resist a parting shot. "But mind, I'm sure you have enough affairs of your own to discuss and settle tonight, so don't waste your precious minutes debating about me."

"You've taught her to be a hornet," commented George to his beloved with some chagrin, "but you've somehow failed to inject any common sense into her head."

"On the contrary," responded Amelia as she shook the dice, "her last suggestion was most apt. My darling, we have some talking to do."

After a good night's sleep and an agonizing breakfast Ursula and George found themselves deposited back on board the *Fortitude*.

Ursula had a stack of romances in her arms. Insurance, she thought, against surrendering to tedium and allowing herself to turn to Richard for conversation or companionship.

"If you really plan to hide away," warned George, "I shall have no one but Uxbridge to talk to. It will be your own fault if I end up in perfect charity with him and take his part against you."

"Not very funny, George," she said.

It was still raining. Amelia stood on the pier, sheltered by an umbrella, waving with unflagging energy. George waved back, solemn and determined.

As the low skyline of Halifax slowly and steadily receded, Ursula watched almost without emotion. What emotion should she feel? she wondered. Her heart, after all, had gone quite dead.

CHAPTER NINE

Ursula could not resist joining her brother on deck to watch as they at last made port one bright and glorious tropical morning.

Scores of small, quick white-sailed Bermuda sloops darted among the larger ships and dotted the horizon like seabirds. The rippling water showed variations in hue that far outdid the range of colours that could be seen in Ursula's eyes. Indigo, turquoise, cobalt, pale green to emerald, laced with white spray and dazzling with sunlight—the sea was all these colours at once, affected by abruptly changing depths and half-hidden reefs.

To Ursula's dismay, but not her surprise, Richard took the opportunity to draw near.

"Pray don't flinch and grimace," he said, "for this intrusion will be a brief one. I haven't given up hope, Ursula."

She continued to scan the horizon and made no reply; whether this was from haughtiness or agitation was left to Richard's surmise. Ursula herself could not have said which with any precision.

"You may not know your own heart," he continued smoothly. "I believe you follow its dictates without comprehending its motives." Oblivious to the fact that she pretended not to be listening, he concluded by saying, "I am convinced you still cherish a hope similar to my own. If not, you would have stayed in Halifax. If you are here now, it is because . . . well, be that as it may, I only wanted you to be assured that my feelings have not changed."

Yes, she thought. Your feelings were dishonest at the start, and they remain so now.

So pleased was she with this barbed reply that she almost succumbed to temptation and spoke it aloud. Only with the greatest effort was she able to turn to George and say lightly, "There's an island out there for evey day in the year," as though Richard were not even present, as though he had not spoken a word.

"You don't suppose," suggested George, "that there is a submerged atoll in the chain that rises volcanically for leap year?" George was willing to play to his sister's humour, but privately he tended to agree with Uxbridge that a continuing *tendre* had to be behind her decision to make Bermuda her destination.

Ursula herself had to consider the possibility and longed to reject it beyond a shadow of a doubt. But she could not, and had to content herself with the fervent hope that her heart was not such a traitor as to lead her astray in such a hazardous direction.

Happily the practical matter of disembarkation soon took precedence over unsettling meditations.

The *Fortitude* was not the first oceangoing vessel to dock at the port of St. George's that morning, but owing to Richard's importance, the governor-general had ordered that the medical examiner board the ship without delay. Passengers and crew were soon declared free of all signs of yellow fever, and while other ships' captains—who had been awaiting clearance for hours—complained of discriminatory treatment, the people and cargo of the *Fortitude* were soon being helped ashore.

Ursula's knees buckled under her at the shock of standing on terra firma again. George caught her from falling and laughed, but his laughter held a nervous, hollow note. In spite of the beauty all around them and the promising appearance of the island, they could not forget for a moment the difficult situation that awaited them.

Ursula was aware of many eyes upon her as she crossed the gangplank and thought how her old frock hung loosely on her frame. She had lost a bit of weight during the voyage. George, with his yellow small-clothes, was quite the London dandy beside her. Of Richard she had only the vaguest impression as she tried to keep from so much as glancing in his direction.

Lord Charles had sent his carriage to meet them. Ursula and George had known all along that they would be compelled, at least at first, to accept the commissioner's hospitality. But there was still a moment of terrible hesitation before Ursula allowed herself to be lifted into the seat and there joined by her brother.

"Don't be frightened," he said. "I'm here."

Ursula sighed. "The closer we get, the more I fear I shall soon go one step too far, take a step I cannot retrace." She knew her predicament was of her own choosing and was grateful to George for not pointing that out.

The viscount sat ahead with the coachman, and Ursula fixed her eyes straight in front of her even though that meant focusing upon the curly-brimmed beaver hat on his head and the strong lines of his back.

She was soon distracted, however, by the new sights all around her and by the soft breezes and sunshine that could not fail to lift her spirits.

The narrow, crooked lanes seemed not so much quaint as unfinished. Ursula remembered that they were casting in their lot with colonials and that she should not confound the island with some mythical tropical paradise. At the same time she rejoiced to see the rows of oleanders that lined the way, never guessing the poisonous nature of the gaudy purple flowers. Leaving the town of St. Georges behind, the carriage jounced along on a narrow path through the olive-dark cedar forest, where the air was fragrant and bracing as a tonic. From time to time they crossed a scarred ridge from which the timber had been cut and cleared and from which could be seen brief and dazzling vistas of white sand beaches and the sea.

Richard had engaged the coachman in conversation, and their voices drifted back to where the Mannings sat in silence.

"No, sur," the coachman was saying, "His Lordship won't set foot in town during the summer months, wot with the threat of yellow jack. No, he sets safe and sound at Fair Haven in the hills." Ursula winced to hear the name of the house. "Right careful he be, as ye'll see," concluded the coachman.

Ursula's heart had been beating with fear and anticipation, but by the time they glimpsed their first sight of a great stone building in the distance, the rough journey had become so tiring that she was quite relieved to be within minutes of the destination. She was stirred by the sudden anxiety of what Lord Charles would look like and what she would say to him when they met.

Her fears were premature, for the company was met at the front door by a Scottish housekeeper whose lips were tightly clamped and whose hair was streaked with grey.

"Ye'll be housed in the west wing till a sennight be passed," was the woman's greeting, and she led them through the house with no further words, their footgear making the stone floors ring with echoes. Servants saw to their baggage.

Inside, the thick walls and the glimpses Ursula caught of interior courtyards put her in mind of an

109

abbey or some other religious structure. It seemed a most unlikely residence for a man whose proclivities were those described by the captain of the *Fortitude,* she thought. She clutched at the hope that the scandal broth was pure fabrication.

Ursula was shown to a room draped in costly silks and overfilled with antiques. She trembled involuntarily at the sight of the large canopied bed. The fanciful bed hangings were suspended from the beaks of a flock of gilded doves, and elaborate festoons hung from devices carved to resemble pineapples.

It had required a great deal of effort and money, thought Ursula, to create something so perfectly hideous.

"If ye be needin' anything . . ." began the housekeeper.

Ursula was glad to have her attention drawn away from the bed and its implications. "Thank you, Mrs. . . . ?"

"McLeod."

"Yes, thank you, Mrs. McLeod." Then Ursula forced herself to ask what was most on her mind. "When will we be seeing Lord Charles?" she asked.

"Ah, be ye in great haste to see yer bridegroom?"

"No," blurted Ursula, and then blushed scarlet at her faux pas.

But Mrs. McLeod's eyes suddenly softened with a look of pity. "There, there, lass," she said, putting her arm stiffly around Ursula's heaving shoulders. *"He* will not see ye till his doctor do give witness that ye've no sign of the infection."

"But we were granted clearance aboard ship. . . ."

"It don't signify, not to a cautious man like Lord Charles."

"Is yellow jack epidemic then?" asked Ursula in alarm.

"It comes from time to time," replied the house-keeper, "especially in this season. Now, *he* finds it impossible to be too careful with his well-being."

With these words Mrs. McLeod was gone, leaving Ursula in amazement. The tone in her voice had been unmistakable. Once she'd left her taciturnity behind, Mrs. McLeod had spoken of her employer with un-disguised contempt.

Ursula wondered how long it would be till Wicken-ham would deign to see her. It was a strange sort of reprieve, she thought, but one she might be able to turn to her advantage. By the time he is ready to see me, she thought, perhaps I shall be gone. She would certainly have time to investigate what possibilities lay open to her.

The three visitors were served their dinner alone in quarantine by servants brought from the nearest vil-lage specifically for the purpose of seeing to their needs. Ursula was particularly pleased with a pie in which an orange-coloured pulp was further seasoned by the addition of salt pork.

"Pumpkin pie, miss" was the answer to her in-quiry, and this was the extent of mealtime conversa-tion.

Later that day Mrs. McLeod knocked on Ursula's door. The girl had been staring at the lime tree out-side her window and trying to turn her mind quite blank.

"His Lordship would like to see you."

"But I thought . . ." Ursula began to protest.

"From a distance, of course. Follow me."

Their steps echoed again on the stone as Mrs. Mc-Leod led to the intersection of the different halls of the building. A carved cedar door had been left open where the west wing joined the main corridor, and through the door Ursula could see a fine drawing room.

The setting sun cast it rays through the window at the far end of the room and dazzled her eyes so that she could barely make out the portly figure who stood there.

From what she could distinguish of his clothing the Hessians and biscuit-coloured pantaloons were unexceptional. The waistcoat was unimpeachable, but the tight-fitting coat was adorned with spangles. The latter ornamentation, particularly on so obese a form, destroyed what impression of good taste the remainder of the costume might have created.

She stared, trying to focus her vision, and saw him bring what appeared to be a white silk handkerchief to his face. As the fabric fluttered, it seemed to waft a pungent odour toward her. The man seemed a large, spreading shadow as he stood there, shielding his nose and mouth behind a vinegar-soaked handkerchief. It was impossible to make out his features or the expression on his face.

"He would like you to turn, dear," said Mrs. McLeod, and Ursula was as startled by the request as by the affectionate term coming from those tight lips.

"To turn?"

"Yes. Pretend you are dancing. Just a half turn. Graceful, that's right. Now another turn, to show him the other profile. Yes, that's what he wants. And again."

When Ursula could face front again, she saw the massive head nodding in approval. Either he had slightly shifted his position, or the sun had sunk farther by now so that it was hidden by the man's shoulder. Ursula no longer had to struggle with the fiery glare in order to see, but the candles in the drawing room were not yet lit, and the man's face remained hidden in shadows. Yet she could distinctly see what he was doing as he kissed the white handkerchief with a loud and open smack. Then he fluttered it in her direction in such a way that Ursula began to shudder uncontrollably.

With a second long-distance kiss Lord Charles Wickenham bade his young bride good night and disappeared behind a carved cedar screen.

The sun had lately risen when a woman's piercing scream shattered the early-morning serenity at Fair Haven.

George came rushing from his chamber, still in his banian. Richard, who had been dressed for hours and reading official documents by candlelight, met up with him in the hall. When Ursula poked her head out from behind her door to ask in a tremulous voice what had happened, both breathed with relief.

"As long as it was nothing that happened to *you*, it cannot be too awful," answered George, and heedless of the quarantine orders given by the master of the house, he hurried toward the main hall.

The first person he encountered was Mrs. McLeod, who was staring with steely eyes at a disheveled woman who tore at her red hair and hung on a half-opened door, swinging with it as it creaked open and closed under her weight. The lady in distress was clothed only in a gauzy nightgown. When the door swung open, George could see a chamber paneled in dark wood, and in the center he glimpsed the foot of an overlarge bed.

At last George made out the words which the buxom creature uttered between screams: "He be taken!"

He approached and, trying to make better sense of her story, pushed her aside and entered the room. The stench struck him right off. The fat old man who lay in the bed had skin as red as a newborn baby's. His breathing was shallow, and his eyes were glassy. Even as George watched in silence, the body let off a moan and shook with a spasm while a stream of black vomit poured from its lips.

"Send for a doctor!" cried George to Mrs. McLeod. She turned and disappeared down the hall, leaving him to wonder whether she'd gone to carry out his instructions or to dissociate herself once and for all from the household.

So that man was to have had my sister, thought George with revulsion. He stood and stared.

Hours later the doctor confirmed that Lord Charles had fallen ill with the dreaded yellow fever, and the quarantine that had lain over the house was reversed: The visitors were now forbidden to enter the main house for their own safety. As Dr. Vere explained, the disease had apparently been brought into the house by the red-headed woman. "She had the fever as a child, she tells me," he explained, "and, having recovered from it, now is quite immune. So she frequently had herself ferried over to ships in quarantine and plied her trade at great advantage and without competition. Without being sick herself, she must have brought the infection with her."

How ironic, thought Ursula, that the man who took such extreme precautions should be laid low by his unruly appetites.

As she alone stood no danger of taking the disease, Dr. Vere ordered the sailors' doxy to remain at Fair Haven and nurse the patient. "At your customary rates, of course," he explained. But privately to Richard he expressed his professional opinion that there was no chance of Lord Charles's surviving. "Which, I take it, leaves you as acting commissioner," he concluded.

In spite of the pall of impending death that hung over Fair Haven, the next few days passed for all three visitors in relative contentment. Richard had set

114

up a spare chamber as an office and held meetings with prominent residents from St. Georges and Hamilton, as well as any of the common folk who might choose to stop by and exchange views. He was formally polite to Ursula when they met at table but made no further attempt to impose his company upon her or to broach any subject of particular interest.

Meanwhile, Ursula and George explored their new surroundings.

"I don't think I wish *anyone* any harm," mused Ursula to her brother one afternoon, "but this is really most convenient."

Wickenham's illness left them to their own devices and without any sense of urgency as far as planning for the future.

"If he could just linger on sick forever," agreed George, "you'd be in no danger of having to marry him, and we should continue to live here very comfortably."

"Oh, dear, we are becoming terrible opportunists, are we not?" Ursula sighed.

She and her brother soon became a familiar sight in the vicinity, wandering the cliffs above the beach and gathering the ferns and wild flowers that grew in cracks in the sharp rocks.

"I've talked a great deal with Richard," began George one afternoon.

They had just taken seats on a flat stone in the shade of a banana grove, and Ursula had removed the poke bonnet that had been protecting her fair skin from the sun.

"About me?" she aked.

"No," he replied. "About his work, politics—the things that men talk about. He's impressed me very much, sister."

"Yes, he is very engaging."

115

"Don't set up your bristles, Ursula," he said cautiously, "but I begin to think your first impression of him may have been most accurate—and that my words against him were spoken too much in haste. I wonder if you do not misjudge him."

"It is not a subject I wish to discuss," said Ursula coldly, and rose to walk farther on and busy herself collecting the herbs that grew wild in the meadows.

"Mrs. McLeod tells me that rosemary steeped in hot water makes the finest wash for the hair," she informed George when he caught up with her. All the way back to Fair Haven Ursula kept up an inconsequential chatter that forestalled George from taking the viscount's part.

In fact, the first days of Lord Charles' illness went by like a country vacation for Ursula. She thoroughly enjoyed her long walks with her brother and started a collection of seashells, but she was equally fascinated by the domestic details of life at Fair Haven. The servants, both black and white, soon grew accustomed to her presence and her enthusiasm. Ursula was always exclaiming with delight at something: at the aroma of coffee beans being crushed by hand with mortar and pestle, at the way meat grew more tender when cooked wrapped in pawpaw leaves, and at the sight of children using scallop shells to skim fresh, heavy cream from the milk. Out in the back of the house young boys sat on the steps, sharpening knives against the bricks, and the brass doorknobs and fixtures were kept at a perfect shine by being rubbed with ash.

And the food! Meat was scarce on the island, but at Fair Haven all were well fed on what the sea could provide. Ursula was accustomed to light snacks of oysters, and to the ever-present boiled cod of the English diet. Even turbot and turtle were common enough fare at the table. But here she sampled fresh fish in more varieties than she had imagined could exist, not to mention the sweet and tender scallops whose shells she had already seen put to good use. Hot bread came to the table fresh from the oven, served on a wide banana leaf, and though she never learned to enjoy cassava or prickly pear candy, Ursula tried each new dish with relish.

It was hard to believe that only days before she had been languishing aboard the *Fortitude* or that she was but lately out of England. Ursula's mood was bright and lively, her enjoyment of life heightened by her scenic walks and by her interest in everything that was happening around her. But sometimes, alone at night, just before she climbed into bed, she wondered how long these calm and happy days could last.

They came to an abrupt end one morning, when Mrs. McLeod appeared after breakfast with a summons for Ursula. "He wants you," she said.

Ursula had almost forgotten the existence of the dying man. Though both George and Richard protested that she should not be exposed to infection, Ursula simply followed Mrs. McLeod to the sickroom. The atmosphere was foul, but Lord Charles was sitting up in bed, smiling. He seemed weak and fatigued, but he was clearly no longer feverish. His red eyes were beady behind his spectacles.

"It's not so easy, you see, to kill off a red-blooded man," he informed her in a rasping voice. "You need not come closer, if you fear . . ." he began. "I called for you because we have much of importance to talk about." He paused long enough so that Ursula was soon vanquished all over again by the fit of nerves she had managed to bring under control.

"Has Mr. Brummell fallen from favour yet?" asked Lord Charles.

"Mr. Brummell?" Ursula asked stupidly, quite disoriented by the unexpected question. Was this the matter of great importance?

"Yes. Mr. Brummell. George. The valet's grandson. The one they call Beau. Do the fools and followers still puff him into his extensive and wholly undeserved reputation? Well, what of him?"

"I have never seen the man," confessed Ursula. She was amazed by the animation that the convalescent displayed. "But I collect he is still prince of the *ton*."

The beady eyes scrutinized her closely. "You have been to London, have you not?" he asked.

"Yes," she said meekly, and instantly regretted her answer. Had she lied and said no, she might have succeeded in gaining Wickenham's contempt. How convenient it would be, she daydreamed, if he were to cancel the wedding plans of his own initiative.

"I detest the man," continued Wickenham, reaching for one of several snuffboxes by his bedside. He lifted one, opened the top, and a strong perfume immediately filled the room, adding its cloying sweetness to the sickroom odor. "Met him once, you see, and he told me my snuff was overscented!" Lord Charles proceeded to take a pinch and then to sneeze so violently that Ursula was convinced his end had come.

"Did I alarm you?" he asked, recovering.

"No," she said, catching her breath. "Only, if you really wish to blow off the top of your head, I should think a pistol would be a more efficient means than a pinch of Martinique."

Wickenham chuckled at this sally, much to the dismay of the girl who had hoped to appall, not amuse, him.

"And what of my dear friend the Countess of Oxford?" he asked, pursuing his previous line of enquiry. "Whom has she taken up with this year?"

"I do not know."

118

"You're not good for much, are you, girl?" he asked petulantly.

"I guess not," was her hopeful reply. It seemed Lord Charles was in the market not for a wife, but for a scandal sheet. Ursula comforted herself that she was entirely lacking in the proper qualifications and would soon be dismissed to go about her own business.

"From thousands of miles away," he lectured her, "I make efforts to keep abreast. When I think of how easy it has been for you, living in the very center of things. . . !" He sighed with such evident disappointment that Ursula felt quite encouraged, but her cheerful optimism was soon dispelled. "However, you'll do," he announced. "You may be no great shakes by London standards, but here you will suit well enough. I am planning your ball for December, and I can predict a sensation in spite of your shortcomings."

Her hopes rose again. If he didn't plan to marry until December, she had five full months to make other arrangements. Surely in that time she would be able to find a position as companion to a respectable lady or as a governess.

"But in the meantime, my dear," he interrupted her happy reverie. "I have been told it has been your custom in recent days to wander off. I have no objection, I suppose. But be advised that I have sent for the seamstress, and she will be here later in the day, so you'd best stay where you can be found. For your wedding dress, of course," he explained. "I've had the satins and laces waiting for months but, of course, could make no further preparations without having you here for measurements." His eyes looked over her body appraisingly with the last word.

"Why the haste?" she asked calmly, "if the wedding is not to be until December?"

"December?" he repeated incredulously, and then

burst into laughter as explosive as his snuff-induced sneeze. This mirth was followed by an attack of wheezing that sorely racked his frame. "No, no, no, my dear," he cried, gasping. "Do you think I could wait that long? In December I shall present you to my friends. At your ball. But we shall be married right away. Until December I wish to have you completely to myself." His eyes roamed over her again. "No, you don't have much conversation, but in other respects you will suit. Yes, you will suit so well that I predict we shall be quite inseparable."

The thought of being inseparable from such a bloated, swollen, disagreeable being would have turned a stomach even stronger than Ursula's.

"But, Your Lordship," she managed to protest, "you are scarcely recovered from a sickness most grave. Surely you cannot be thinking so soon of a wedding!"

"Your concern for my recovery is most touching," he answered with a wet sigh. "My illness was indeed most grave—and almost led me to that very place."

"You need time for a full recovery, my lord," she argued.

"Nothing will help me recover so well as our marriage," he answered calmly. "It will give me a renewed reason to go on living. You, my dear, will restore my will, and bring back . . ." He paused and passed a dry tongue over fat lips that had grown parched and split with the fever. "Yes, you will bring back the vigor of my blood."

He dismissed the girl with an imperious gesture, and Ursula fled down the halls.

CHAPTER TEN

"Why not marry him?" asked George when Ursula rushed to him in tears. "Call the vicar right away, and have him read the service right by the sickbed."

"How can you make so hideous a joke?" Ursula cried.

"I'm quite serious, darling," her brother replied. "I doubt he'll survive this bout of illness, so just think what you'll inherit."

"He appears quite on the way to recovery," she advised him miserably.

Even so, it will be a long time until he is strong enough to expect to . . . exercise his, uh, marital rights. By then anything can have happened. So why not?"

"Because it's too awful for words!" was her final reply before she fled from George and sent urgent word to Dr. Vere. Surely the medical man would not permit the marriage to happen.

Dr. Vere was out in the countryside, making calls, and Madame Yvette, the seamstress, arrived long before the physician. She was an aging Frenchwoman of great dignity who had fled her country during the bloody days of the Revolution and settled at San Domingo. During the slave revolt of '91 she had gone into exile yet again and had made Hamilton her new home. Though her English was excellent, her stormy life had left her with a melancholy disposition and little interest in light conversation. She held out the white satins and laces that Lord Charles had purchased and wordlessly opened a small casket to show

Ursula the hundreds of seed pearls with which the dress would be ornamented.

Ursula submitted to the fitting rather than open her personal life to discussion. Her silent hopes of deliverance remained fastened on Dr. Vere.

Suddenly the silence was broken. "Leave us," said a commanding voice from the doorway.

"What right have you . . . ?" began Ursula, staring at Richard and noting the high colour of his cheeks. "Stay, Madame Yvette."

The dressmaker looked at Ursula and then at the man in the doorway. She saw without a doubt that he was the one who would brook no argument, and without removing the pins from her mouth, she bowed her head almost imperceptibly and moved slowly from the room.

"You will not go through with this!" cried Richard as soon as they were alone.

"It's none of your concern," answered Ursula coldly, withholding the fact that despite all appearances, she still had no intention of going through with it. She spoke emphatically, but something stirred within her. Maybe it *was* his concern. Maybe there was still some way . . .

"What is wrong with you, Ursula? You will give yourself to that fat, depraved toad and overlook how many grievous faults? But can you not find it in your heart to forgive me for the foolish display I made of myself only one night? Look at me, Ursula!" he cried at last, aware that she was staring right through him.

Indeed, though she had sat at table with Richard every day, it was quite true that she had not truly seen him since the night of the incident. Ursula turned her face away, but not before their eyes met for just an instant. His look was deep, searching, and full of despairing love. They held enough fire to melt her thickest ice.

"Ursula!" he whispered, and these quiet syllables reached her in a direct and disturbing way. For days she had heard his words only faintly, across an unbridgeable gulf of her own creation.

"Why are you fighting me, my darling?" he asked, and for a moment she asked herself the same question.

Because of the uncertainty, she answered herself. Because love, true love, isn't joy. It's tyranny.

"I know I behaved badly," he was saying. "But please try to understand. I joined the sailors in drink because of the conflict in my heart. The words you heard were spoken by the rum, not by my heart, which was yours all along. The struggle was with myself, for Mr. Crandall was quite right in his way. I was most perturbed by the impossibility of our situation. I could not be loyal to you and to Lord Charles both. I could not behave properly both to you and with regard to the work ahead of me. But Ursula, you won without contest. . . ."

Love is tyranny, she was thinking, and I love him. If I marry Richard, I shall be entirely his, and my life will then consist of an awful suspense, until the moment when he betrays me. No one else will ever be able to hurt me that deeply, in my spirit, that is, because no one else will ever touch me there. . . .

"Ursula, I don't promise you happiness at every moment," he said, as though reading her mind. "For though I will strive never to hurt you in any way again, and even if we never quarrel again, there's no telling what troubles the future may hold. The storms ahead are a mystery to us, Ursula, but there is no doubt in my mind as to the happiness we could share. Maybe

123

the sailing will always be bright and clear, but if I must go through the tempest, I want to do so with you by my side."

Whatever is wrong with me? wondered Ursula. I turned from him because I thought he had no intention of taking me for his bride. And now that I can see he really does love me, why am I so frightened of that love? What reason have I now to refuse him?

In her confusion she softened and gazed at her suitor with perplexed hesitation. They faced each other a moment, inches apart but not touching, until Ursula knew she was melting, and Richard knew it, too.

I have no reason to refuse him, she realized at last. And no reason to be afraid. It is I who should be begging pardon, it is I . . .

Their lips met, and Ursula shuddered with relief and delight. Even the violence of Richard's longing—she could feel his need for her surging beneath his tenderness, at war with his gentle self-control—even the urgency of his passion could not frighten her now.

"Begging your pardon. . . ." These words, spoken in a stern and humourless voice, broke the enchantment and restored to both Ursula and Richard an unwelcome awareness of their surroundings.

Dr. Vere stood in the doorway, a look of cold and critical surprise only too evident on his usually bland features.

The lovers stood hand in hand. Ursula's eyes were downcast, and a soft blush spread over her face, but Richard, at his most arrogant and commanding, stared the doctor down. "Yes?" he asked coolly once he had made the medical man avert his gaze.

"Lord Charles has suffered a relapse." Dr. Vere tried to keep all emotion from his statement. When there was no response to his words, he stuttered out a further explanation. "It is not infrequent in these

124

cases for the patient to enjoy a respite of a few days, which appears at first to be a full recovery. . . ."

"The prognosis?" asked Richard after an awkward silence.

Dr. Vere paused and studied the two faces before him. "I am not certain I wish to communicate my prognosis to you," he said, shocked at his own daring, "as I am not convinced you have the patient's best interests at heart."

Ursula's flush was now one of anger. "I assure you, Dr. Vere," she said as steadily as she could, "I wish Lord Charles no harm. There was never any possibility of my becoming his bride. And so, you see, his full recovery will not stand in the way of my marriage to the man I love."

How stupid I have been! she thought.

Again the doctor hesitated, then seemed to make up his mind and left the room without another word. But at the door he turned back. Ursula and Richard had not resumed their embrace. They stood side by side, their eyes still fixed upon him. "Short of a miracle," said Dr. Vere slowly, "Lord Charles doesn't stand a chance."

Lord Charles Wickenham was buried four days later. Ursula and Richard stood together at the ill-attended service, but they had seen little of each other since their reconciliation. Richard had been busy with government business in town and in finding them a first home. For though Fair Haven was reserved for the use of the commissioner, and Richard could have properly made it his residence, the massive building held too many unpleasant memories for both of them. He and Ursula would start their life together in a fresh and uncontaminated spot.

Ursula spent hours in discussion with Madame

125

Yvette, convincing that lady to modify the style of the wedding dress which would now be used for a happier occasion than intended. The original pattern was lovely, but Ursula hated to think she would be married in a gown that had been commissioned by the dead man. She would have replaced the material altogether, except that it would mean a terrible extravagance, and besides, white satin was not easily available on the island and had to be ordered specially.

If Ursula and Richard were incomparably happy and filled with anticipation, George was almost as joyous. Of course, he was pleased that his sister's problems had reached such a fine resolution, but there was another reason for his good humour: He had already booked his passage back to Halifax. Right after the wedding he would bid his sister and her husband farewell and return to his Amelia as quickly as the winds could blow.

The third week of July Ursula Manning and Richard, the Viscount of Uxbridge, were married in the Devonshire Parish Church.

The pews were packed, and the vicar was not so puffed with self-importance as to imagine that all of Bermuda's polite society had come to hear his sermon.

The bride was resplendent. The fine ladies of Bermuda cast envious eyes on her gown, especially on the painstaking white-on-white embroidery in a fleur-de-lys and heart motif, representing purity and love. Being practical ladies, they limited their envy to Ursula's attire—for with money they knew they, too, could someday purchase equal finery. Her natural beauty would be forever out of their reach, and so they wisely acknowledged her supremacy without resenting it.

There was a wag or two at the church service who

could not resist commenting on the fact that Richard had "taken the old man's job and his bride as well." But Ursula and Richard were oblivious to gossip, as well they might have been since none of it was meant with malice.

Ursula was in a daze throughout the ceremony, but as she entered the church, something seemed vaguely familiar. Then she realized that several ladies were wearing exact copies of her silly puff-sleeved frock. Richard had been right, she thought dreamily. Her out-of-date fashion had been taken for the latest London style. Perhaps this was a strange preoccupation for a young lady right in the midst of being married to her beloved, but to Ursula the words "Richard was right!" ran through her head again and again with joy.

When they stood together at last before the altar, she knew without any lingering doubts that love was no illusion and that Richard was her one and only love.

"It's not a manor house. It's really more a cottage," began Richard somewhat apologetically as their hired coachman pulled on the reins and drew the carriage around in front of a small rustic house on the cliff.

"But it's perfect!" cried Ursula. The small wooden home was situated in complete privacy and yet commanded a perfect view of the beach below. There was no formal garden, but wild flowers in a riotous profusion of purple, yellow, and blue made the scene cheerful and bright.

Richard leaped from the carriage and helped Ursula down, holding her in his arms much longer than was strictly necessary. Then, after dismissing the coachman, they watched the carriage return toward town. Richard reached for Ursula's hand, and they stood side by side a moment to watch the sinking sun, while Ursula let her head fall gently onto her husband's shoulder.

Husband! she thought. What an amazing word.

"There's no one to greet us," he said at length, "as the couple I've engaged as servants won't arrive until late tomorrow. However, there's an outbuilding in the back—they call it the buttery—which serves as a pantry, and where if I'm not mistaken, Mrs. Kinneally has left us some cold supper should we want . . ." His voice trailed off. After all, of what matter were such unimportant details? What use were words?

He embraced her tenderly yet hungrily and felt her whole body strain against his in trusting love. In a moment she was in his arms again, and he carried her, with long, sure strides, into their home.

The cottages was clean and neat, and someone had left masses of roses in every room. The dying sunlight poured in through the windows, casting shadows of ruby and gold around the rooms, for only in the bedchamber were the heavy curtains drawn.

It was there, after he had lain her gently upon the four-poster bed, that Richard seemed to hesitate. "You're not afraid, are you, Ursula?" he asked, lightly caressing her cheek.

Afraid? She had thought often of this moment. She had heard she might experience discomfort . . . but Ursula felt she would gladly walk through fire for this man. What would be a small discomfort to show her love? And as she was swept by waves of longing, she suspected the stories she'd been told had really very little to do with what was about to happen.

She turned her head slightly, suddenly abashed by the eagerness she was certain could be read in her face.

"Ursula?" He was uncertain of the meaning of her movement.

In answer, it was she who reached up and drew his face close to hers. As they lay full-length, side by side, his arms released her only for as long as it took to carefully undo Madame Yvette's confection and to remove his own clothing.

She was overwhelmed by the sudden sight of him and threw her arms around his neck. "I love you!" she cried, pressing herself against his warm chest so that she could hear the pounding of his heart.

How strange it was that she had never told him that before!

"I love you!" she cried again. How strange and wonderful that she could say those words so freely, that they could lie together naked, that there were no barriers between them.

They cried out together in love and joy as he made her his.

CHAPTER ELEVEN

Richard sat dressed in a flowing India cotton banian and watched intently as Ursula set the pot of water to boil for tea and then walked out the door toward the buttery. He began to rise and join her, then restrained himself. He was torn between the desire to be near her at every moment and the pleasure of watching her slender figure move gracefully down the path, the morning breeze shifting her nightgown, now making it billow and now making it cling, while the sun, slanting through the fabric, clearly revealed the outlines of her body. Though it held no more secrets, Ursula's body retained a freshness and a mystery he could not explain to himself. What a joy it was to see her drop momentarily out of sight while he was secure in the knowledge that the buttery door would open again directly and she would be returning to his side.

Ursula's feelings held the same sort of pleasant conflict. She didn't wish to be parted from him for an instant either, but she could feel his eyes following her, and that gave her a gentle thrill. She was so full of happiness this morning that while she would have loved to remain cradled in his arms for hours more, she also longed to run free and laugh and drink deeply of the fresh air of the cliffs. She paused for a moment, feeling the refreshing coolness of the morning dew on her bare feet.

Richard was smiling at her when she returned with the tray of bread and cold sliced tongue, and it seemed he hadn't taken his eyes from her for a moment.

"It looks as if the revolution has come," he said, standing and greeting her with a kiss.

She looked at him quizzically.

"I never thought I'd see the day," he explained, "when my viscountess would creep out of the scullery —barefoot—to serve me breakfast."

"Well," she replied in the same teasing tone, "I always thought a viscountess would live in a huge manor house or a castle—yes, preferably a castle—and would have a beautifully appointed chamber all her own. Little did I dream I would have to share my sleeping quarters!"

"I promise you, my darling," he said, pulling her over to sit upon his knee and wrapping her tightly in his arms, "once we return to England and I take you home to Collingwood, you may have a whole wing of the building to yourself, if you choose, and you need never even see me again."

"No, Richard," she cried, "not even in jest! Don't say such a . . ." and she punished his thoughtless lips with kisses.

"Do you smell something strange?" she asked suddenly, breaking their kiss.

Richard sniffed the air; then they both looked at each other and laughed before Ursula jumped up and snatched the scorched teapot from the fire.

"The water's all evaporated, boiled away," she reported with a sigh.

"Fortunately, the Kinneallys will be here later; else it's clear we both should starve to death," Richard smiled.

"I shall put up more water," she retorted, taking offense. "And in any case, if you are famished, the tongue and bread are laid out . . ."

But at this moment their eyes met.

131

"Do you really want breakfast now?" she asked shyly. He needed no further encouragement to sweep her up in his arms and leave the tray of food untouched upon the table.

"Are you sure you don't mind?" Richard was asking a few days later as they climbed the long steps leading to the most imposing house in St. Georges. Ursula looked up at the unusual scalloped gable, taken by its charm, before answering.

"Your exclusive company hasn't yet grown tedious, my lord," she said, and bobbed an exaggerated curtsy, "but I agree we could hardly have refused the governor's invitation."

"Who knows? We may even find the evening agreeably amusing," he said. "And after this supper I promise you a few more days of seclusion before I turn to my work in earnest."

The guests were enjoying fine Canary wine in the drawing room when the viscount arrived with his bride. Conversation almost stopped when Richard and Ursula entered the room.

The company had been eagerly awaiting their arrival. On the island everyone knew everyone else, and there was rarely enough news or gabble to keep social discourse animated. Without exception the prominent residents had been waiting with great anticipation to meet the newcomers fresh from London.

Ursula soon felt hopelessly provincial. Of course, the Bermuda ladies were more provincial still, but they were so eager for her to tell them all the latest of life among the *haut ton*—of which Ursula knew pitifully little—that she felt she must surely be a terrible disappointment to everyone.

As it turned out, the ladies hardly gave her a chance to speak but rivaled one another in seeing who could

132

complain most grievously over how frightful it was to spend one's life buried away from refined society. Ursula thus gained the reputation of a sensitive and sympathetic listener.

The governors wife was particularly taken with the young guest. When Ursula complimented her hostess on her gown trimmed with ecru lace, it gave that estimable lady the opportunity to reveal the depths of barbarity to which a lady had to sink in order to make do in Bermuda. "There's nothing but white lace to be had in the stores, my dear," she said. Then, lowering her voice to a whisper, she added, "I dyed this trim by dipping it in coffee." The governor's wife smiled with satisfaction, certain that no one else present could provide a more primitive anecdote.

Richard was also learning that the Bermudians were franker of speech than their London counterparts and seemed to take a sly pleasure in confessing their foibles. Even the lions of Bermuda society displayed a refreshing naïveté. One distinguished gentleman openly drew Richard's attention to his snowy white cravat and then explained that his servants were incapable of getting any clothing clean. "I keep a bolt of white cloth," he confided, "and cut my cravat from it fresh every day."

Supper was guinea hens and a Virginia ham. The latter had been smuggled from the United States, and the British governor found it necessary to make apologies to Richard even as the meat was being carved and the delicious aroma rose to tantalize the diners.

"You'll find, as I have found, that the Bermudian is a loyal subject of His Royal Highness," sputtered the governor, afraid his words might seem hypocritical. "But you must realize how many islanders have close family ties to citizens of the United States, especially in the Carolinas and"—with a gesture to the ham—

"Virginia. Of course, the Bermudians aren't alone. I'm sure many Englishmen—and Americans, too—regret this war. . . ."

He chose not to mention the matter of economics, but no one present ignored the fact that the island lacked sufficient agriculture and livestock to feed its population. Food from the American states had been essential to Bermuda's well-being, and the trade interruptions caused by the war had made many an islander go to bed hungry at night. The fact that the British governor-general, the king's representative at St. Georges, could serve Virginia ham at his table was a clear indication of the difficulties that would be involved in enforcing an embargo.

"How long will you be staying in Bermuda?" asked the governor to change the subject.

"Just as long as it takes to complete my mission," said Richard with a wan smile. "That is, until I've wiped out piracy . . . and smuggling."

There was nervous laughter, which was interrupted by the governor's earnest request that the viscount study the matter without preconceptions. "To separate out, in your mind, if nowhere else, the crime which springs from greed and that which grows out of necessity."

Following this speech, the conversation turned to subjects more appropriate to the supper table: the likelihood of another summer storm and the latest London fashions.

After the meal had been thoroughly and enjoyably consumed, the folding doors were opened again, and the guests returned to the drawing room, the viscount and the governor drawing apart from the others. While the rest of the company drank with greater abandon and made merry, Richard and his host resumed their serious conversation.

"What progress have the abolitionists made in Parliament?" asked the governor, as soon as they were out of earshot. The subject of slavery was too delicate for general conversation.

"It will happen," said Richard evenly, "though I doubt in our lifetimes." Then, regarding the governor squarely in the face, he added, "As a member of the House of Lords I shall continue to vote for the abolition of slavery whenever the issue comes up."

The governor's eyes did not drop. "Yours is not a popular view here, but"—and his voice grew quieter still—"I confess that I share it."

"Will it be a difficult adjustment for Bermuda?" asked Richard.

"I don't think so. At least, it should be easier here than elsewhere." At Richard's questioning look the governor explained, still speaking in a fast but hushed tone, "We have no plantations here, you know. The terrain is little suited to massive agriculture. In Bermuda a slave is quite a different kind of investment, you see. Suppose I were to own an African—which I don't. What I should do is what the other Bermudians do: have him taught to read and write and work accounts, or else apprentice him for carpentry, shipbuilding, shoemaking, or some other useful trade. Then, you see, while I sit home idle, I send him off to work and live happily off the wages he is compelled to bring me."

"What a system!" murmured Richard under his breath.

"As a result, you are living in a society where the black slave is educated and industrious and knows how to apply his time and his skills," concluded the governor. "Here the free white man flaunts his own ignorance while he lives off the spoils. If freedom comes, I rather expect life in Bermuda will go on the same as ever, with the Africans seeing that all runs smoothly, the only difference being that they will have their wages to themselves, and their idle masters will be reduced to begging . . . or, one hopes, to recovering the long-forgotten ability to work."

Sudden peals of feminine laughter disturbed the reflective tenor of this discussion. Richard looked up, and he and the governor exchanged amused glances. Ursula was teaching the governor's wife how to waltz.

They spent the night at the governor's house, and in the morning Richard arranged the purchase of two horses. By the time the sun was high in the sky, Richard and Ursula were heading home, he on a grey stallion and she sidesaddle on a roan mare. When the narrow way permitted, they rode side by side, sometimes brushing against one another, not entirely by accident.

"Supper wasn't too terrible," he said at last.

"Oh, no, not at all," answered Ursula. "I quite enjoyed it. In fact, I've almost forgotten what it means *not* to be perfectly happy at every moment. I noticed you and the governor had quite a lot to talk about," she continued, now hesitantly. "I suppose that means he is stealing you away, and you will soon abandon me in favor of your work. . . ."

He reached over and touched her arm. "It's true I'll soon be extremely occupied, but I shan't abandon you at all, goosecap. That's one reason for your mare, though," he said. "While I'm pursuing investigations, I shouldn't want to think of you as a virtual prisoner at the cottage. Our seclusion has been very romantic, but it will hardly seem so when you are home alone. There are people you can visit not a far horseback ride away."

"And I suppose Mrs. Kinneally and I shall become the best of friends?"

"I'm sorry," he said.

"Oh, no," she hastened to explain. "I didn't mean that in ill humour. She's really quite wonderful. Anyway, I'll wager no woman ever has her husband to herself. I'd rather share you with your work than with some London light-skirt."

"You may find that work is a more jealous mistress," he said thoughtfully. "I'm certain there's many a London gentleman who visits Harriette Wilson once each sennight without his good wife's even remarking upon his absence from the house. I hope you'll be patient and understanding."

"Richard, I'll be proud of what you accomplish," she said quietly. Then, with a smile, she added, "I'm also certain there will be moments when I'll miss you terribly and I'll absolutely detest you for your commitments."

They rode awhile in silence.

"I wonder what is happening in Halifax," said Ursula at last. She and Richard exchanged happy smiles and then simultaneously spurred their horses on to greater speed in their eagerness to be home.

"Richard?" she asked one night as they lay together, drifting toward sleep. "What are you going to do?"

"About what, darling?"

"The smugglers and the pirates."

He was silent a moment. He trusted Ursula completely, but his own mind was uneasy over the task before him. He had succeeded in learning the names of the ringleaders. Though their ships had hundreds of hidden harbours on scores of islands in the archipelago, Richard knew which sites were most frequented.

It would not be hard to apprehend at least a few of the criminals and make an example of them as a warning to the others. His hesitation came from a realization of the poverty suffered by the islanders. He had learned that for many years the only way to earn a labourer's wage was to mine salt from Turks Island. Then, ten years ago, the crown had given that island with its resources into the jurisdiction of the Bahamas and had, with a stroke of the pen, deprived many Bermudians of their livelihood. Perhaps that was why so many Bermuda privateers used Turks Island as their base, he thought—because resentment at this ill treatment must still rankle.

"The thing is, Richard," whispered Ursula, as if reading his mind, "they're so terribly poor."

"Yes, I know," he said quietly.

"Do you?" she asked. "I've been out riding day after day, visiting with people. I wish you could come with me and see the pitiful frame houses, shacks really. The women cook all the meals out of doors to prevent fires. Even so, the plots of land are so small that they cannot go very far from their dwellings. With any gust of strong wind they run the risk of seeing their little homes going up in flames. Oh, Richard," she continued, "they have no meat to eat, and few vegetables. And no soap to wash with. You might think it quaint— do you know they wash with these funny leaves called dock leaves? The women I've met—oh, they try so hard to make their homes decent. They hurt their hands crushing these dreadful sharp leaves they use to scrub their floors with, and they put down empty corn sacks for carpet. But it's no help. How can you disguise misery?"

"There are poor people in England, too," Richard reminded her.

"I know, but it still seems they must have more hope because there is work in England and there is food. There may not be enough for everyone always to live well at the same time, but people at home can see opportunities, don't you think? While here, aside from piracy and smuggling, what can a Bermudian think to do?"

"If I knew the answer to that, darling, I would know what to do." He kissed her gently and held her close. It was hard, he thought, to believe that some people were suffering at the very same moment when he could lie in his own home and feel Ursula's warm and peaceful breath against his throat.

A sennight passed, and Ursula came to regret the sympathy she had expressed for the islanders. One afternoon Richard seemed distracted and out of sorts and finally drew her to him to say he'd be leaving at dusk for an island in the Caicos.

"A sloop will call for me down on our beach," he explained hesitantly.

She looked at him with uncertainty. "It sounds mysterious."

"I've arranged a rendezvous with some of . . . of the men we've discussed."

That was all he said until later, when she came upon him cleaning his pistols.

"Richard, you will be in danger!" she exclaimed softly, filled with terror.

He stopped short and balanced the gun a moment in his hand. Then, putting it aside, he said, "On second thought, I'll leave these behind. Let them see I come in good faith—alone and unarmed."

She threw herself into his arms, fighting against her tears.

139

"Please, not so desperate, my love," he whispered as she tried to lead him to their chamber. "You act as though you don't expect me to return."

Hearing her fears put into words broke the last wall of Ursula's resistance, and she dissolved in abandoned weeping.

"I shall have to wait and comfort you on my return," he said sadly. "It's time for me to go." Kissing her lightly, he started to leave. Then, turning back to her, he looked at her hard and long. He took her in his arms as though he'd never let her go. But a moment later he was gone.

The only land access to the beach was down the escarpment which formed part of the property that went with the cottage. The shimmering expanse of pink sand was cut off from the rest of the coastline on both sides by marsh and mangroves. There was no one to see Ursula as she gingerly let herself down the slope, clutching now and then at sea grasses to keep from falling. Her slippers soon filled with sand, and she took them off and continued barefoot. The sun had but lately risen, and the sand was still wet and cool. The pink glow in the sky gradually faded while she shielded her eyes from the sun and watched the horizon.

An occasional seabird flew by, crying, its call almost as piteous as the state of Ursula's heart. The sky turned smoky and then to day—an exhilarating Bermuda day with blue skies and fluffy white clouds—and still there was no sign of Richard.

In the distance she could hear the sighing and moaning of the water in the tidal swamps, and the sound made her shiver.

Three months, she thought. It was three months since the *Fortitude* had dropped anchor in St. Georges

Harbour. Those months had flown by with such haste that they seemed to have lasted less time than it had taken for the sun to move from the horizon to its noontime place overhead.

How silly Richard would think her to be keeping vigil on the beach instead of occupying herself elsewhere. What a goosecap she was to worry so.

She tried to tease herself out of her tremulous mood of mounting anxiety, but no words or thoughts could be of any help. The only thing that could give Ursula's mind ease would be the sight of Richard, safe and unharmed before her. In her mind's eye she saw again the dark wine stain on his cuffs. Had it been a warning?

Twice she saw what seemed to be an approaching sail, and blinking again, she saw the sail disappear. Mirages perhap, called up by her sun-dazzled eyes. Then a third time, a white speck on the horizon. She blinked, squinted, and turned away, then looked again. The speck did not disappear.

"Let it be Richard, and let him be safe!" she cried softly, and stood to see better as the speck loomed larger, continuing its miraculous approach.

It seemed that years passed until the sloop drew up to the shore and Richard jumped to the beach. He helped set the small vessel adrift again and waved good-bye to the captain as the sloop changed its direction and let the wind take it. Only when the sloop was gone did Ursula dare stir from where she stood frozen. She ran, laughing and crying, to her husband's arms.

His eyes lit up at the sight of her. "You didn't have to wait for me here," he said between deep and satisfying kisses.

"I was so worried."

"I'm so sorry."

"It doesn't matter now that you're back."

The words didn't matter, only the closeness and relief.

Calmed at last, they walked hand in hand over the sands while he told her of his night's adventure. "It all went well," he said, "although I'll allow I suffered a few moments' anxiety when I was delivered into their camp. These are not all just the poor, starving men of whom we spoke, my love. By the light of their campfire I saw some faces I should not like to meet again." He felt her shudder at these words and regretted dramatizing the danger he had run. "But I listened to their complaints and told them what I intend to do. We are returning to England, darling, within the month. There is little for me to do here. The work must be done there, in London, where the power lies. I shall take with me a report and recommendations."

"But what will you suggest?"

"Up until '08," he explained, "a lot of these men were employed building ships for the British Navy. I see no reason why the business should have been let elsewhere. The Crown needs ships and shipbuilders, and the Bermudians need work. I shall strongly urge their suit in London. . . . I am not deceived that all the buccaneers will cease their predations while awaiting news of the success or failure of my mission, but I expect I had an effect on at least the less hardened of them. At any event," he concluded, "I let them know in no uncertain terms that if they are to enjoy the King's largesse in the matter of contracting for vessels, they cannot at the same time expect mercy or immunity from punishment for their crimes."

"Well done," said Ursula, kissing him on his cheek and laughing to feel the bristles that had resulted from Richard's being deprived of his morning shave. "I hate you for putting yourself at such hazard, but I love you even more for making me so proud."

A sudden wave splashed over the beach and reached their feet. Richard swept Ursula up in his arms to protect her, and then, rather than release her, he carried her to a soft expanse of sand in the shadow of the cliff.

"Richard! Surely you don't mean to . . . here?" she said, amazed.

"To do what?" he dared her, laughing. "We shall have to be civilized Londoners soon enough," he added, overriding her objection, and as he knelt beside her and began to undo her bodice, Ursula did not protest again.

Later they lay exhausted in each other's arms and watched the sky and sea. Richard ran a hand through Ursula' damp hair. "The sun has turned your curls to gold," he said. "Exactly the colour of a new sovereign."

They kissed softly, and he left his hand on her breast.

"Will you be glad to go home?" he asked.

"This is home" she replied.

"Then will you be sorry to go?"

"Being with you is being home," reflected Ursula. "Yes, I miss England. But we've had such a wonderful life here. . . ."

"This afternoon . . ." he began, and they held each other closer. "Do you see the colour of the water?" he asked abruptly. She raised her head just a little from his warm chest and looked out at the waves.

"I've never seen a colour like that before," she answered.

It was too deep to be azure, too light and sunfilled to be indigo. It was neither turquoise nor any other shade of blue.

"I've seen beautiful colours before, but never anything like that," he said. Their fingers twined tightly. "You must have been very worried indeed," he continued. "Please don't blush when I tell you this, my love . . ." He hesitated again. "The moments I've held you in love have been the happiest moments of my life. But this afternoon, as I lay with you here, it was different, unlike anything before. It was more . . . I think of the colour of that sea, the golden light on your hair. What happened between us this afternoon lying here in the sand—I hardly know how to explain . . ." He concluded the thought as his voice became choked. "Whatever may happen, I'm going to hold this feeling in my heart as long as I live."

Then his passion burst into a renewed fire, and Ursula was soon trembling joyously close against him again.

CHAPTER TWELVE

The *Coronet* was a small and saucy craft by comparison to the *Fortitude*, and Ursula was delighted. For if Fair Haven could be considered the terra firma equivalent of the *Fortitude*, then life aboard the *Coronet* might be much like life in the cottage on the cliffs. Even the sailors made her smile. Unlike the men of the *Fortitude*, whose drinking and crude talk had, in her mind, led Richard astray, the crew for this voyage seemed fresh-faced and full of innocent gaiety. Several of them had just barely returned to ship in time for weighing anchor. Ursula and Richard had stood by the rail and spotted them dancing with village girls to the music of a fiddler on a greensward not far from the harbour. The captain tolerantly but firmly sent a sloop to collect the truants, and though the sailors must have been reluctant, they obeyed the summons directly.

The *Coronet* carried few guns, and it was easy to forget a war was raging. A score of British ships of the line were going through maneuvers along the coastal reefs, but in the bright sunshine it seemed a holiday display rather than a serious naval exercise.

"Farewell, Garden of Eden," said Richard as the white roofs of St. Georges grew ever more distant.

"Paradise Lost," echoed Ursula, but she sighed with pleasure as much as with nostalgia. On this voyage she had nothing to fear. No terrible fate loomed ahead. She rested her head on her husband's shoulder. Yes, she had everything she wanted in the world.

"I do hope you and Lydia will get on," Richard said at last, referring to his sister, who had taken up residence with him at Collingwood following her husband's death in the Peninsular campaign. "Life in the country can be pleasant enough," he hastened to assure his wife, "and I don't doubt but that you'll go into raptures over the West Country once you've become accustomed to it. But Lydia has become a bit of a recluse, I fear. Oh, she puts on a gay enough face and tries to take an interest in things, but I suspect her life is really very bleak. Except for her son, of course. How she loves that boy!"

At the mention of his nephew Richard regarded his wife shyly, and she blushed, reading his mind. No, there had been no symptoms, unless there were ways of telling which she, in her ignorance, did not know. There was time enough, she thought. Anyway, she was bringing Richard back from Bermuda, and surely one prize at a time was sufficient.

"I'm certain Lydia and I shall be friends directly," she replied, turning to a less embarrassing topic.

"Yes, of course, though I warn you, she is not as steady as she should be." He paused, considering how to express his doubts without seeming to criticize his sister. "I'm her brother, and I trust that makes me sensitive to her true value and not merely blind to her faults, but . . . I believe you will end by being an excellent influence on her."

"In what way?"

He paused again. "Some people consider her haughty, but I can assure you, she is actually painfully shy."

Ursula laughed and took his arm. "So you see through your sister's imposture just as I always maintained to see through my brother's."

Richard smiled, too, at the mention of George. They had lately received a letter from Halifax. A wedding was not far distant, for serious Mr. Crandall had been

146

swayed by all of Amelia's persuasions. It was George who had insisted on postponing the wedding for six months, during which time he hoped to prove himself worthy of his good fortune.

"It was very lucky his meeting up with the Crandalls that way," commented Ursula. "In England I'm sure my brother would have continued to consider work beneath his dignity as a gentleman. And he could not have continued to live off Uncle Alfred's limited largesse forever."

"He would have married an heiress," insisted Richard.

"If one would have had him with his silly cynical temper," she answered. But George's affairs seemed nicely settled, and there was little point to dwelling on his old faults, so Ursula turned the conversation back to a subject of great interest to her: Richard's home. She found it hard to believe that any place could be as mystical as Richard described the landscape around Collingwood, midway between the Quantock and Polden hills. She had always thought a bog would be a nasty bit of business, but Richard assured her it had its own mysterious and awesome beauty, being neither water nor land.

He told her about the rhines, the irrigation ditches along which grew endless groves of pollard willows. She could imagine the knobby reflections of the tree trunks on the untroubled surface of the water. And he compared the tawny colour of her hair to the withy reeds which the farmers dried to use in weaving baskets.

What fascinated her most was to learn that Glastonbury Abbey was just across the Poldens from Collingwood. "But the hills are trackless," he told her, "and no one ventures into them save Pocock, our legendary highwayman."

"Is he legendary because his exploits have been

turned to legend or because he does not exist?" she asked, a little anxious at the thought of living in close proximity to a notorious criminal.

"Having never met up with him," confessed Richard, "I can't say. But the farmers and their men love to tell of him. They'd have it he is a bit of a Robin Hood, sharing his booty with the needy."

Some people said the mortal remains of King Arthur and his ill-fated Queen Guinevere had been laid to rest in Glastonbury Abbey. And, Richard added, it was believed that the valley north of Glastonbury was the very site of Camelot. There could be found the very island to which the dying King Arthur had been carried by the Lady of the Lake to await the day when he should return to lead his nation.

It was curious, Ursula thought, that Richard could speak of King Arthur as though he actually knew the man, while he hesitated to acknowledge that Mr. Pocock was a living, breathing entity.

"My family's fortunes are closely tied with the abbey," Richard explained. "We began our rise during the reign of Henry the Third. A male of my father's line abandoned his family and took up a cloistered life there. His wife and children were soon reduced to the utmost privation and despair, while in the abbey some came to say my ancestor was a saint. Word of his holiness and of the miracles he was said to have wrought reached the ears of the king. Fortunately he also received word of the misery of the holy man's family. King Henry did not want it bruited about that Providence had failed to provide for the wife and infants of a saint, so he took the role of Providence upon himself. He gave them royal favour, land, and title, and the family has continued to advance nicely with the years."

"Listening to you talk is like reading a romance," declared Ursula when he had finished. She maintained her funning tone, but inwardly, the closer they drew to England, the more Ursula wondered if she would be able to behave as a viscountess ought. Indeed, the way of life in which Richard had been born and raised was as remote to her as a fairy tale, and she hoped she would not bring shame upon him by her ignorance. It was one thing to be a barefoot viscountess in a cottage on a distant island. She had charmed him with her simplicity in Bermuda, but back in England naïveté would be a liability devoid of charm.

Just look at me, she scolded herself. I'm doing what I always do, creating problems to worry about. Why can't I simply enjoy today's bliss without worrying about tomorrow?

The morrow dawned bright and clear, and even when sails were spotted in the distance, no one was alarmed. Soon it became apparent that the other vessel was proceeding toward the *Coronet* at full speed.

"It looks to be flying the Union Jack," said Richard, squinting to distinguish the flag on the stranger's mast. "But you'd best get belowdecks, just in case."

"Only if you'll come along," she insisted. "You're no longer in the Navy, and I shan't allow you to risk your life if there's trouble."

"If there's trouble," he replied, "lives will be risked whether you will it or no." He regretted his frank words when Ursula turned pale, and so he protested no longer but accompanied her to their cabin.

"You'll soon regret your choice of a wife," murmured Ursula ruefully, "now that you see you've married a watering pot who has a spasm at the slightest provocation."

"I would hardly call war a slight provocation," replied Richard, uncertain whether to reassure his wife that there was no danger or whether to insist that they did indeed run great peril and so she should not feel foolish for her fears.

"Before many months go by, I warrant I shall deteriorate still further," she continued, "and you will have to be ever at the ready with my smelling salts. For now I see I am indeed the sort who becomes subject to the vapours."

"There you are wrong, my dear," he said, hoping to tease her out of her mood. "And I warn you, while I would fight off a whole pirate band single-handed for your sake, I refuse unconditionally to hover by your side with the restoratives you describe. I leave fits of the vapours to people like my aunt Isobel. I put you on notice that I expect better from you."

This dialogue was halted by an urgent pounding on the door. Richard gave Ursula a look that said, "Courage!" and went to open it. At first he opened the door only wide enough to see who was the source of the insistent summons, but almost instantly he flung the door wide. Beyond him Ursula caught a quick glimpse of a naval officer whose resplendent uniform was in sorry contrast with his drained and haggard face. But even as she watched, the deadened eyes lit up, and her husband and the stranger were embracing each other heartily.

"My dear fellow," cried Richard, "though I see I must now call you captain. To think I brought my wife below to hide her from the enemy when all the while it was my dear friend who came in pursuit!"

The officer bowed low upon his presentation to Ursula, but she noted with alarm that he avoided looking directly at her.

"John Steele and I served together in '09," Richard explained to Ursula, "and a better man you'll not find."

Steele nodded his head almost imperceptibly in response to this compliment, but his manner became animated when he turned to Richard again to say, "I could scarce believe my good fortune when I asked your captain for the names of passengers and learned you were aboard."

"It's a strange meeting, so far from home," agreed Richard.

"And at a bitter time."

Richard looked at his friend closely, noticing how drawn and white his face had become.

"We were overtaken by an American ship late yesterday," he explained without waiting to be prodded into an explanation. "I fear they got the better of us. They didn't capture the ship, but more than a third of the crew had to be buried at sea, and five other men lie grievously wounded. I haven't much hope for them."

"You've been wounded yourself, sir," broke in Ursula, abruptly realizing the cause of the man's unnatural pallor.

He turned to her, and his eyes flickered a moment before he replied, "Some loss of blood, but no serious injury." His gaze flinched a moment, but then Steele stood straight and regarded Richard directly. He spoke slowly. "I came aboard to seek reinforcements. I am empowered to impress such members of this crew as I need into His Majesty's service. I've taken a few, but they are young, all untrained and untried. I can use them for navigation and piloting, but, Richard, I need fighters."

Richard used all his willpower to keep his eyes

from looking away. "As you see," he replied as slowly and steadily as his friend, "I am a newly married man, taking my bride home to England."

"Regardless of that circumstance," said Steele, "I have the power to command you to join me."

They stared at each other in a silence broken only by Ursula's gasp of horror.

"I fought the French with a will," added Richard, "but I have no quarrel with the Americans."

"When they open fire upon you, you will have a quarrel with them," replied Steele coolly. "You are not alone in not favoring this war, but . . . I would not ask you, Richard, were I not in such dire straits," continued the officer. "Come with me willingly, and I give you my word of honour that at the first opportunity I shall release you. I may put myself in difficulties for this private arrangement, but I urge you to accept it. I shan't leave the *Coronet* without you, and if you force me to impress you formally, I fear you may be a naval man for some time to come."

"I have already done my duty to the Crown," answered Richard stubbornly, afraid to face his wife but aware that the issue was already decided.

"Patriotism is not a debt that one can discharge."

Except for the sounds of footsteps overhead and the slapping of waves against the hull, the room was silent.

"I recognize my responsibilities," said Richard at last. "Now leave us, please, while I say good-bye to my wife."

Steele bowed stiffly and withdrew. Ursula watched the door close and continued to stare at it, imagining the face and figure of the man who had appeared out of nowhere to disrupt her happiness. He might be an Englishman, the very flower of the king's Navy, but to

Ursula, Captain John Steele was the enemy. He was the enemy from whom she had tried to protect her husband, the enemy from whom she had hidden, in vain.

CHAPTER THIRTEEN

From the moment that Captain Steele had appeared to claim Richard, the days and nights ran together for Ursula. Without her husband it seemed that nothing mattered or made any sense—not the endless voyage or the trip by coach to Collingwood.

One moment she was lost in a world of confused worry and grief, and the next her new home was revealing itself in all its spired, turreted, and overpowering Gothic glory.

Even before she stepped down from the carriage, the front doors to the house were flung open, and a crowd of people and a dozen dogs came spilling and scrambling down the steps. Ursula found herself being embraced by a plain, nervous lady whose most distinguishing—and not terribly flattering—features were a pointed little chin and two dark eyes that darted about rather than meet anyone head-on.

"I'm Lydia," she cried, "and I am so happy you are home. But where is Richard?"

Before Ursula could answer, she was being hugged again, this time by thirteen-year-old Edmund. "Welcome home, Aunt Ursula," said the boy warmly, and in his easy smile and expressive eyes Ursula at once saw a resemblance to her missing husband.

Her sad account of Richard's impressment cast a hush over the welcoming party, and among the staff of fifteen servants there were few dry eyes. But then the residents of Collingwood, all hoping to cheer their new mistress, bravely rallied their spirits. Ursula was swept off the front steps and across the threshold in a swirl of well-wishers.

154

I'm home! she thought. The happy feeling was so strong that for a moment she stopped grieving for Richard.

The interior of the house was a delight.

"Richard told me you inhabited a Gothic monstrosity!" Ursula protested. "It's not that way at all!"

She had resigned herself to living in a dark, oppressive castle, trusting that love would brighten its heavy, overpowering rooms. But there was a light and airy feeling to Collingwood's turrets and spires, and as there were few trees to block the sun, the natural light flooded in from all the mullioned windows and transformed the interior into a scene of great cheer.

"Oh, I'm so glad you have joined us here!" exclaimed Lydia for perhaps the hundredth time as she saw Ursula installed in a bedchamber with a lofty ceiling and a pastel floral design painted on the white walls.

It was like having a sister and for the first time in her life being part of a large and loving family. Ursula was so filled with joy that she almost felt guilty for being happy while Richard was in danger far from her side.

"You'll have to share my abigail for the time being," chatted Lydia, "as Richard gave me no word, and I thought you might have already engaged someone." She rattled away about domestic concerns. "And I had planned an entertainment for tomorrow night to welcome you both home. Please do say you won't be shocked, darling, if I tell you I do not plan to withdraw the invitations. Richard would want you to meet his friends and neighbours, and I feel sure we shall contrive to ease the burden you must be carrying within your heart. You are lonely and have been grievously used by the war, but there's been no tragedy, my dear sister, and I shall see that when Richard returns, he will hear that your spirits have never flagged."

Ursula could not fit in a word, either of protest of acquiescence, for Lydia babbled on. "To mope is to admit defeat, Ursula. We shall smile and dance and let the whole world see that we have faith in the future and that we do not doubt our happiness is secure."

Ursula followed Lydia down long halls lined with marble statuary and suits of armour. Wherever they went a dozen puppies scampered after them, yelping and dodging about the ladies' feet. Even the faces that stared down from their canvases in the portrait gallery seemed to be smiling at them.

Once the ladies and their entourage of household pets reached Lydia's pink and silver bedchamber, Lydia flung open the door to her wardrobe, and while Betsy, her abigail, hovered anxiously waiting to be of assistance, Lydia took out armfuls of dresses and tossed them carelessly on her bed.

"Here, Ursula," she cried gaily. "As you can see, I've dresses aplenty, and hardly occasion to wear them all, even should I change four times a day. Really, Ursula," she added seriously, "Richard wishes to cheer me, and so he showers me with gifts. It's not so much want of imagination—you mustn't think I speak in criticism. Richard would do anything, as no doubt you know, to brighten the lives of those he loves. But I'm nowhere near as unhappy as he seems to think me. Hence, I have received more gifts than I have need for." Lydia's eyes darted from Ursula's face to the pile of dresses. "So help yourself to what you will. Until your new things arrive from London, share my clothing as sisters will. . . . Here, this tunic looks as though it were made for you!" exclaimed Lydia, regarding her sister-in-law with admiration as

Ursula held the lilac and silver-bordered silk against her body. "My face and build never did the gown justice, and I've never worn it. So please, don't just borrow it. It's yours."

"Thank you." Ursula embraced her happily and let Betsy help her into the tunic. She was surprised at how much pleasure she felt at seeing herself in the glass. Rather than change back into her old and faded frock, she wore the new tunic as Betsy carried the other gowns, and they hurried down the hall to hang them in Ursula's wardrobe.

"Our party tomorrow will begin out of doors," Lydia was saying as they retraced their steps through the passages. "But everyone will return to the house to change, and I think what you're wearing now will be perfect for dinner and dancing."

"Dancing, too?" Lydia had apparently planned a most elaborate entertainment.

"Yes, I have just this moment decided so. You need to be cheered, my dear, and I shall send directly to Langport for the musicians. The allowance Richard left me is more than enough," she explained, "and I have few enough excuses for extravagance."

A sudden slithering movement in the shadows made Ursula gasp with fright, and Betsy shrieked and dropped the gowns she was carrying. "A rat!"

Lydia just laughed. "Don't go into a spasm, Betsy," she scolded. "It's just Guinevere, I'll warrant."

Sure enough, looking more closely, Ursula spotted a small spaniel lying at the feet of a suit of armour. The little tail did not wag, but rather quivered, and the red-brown eyes implored.

"She was the runt of the litter." Lydia went on, "and born with a bad leg besides. I wouldn't let the poor thing be drowned, but my benevolence hasn't won her love. She's afraid of other dogs, of people . . ."

Even as Lydia spoke, the little dog gave a low yelp and sprang up to greet Ursula. The little paws caught on the tunic, and before anyone could react, the silk rustled and tore.

"Oh, no!" cried Lydia. "This is the outside of enough! It's one thing to be ungrateful and unfriendly, but I'll not tolerate a destructive animal."

But Ursula had scooped the puppy up in her arms, and Guinevere was happily licking her face. "But she's not at all unfriendly," she argued, "though she hardly seems queenly enough to carry a name like Guinevere. I shall call her Gueevie for short, and if you'll let me keep her as mine, I promise I shall turn Gueevie into the sweetest, best-behaved canine at Collingwood."

Betsy stooped to pick up the dresses she had let fall, and she chattered away, promising to try to mend the tunic so that it would be suitable to wear for the party. As for Ursula, her face was buried in Gueevie's fluffy hair. She was delighted by the warm, squirming body that whimpered with puppy joy.

"How rude of me!" Lydia's voice broke into Ursula's thoughts. "You must be exhausted after all your traveling. I quite insist that you take a nap while I see to arrangements for tomorrow. Betsy, see that Guinevere is given a good bathing. I can smell her from here. . . ." She made up her mind abruptly and spoke again to the abigail. "Give me the dresses, and you take the dog. Lady Ursula shouldn't have to carry the dirty creature about before she's been washed and brushed."

"Who needs washing and brushing?" demanded Ursula with a light heart. "Do you mean me or Gueevie?"

"Really!" exclaimed Lydia. "But come, give the dog to Betsy," she coaxed.

The exchange was affected over Ursula's mild objections, but at the sight of her mahogany bed with its silk coverlets and fluffy pillows she realized how dreadfully tired she really was. Fully appreciating Lydia's good sense and courtesy, she gave her a kiss on the cheek, patted Gueevie, and prepared for bed.

How wicked of me, she thought just as she fell asleep. My husband is at war, and here I am, as if without a care in the world.

"Have you a riding habit?" asked Lydia at breakfast the next morning.

When Ursula shook her head, Lydia laughed. "What a question! Of course, you do. But it's hanging in my room. You do ride, don't you?"

Ursula was vastly relieved to be able to answer this question in the affirmative.

"Betsy assures me that her sister is a cheerful and capable young person who would serve you very well," explained Lydia, "so unless you have any reservations, we shall ride over to the tenants' cottages and engage young Lucy to be your abigail."

"Have you really the time to spend on my concerns?" asked Ursula.

Lydia assured her that she was quite at her disposal until late in the afternoon, when she would need to be in the house to supervise preparations for the supper and the ball.

"If you really have the time," said Ursula hopefully, "I should love it if you could show me some of the grounds."

Ursula was soon dressed in a grey velvet habit, hugging Gueevie on her way out the door.

Outside, Lydia introduced Ursula to her mount— not a horse, but rather a shaggy moor pony, which, Lydia explained, was known for its natural ability to find its way safely across the moors, skirting the bogs by instinct.

"I don't mind going out with you today," explained Lydia as they set off, and Ursula could not help but compare their bumpy progress to the canters she had enjoyed on her own roan mare. "Because Richard and I grew up here and know the lay of the land. Until you are more familiar with the countryside, you really should not venture forth alone."

"Oh, I'm not afraid of Mr. Pocock," Ursula laughed.

"No, I don't refer to highwaymen or to churlish tenants. I'm talking about the bogs, quicksand, and sudden floods."

How did people live in such an environment, Ursula wondered, and how did they learn to love it?

The day was cold, windy, and not conducive to a full enjoyment of the natural scene. After they had been riding for only fifteen minutes, Ursula's cold and discomfort were such that she thought of asking Lydia to turn back. But she resolutely held her tongue and tried to keep her teeth from chattering while her grip on the reins grew numb. In the next few minutes her senses became suddenly keen and better attuned to the world around her. The cold wind carried with it the sweet and pungent scent of apples and the thick, homely smell of turf fire. As they rode along the water channel, her attention was drawn by thick clusters of green foliage that remained underwater and lent the shallow rhines an illusion of great depth and colour.

Perhaps this was the secret of the moor's power over the senses: Its beauty could not be discerned from a distance. The moor could be known only at close hand by its details, its intimate life. The visitor must be drawn deep into the life of the moor to know it and, in that drawing deep, would come under the sway of the land.

"Trees!" exclaimed Ursula at last as they came upon a more conventional rural scene: an apple orchard in autumn. Steady, penetrating mists had begun to envelope the countryside, but the families at work on their ladders and with their baskets seemed oblivious to the inclement weather. Perhaps, Ursula thought, in this part of the world a day like today is considered fine. The apples made a rattling, drumming sound as they were shaken from their safe perches by the workers and came tumbling to the ground.

"We'll be here tonight for the wassail," said Lydia, drawing up, "but I thought you might like to see the scene by daylight."

"The what?"

"The wassail. The farmers will be celebrating the apple harvest and the good hard cider that comes from it. We'll join them briefly before our own entertainment and then leave them to drink their tanglefoot."

"Lydia," exclaimed Ursula in delight, "I do hope you won't think my words rag-mannered, but in some ways this corner of my own land is as foreign and strange as Bermuda seemed at first."

Lydia laughed. "It's true, my dear. Why, we don't even speak the same language here. At least the common folk don't. Their daily talk retains much of the Saxon."

Spotting another curious object, Ursula demanded, "Lydia, is that a rowboat tied to the apple tree?"

"You would not get the workers in the fields hereabouts without one," replied Lydia. "Floods come with little warning."

"But there's no water in sight!"

"We know the land with senses other than sight," Lydia told her. "The ground is saturated. The sea is far off, but a constant threat, with nothing to stay its course. No man, woman, or child ventures far without knowing where to find a boat or a spot of safe, high ground in case it happens. . . . But let's go on. Time is passing, and we have business to attend to."

Ursula would dearly have loved to venture closer to the people who worked in the orchard and whose voices, some raised in song, could now be heard under the drumming of the crop.

Instead, they skirted the orchard, and Ursula watched with continuing interest as the landscape changed to vast fields of purple thistles, which to her perplexity grew in such ordered abundance that they seemed to be cultivated.

"Why cultivate thistle?" she asked.

"It's not thistle, but teazle," replied Lydia, "though some do call it fuller's thistle. It's very useful for scouring cloth and working up the nap of textiles. Laugh if you will, but teazle is the great cash crop of our people. Besides," she added, "the water that collects among the leaves takes on a medicinal virtue from the plant and soothes most inflammations of the eyes."

So engrossed was Ursula with the interesting things she was learning about her new home that she had all but forgotten about the cold and damp. Finally they came upon the cottage of Betsy's family. Two red oxen, freed from the yoke, grazed lazily near the door, swishing invisible flies away with their damp tails.

"Well, if Jack isn't ploughing today," said Lydia somewhat tartly, "it means he is either working in the apples or sleeping off too much tanglefoot. But as I hear no snores from this distance, I think it safe to say the man's at work."

"Oh, I didn't think of that!" cried Ursula. "If they're all in the orchard, we've come here in vain."

"The mother is a cripple," said Lydia. "She'll be home."

Mrs. Tuckey was indeed at home. Once the ladies had tied their ponies to the post and Lydia had called out curtly at the door, the woman appeared. She had a shawl over her large frame and a cap on her head. Her disability was clear to see: a withered leg that she dragged as she walked, leaning on household objects for support, and a twisted arm that looked as though it could serve little purpose.

"Come in, come in, will 'ee," she said in a tone showing respect, but devoid of animation. "And a cup of some'n hot I'll gi'e 'ee. To think of ladies ridin' about i' the cold and damp. Makes me shiver, it do, just to think on't."

To show her hospitality, Mrs. Tuckey offered not tea, but hot brewed mead to her guests. Despite her handicaps, she managed to serve them in a most solicitous manner, and once the ladies seemed to have relaxed, Mrs. Tuckey asked what was most on her mind.

"And my Betsy, how be she?"

Ursula was ashamed at once that they had not thought to include Betsy in the morning ride. She wondered how often the girl was able to visit with her own people.

"She is very well," said Lydia, offering no further news. "But it's Lucy I've come to see about now."

Ursula could at last understand from what Lydia's unflattering reputation derived. Her sister-in-law was careless and thoughtless, rather than intentionally mean, but Ursula could not but find this flaw unfortunate.

" 'Tis onlucky then," ventured Mrs. Tuckey, to whom most of life's events were probably "onlucky" ones. "For she be gone to the orchard and packed her a bit of cheese I did this mornin', so she hain't reason to be comin' home till late."

"The matter is one I can well discuss with you," Lydia interrupted. "My brother's wife requires the services of an abigail. Betsy has proved quite satisfactory to me in spite of her lack of experience and prior qualifications. So if you choose to send your other girl to Lady Ursula tomorrow morning, she shall have a place at Collingwood."

Mrs. Tuckey broke into tears. "Milady," she sobbed, "my sperrit is glad on't, but sad on't, too, if 'ee'll know the truth. For to be left here hard alone with that man, that be an onlucky fate for I, see? But to think my girls, the two little maids of 'en, both be out o't, and safe in a fine grand house with such ladies as 'ee be . . . I'll gi'e thanks for this milady every night. And I'll send the girl to you at daylight, that I will."

Ursula wished to reach out and take the unfortunate mother's hand, but Lydia stood abruptly and, leaving a golden guinea on the cluttered table, told Ursula it was time to be off.

There were lowering black clouds on the horizon by sunset, and so the gentlefolk who had gathered on horseback to watch the wassail of the orchard waited only long enough to see Toby Hawkins dip a piece of toast in cider with a most exaggerated gesture and then climb and leave the soggy trophy on the highest branch of the tallest tree. As the farmer folk, led by Toby, burst into song, the fine people of the county nudged their beasts and rode off. They had a party to attend, after all, while the good people of the fields would soon indulge their own taste for pleasure beneath the canvas tent which Lydia had ordered erected. Snorting casks of cider—also Lydia's gift—awaited the revelers.

Collingwood became a center of bustling, flurrying activity as the guests returned to its welcome comforts. Their valets and ladies' maids drew hot baths, arranged curls, and put the finishing touches on the fancy dress their masters and mistresses had brought from home.

Lydia insisted that Betsy see to Ursula first. With the abigail she sent over a casket filled with amethyst chains. By skillful arrangement the chains helped disguise the mended portion of the lilac tunic. "Yes, they'll all see why His Lordship waited so long to wed," commented Betsy. "Twill be no mystery oncet they zee the beautiful bride he found him."

Then, realizing that her appearance would be a reflection on Richard and his honour, Ursula took a sudden interest in her image in the glass and tried to pinch some colour into her wan cheeks.

Downstairs, Ursula was surprised by the glittering assembly of lords and ladies dressed as if for a night at the Royal Opera. Most surprising of all was Lydia, who slowly descended the curving staircase, graceful as the sweep of her white silk gown. She was as breathless and tremulous as a leaf in the wind and would have looked for all the world like a maiden at her presentation ball were it not for the low and unmaidenly cut of her gown. Four men immediately rushed to greet her and planted kisses, quite unabashedly, on her small hands and pink cheeks.

Lydia sensed Ursula's perplexity over her behaviour, for shortly afterwards, while the guests helped themselves to cider and port, and while Lydia led Ursula around the drawing room to make introductions, she spoke softly in her ear. "Darling, everyone here understands our situation, that circumstances have left us bereft of our husbands—me forever and you for a short while. We are among friends, good and true friends, and there is nothing wrong if they show their admiration and let us know we are still young women. You needn't fear the attentions of anyone in this room. They are all dear friends of Richard's, and if they flirt

165

with you, it's as much out of affection for him as a natural response to your beauty."

Somewhat reassured, Ursula went in to supper on the arm of Bertram Moorhead, whose carriage and demeanour made it clear he was not unaware of the effect he had on the ladies, with his imposing head of thick black hair, his penetrating grey eyes, and a low, seductive voice that made the most common pleasantries sound like intimacies.

Indeed, as they sat together at the table, enjoying pigeon pie and asparagus, roasted sweetbreads and a garnish of local cucumbers, Bertram spoke of frivolous matters with an intensity equal to Richard's when speaking of his innermost hopes and dreams.

Bertram's eyes never left her face, except to glance now and again down to her bodice, to watch her tiny hand bring the fork to her lips, and then to linger on those lips until Ursula was too dismayed to chew or swallow.

Objectively Ursula agreed that Bertram was an attractive man, but more than loyalty to Richard kept her from feeling the least bit attracted to him. She was frankly repelled by the way he overtly used his compelling force. Lydia had assured her that the guests could be trusted, and without that assurance Ursula might have become openly rude to her table companion.

"I saw the most interesting wager being won today," Bertram was telling her in his smooth and hypnotic voice. "A labourer laid his whole week's wage on a claim that, with his hands tied behind his back, he could kill a hedgehog with his face." As Ursula made no response whatsoever, he simply continued with his anecdote. "He wasn't an extraordinarily handsome man, but still, hardly frightful enough to kill a beast just by looking at it. I hate to take advantage of a workingman in his cups, but I'll allow I was one of many who laid odds against him."

Ursula's fork was in midair, but she let her hand drop back to her plate. It wasn't that her attention was so caught up in the story, but rather that the event seemed so grotesque that it had quite stolen away her appetite.

"His hands were bound, he lay down on the earth, and the hedgehog was produced and set before him. He grimaced most fearfully—the man, that is—and then set to attacking the creature with his nose, if you can imagine! At that moment I realized the man was a madman, and there was talk of calling off the bet entirely. His face was soon torn by the bristles, and though he was bleeding profusely, when a friend attempted to put an end to the trial, the bleeding man become enraged and insisted on his right to continue. Meanwhile, the hedgehog, had curled up into a prickly ball and withdrawn its head. It was winning the fight by refusing to engage in combat and allowing its human foe to destroy himself against its quills."

"Mr. Moorhead, I don't think I can listen to more . . ." Ursula interrupted faintly.

"Very well, I shall spare you more description and jump ahead to the felicitous ending. At last the hedgehog grew tired of this incessant prodding, uncurled itself, and stretched out its little neck. The labourer, who had been waiting long for this very opportunity, reacted in the instant and bit off the creature's head. He won his three shillings."

Bertram laughed heartily.

Feeling ill, Ursula watched the savoury dishes go by. When the veal fillet with mushroom sauce was served and Bertram explained how the calves were raised in the dark and fed on a concoction of milk laced with local mead, she nodded and said, "How interesting," but could not bring herself to eat another bite.

Dared she plead a headache and escape to her room? Ursula feared not. She surely would have fled from Bertram alone, but Ursula wished to make a good impression on the other neighbours who had traveled long distances in the cold to meet her. She bore her agitation in silence and with great self-restraint.

When they rose from the table, the guests were ushered into the ballroom. The musicians were already tuned up and in the gallery, and they began the night with several country-dances.

Ursula had dreaded the thought of the dancing, but she soon discovered that in the rhythms and music she found some release from the terrible tensions that beset her. The faster the music, the better she felt as though she could throw off her nervous agitation through physical exhaustion.

Then, at a sign from Lydia, the waltzing began. Ursula had diligently sought the company of an old and fatherly country gentleman and had danced and conversed with relative contentment in his safe company. But with the strains of the waltz, he apologized that he did not know the step, and before she could forestall the move, Bertram had claimed her and swept her onto the dance floor.

She held herself stiffly, and when his hands took undue advantage of her proximity, she purposefully put her natural grace in abeyance long enough to tread most clumsily on his feet.

Seemingly oblivious to any rebuff, Bertram whispered in her ear "I know how you are suffering now. I shall mention your husband in my prayers each night, my dear, but while he is gone, remember you have a friend in me. Come to me for whatever you may need, and you will not find me lacking."

"I trust your intentions are good, if you say they are," she replied at last, "but I assure you, I am quite well and need not trouble you for any attentions whatsoever."

He smiled and drew her closer.

This is intolerable, Ursula thought at last. Pleading the headache, which, in fact, was throbbing painfully behind her temples, she tore herself from her unwanted partner, bade the visitors an apologetic good night, and withdrew.

She locked her door, prepared hurriedly for bed, and climbed beneath the coverlet with Gueevie in her arms. Despite her inner turmoil, she fell directly asleep but was wakened shortly thereafter by Gueevie's anxious whimpering. Ursula rubbed her eyes and listened. There was someone at the door, a gentle knock.

"Ursula?" It was Bertram's voice. She heard the sound of the doorknob being turned and gave silent thanks that she had thought to turn the key. "Locked!" muttered the voice in irritation.

Filled with horror and despair, Ursula clutched her puppy to her and passed the night trying in vain to recapture the sweet oblivion of sleep.

CHAPTER FOURTEEN

In the morning Ursula would have liked to stay in bed and hide, but with a houseful of guests that seemed impossible.

Still, she was paralyzed into inactivity as she reviewed the night's events over and over. Had she done anything to encourage that awful man to think he could visit her room? Her knowledge of the gentry's social code was so sketchy that she concluded she might well have made a misstep somewhere during the evening without realizing it. Perhaps she should have delivered a sterner setdown during the waltz.

Ursula was so inexperienced that she could barely conceive of a stranger's behaving to her in such a way without her having given some sort of provocation. She was too innocent to believe in her own innocence.

Was it possible, she thought at last, that she had merely imagined the sounds at her door? Had Bertram's voice been but a product of her feverish agitation? That must be the case, she told herself desperately and proceeded to convince herself of the truth of that theory.

I was asleep, she reminded herself, and roused myself only because of Gueevie. Most likely I wasn't fully awake. I heard some sound in the corridor and, dreaming, imagined it to be what I most feared.

Then the ghostly memory of a nighttime knock upon her door was driven from her mind by a new and very real rapping. She might have failed to respond to the sound, fearing to find Bertram at the other side of the door, but the voice that reached her ears was feminine in register.

"Speak up, girl," came Lydia's distinct tones. "Speak clearly."

Ursula unlocked her door to find her sister-in-law standing in the hallway with a young, apple-cheeked, and blushingly shy young girl who was, without doubt, Lucy Tuckey.

The poor young servant was overwhelmed with confusion at the warm and almost joyful greeting she received from her new mistress. No one had ever looked so happy to see her before. Lucy Tuckey could not have known that she stood like Deliverance in Ursula's doorway. Not only was she a much more welcome sight than Bertram would have been, but she also armed Ursula with a credible excuse for remaining closeted upstairs awhile longer.

Lydia left the two women alone together at Ursula's request and drifted toward the parlour, where the board had been set for breakfast with mountains of breads and dainties, hams, and oysters. Most of the guests had risen with hearty appetites and were doing justice to the spread, forcing themselves out of their over-stuffed armchairs only long enough to replenish their plates. A dozen pairs of eyes turned to mark Lydia's entrance, and she basked in their admiration.

"Why don't you find Ursula and fetch her downstairs to join us?" suggested Lydia after taking a seat near Bertram. "Otherwise, I fear she'll spend the entire day with her new abigail."

Engaged in stuffing his mouth, Bertram merely shrugged at her request.

"You surprise me," said Lydia. "Last night it seemed she evoked a great deal of admiration from you."

"I did not evoke a comparable sentiment in her," he replied, swallowing an oyster.

Lydia smiled and touched his arm. "She is excessively timid, that's all. But reticence is certainly out of character for Bertram Moorhead."

"She seems virtuous," he mumbled.

"Once so was I," returned Lydia with a nervous giggle. "Everyone *begins* as virtuous."

Meanwhile, the subject of this exchange had dismissed Lucy and was sitting dreamily at her writing table, composing a letter to her husband. Although she knew the missive might never reach him, as deliveries to war vessels were uncertain, she felt in close communion with him as she wrote to him gaily and fondly.

She was interrupted from her sentimental task by a male voice, but there was no cause for alarm. It was not Bertram, but Edmund, whom Lydia had dispatched in Bertram's place. Ursula had already conceived such a great fondness for her nephew that she willingly put aside her letter and followed him downstairs.

"Mother doesn't usually allow me to join in adult parties," he explained, "but today I'm to be treated as a man. But honestly, Aunt Ursula, I find adult company rather tedious at times."

"Then why come for me and add still another adult to the assembly?" she teased.

"You could never be tedious," he insisted, and Ursula smiled at him, aware that he spoke out of youthful earnestness, rather than gallantry. She didn't know how she had captured the boy's loyalties, but she was glad she had done so.

When Ursula and Edmund entered the drawing room, Lydia was seated on the sofa with one of her admirers. Her hand was familiarly placed on the man's arm, and they seemed to be deep in conversation. However, the moment the late arrivals had entered the room, she immediately rose to her feet and hurried to sit with her son.

"She certainly quits her friend most abruptly," commented a buxom red-haired woman to Ursula as she gestured with her eyes to the gentleman Lydia had left on the couch. "I rather expected they would be making an announcement."

Ursula made no response, not knowing what was expected. She felt strangely cowed by the red-haired woman. The woman had been introduced as the Lady Amabel, but her bearing, her voluptuous figure, and a certain free air about her put Ursula in mind of the sailor's doxy who had brought about the death of Lord Charles. It was strange to think of her as a member of the aristocracy.

"I could have told you that there would be no such announcement," said Bertram, having overheard the comment and taken the opportunity to insinuate himself between the two ladies. He put an arm around Ursula, and much as she wished to remove it, she hesitated to appear a foolish Puritan in front of Lady Amabel. "Lydia loves her boy," Bertram went on. "She will never marry again. No matter how rich or well-meaning the man may seem, she will never trust anyone to be a stepfather to Edmund. She'd rather see to his future herself, the best she can, than take a chance of his falling upon the mercy of some man with no blood tie."

"A noble sentiment," said Lady Amabel somewhat caustically, "but rather exaggerated, don't you think?"

As this question was addressed to Ursula, who was embarrassed to remain mute again, she tried to answer in diplomatic fashion. "I hardly know anyone here well enough to pass judgment . . ."

"Ah," responded Bertram, "but you shall get to know some of us very well very soon."

"Yes," she replied frostily. "I trust that I shall soon

be on intimate terms with Lydia and Edmund." She stressed their names as if to exclude anyone else from the list. Her point was not lost on Bertram.

"You are a very young woman"—he smiled—"and it's only natural that you still fear men like any schoolroom miss. You may suspect, in some secret part of your mind, that we are really very nice, but those girlish fears that society instills in you take time to overcome. You are too intelligent and lovely to devote yourself to the company of a child like Edmund when there are mature minds around you. So you may rely on me, Lady Ursula. We shall defeat your silly fears together."

"Frankly, Mr. Moorhead," replied Ursula as her temper grew hot, "I am not afraid of you because you cannot possibly do me any harm. You could hurt me very much if I trusted you, but I don't."

Lady Amabel smiled, with the first genuine warmth and respect she had shown, it seemed.

Rather than turn pale or turn away incensed, Bertram burst into a merry peal of laughter. "Ursula, my dear, you are stupendous! I see we shall be the very best of friends!"

"You mistake my meaning, sir," she said coldly, "when I thought I had made it uncommonly clear."

"Uncommonly clear indeed!" he exclaimed. "And you are uncommonly wonderful. I shall fetch you a fresh cup of tea."

"Well spoken of you," came the compliment from Lady Amabel, once Bertram had moved away to the sideboard. "You two will get on famously."

"But I don't mean to get on with him at all."

"Really, Ursula," returned Lady Amabel, "Bertram is a terrible rake and scoundrel, but so was Richard, and it seems you knew how to tame *him*. You have won an unprecedented respect from Bertram. There are many sides to his personality, and you have dazzled him with your frankness and wit. Your words have shown him he must give up all hope of a dalliance, but he is now, no doubt, intent on becoming your friend, and he will not be easily shaken from his course. Believe me," she added, "he is capable of disinterested friendship, though such noble sentiments are not easily inferred from his conduct."

"Perhaps I have been overly harsh," agreed Ursula tentatively. "I have been told before what you are telling me now." She wondered whether to mention the incident of the previous night. But what difference did it make? There could be no doubt that Bertram had anticipated that she would be an easy conquest. The only question remaining was whether, having failed in his initial ambition, he would happily settle for a different sort of relationship.

The afternoon passed with eating and drinking. Some of the men went for a ride, but the drizzle kept the ladies from venturing out of doors. During a game of charades comparisons were drawn between Ursula's countenance and that of the sphinx. Indeed, Ursula had withdrawn into a private world of her own, where she was working to untangle her confused feelings and ideas. She recalled how distrustful she had once been of her own dear husband and chastised herself for being too hasty with her suspicions. Perhaps, she reasoned, her problem stemmed from her close relationship with George. All her life she had known not to take George at his word. In his case she had seen a finer character than the one he presented outwardly. Perhaps, she reasoned, that is how I perceive all people—as being in essence quite contradictory from their words. When people present themselves as honourable, she thought, I immediately expect dishonourable conduct.

Gueevie spent the day curled up in her mistress's lap, and Ursula directed many of her silent thoughts to her pet.

The guests took their leave, at last, before the time of day when the sky was said to "pink in." Suddenly Ursula and Lydia were left alone together.

"Your loyalty to my brother makes me rejoice," said Lydia, breaking the silence that hung between the two women.

Ursula looked up in interest. "Then did you observe my loyalty being challenged?" she asked. If Lydia had been aware of any improper advances, then Ursula knew she had not been imagining her fears.

"Of course. But you are so innocent, my dear." Lydia sighed. "Richard knows you are loyal to him, but he would never expect you to lock yourself up in prison while awaiting his return."

"I don't quite understand you, Lydia."

The shadows deepened in the room. Lydia rose slowly and rang to have the candelabra lit. "Would you care for some more tea? Or perhaps a glass of port?" She did not immediately return to the subject at hand but stood a moment smoothing out the folds of her sprig muslin. She did not speak until the candles were ablaze and the servant had quitted the room.

"We have only just met, and I don't wish to risk your good opinion, sister," she continued at last, "but you grew up without a mother and without close and intimate friends. Your idealism and romanticism are very charming, but really, dear, you must learn to live in the real world."

"You must speak more clearly, sister," said Ursula, growing uneasy.

"An unmarried girl is held to one standard of behavior; a married woman to quite another. It is expected for you to accept an admirer to fill your days—

and your needs—while your husband is unaccountably away."

"Lydia, please!" cried Ursula. She had sensed where the conversation was leading, but to hear the words said aloud was a shock.

"You will think very ill of me, I'm sure," said Lydia, now burying her face in her hands. "It's passing strange to have an innocent like you here. I cherish my late husband's memory, and I shall not remarry because of the jeopardy I fancy my son would run in another man's household. But I am still a woman, and there are times, especially at night, when a woman needs a man. Don't you agree?"

"I need Richard," said Ursula slowly. "Not any man."

"That was what I thought at first"—Lydia sighed—"but I soon learned it was a foolish idea. Time will pass so much more quickly for you if you accept attentions from someone. Bertram was quite taken with you, Ursula."

Ursula stood at last, flushing. "Lydia, I shall not listen to this." Then, afraid of hurting her sister-in-law, she ran to her side and grasped Lydia's hands. "Darling Lydia, I don't judge you. Your husband is never coming back, and you are right to think of Edmund's future. But my husband will return, and I shall wait for him."

"But you needn't hold yourself from other men while you wait."

How strange my life has been, thought Ursula. I am certain that other girls spend their lives hearing speeches about virtue and chastity. Yet I have heard just the opposite from my brother and now from the sister of the man to whom I am married. Am I right to hold such strong views or am I merely being contrary?

"You needn't . . ." began Lydia again.

"Oh, but I must," replied Ursula firmly. "I shall wait for Richard, and no other man will touch me. Don't you see, Lydia? If I accepted attentions from any other, it would be as though I were admitting to myself that Richard will never return. No, no one will touch me until Richard has come home."

"He need never know," urged Lydia. "And if you are worried about . . . children, let me assure you we are not all as naïve as you. A man like Bertram is experienced in avoiding such unwanted complications."

"Why, Lydia?" cried Ursula, her nerves now wrought up into a terrible state. "Why do you push me to do what I know is wrong?"

"For your own good, my dear. Do you think Richard is waiting faithfully for you? He is facing danger every day, and when the ship pulls into port, don't you think he seeks some comfort and release?"

Ursula turned pale, less at the thought of betrayal than at the idea of the danger Richard was facing.

"He is used to having his own way, my dear," continued Lydia. "Didn't you think it strange he allowed himself to be torn from you so easily? No, he must be independent and lead his own life. But my brother is fair and just. He would not demand a greater standard of fidelity from you than he is willing to abide by himself."

"Lydia, promise me you shall not speak to me of this again!" cried Ursula in despair.

"I love you too well to keep silent, sister," replied Lydia. "But no one will force you. You will see, as time passes, the truth in what I say. And when you wish to take a lover, you will do so in the full knowledge that no one here will condemn you. Rather, we shall all rejoice for your happiness. No one will ever breathe a word to Richard. He will have his secrets, and you will have yours."

Seeing that she could not persuade Ursula, Lydia wisely closed the debate. "I shall say no more, darling," she conceded with a sigh. "For now."

CHAPTER FIFTEEN

In November the teazles were thinned and brought in. Ursula rode out with Bertram and watched the men cutting and gathering the purple heads. As if by magic, they seemed to fly off the stalks into waiting hands. Bertram called over one of the men to show Ursula the curved blade that was used for the cutting. It was so tiny that it was almost invisible in the man's big-boned hand.

"I wears gloves, milady," the worker explained cheerfully, "not fer the calluses, 'cos 'ee can zee I got enough of 'en a'ready, but fer the blood." She started at the word "blood" but realized almost immediately that he was merely referring to the thick black sap that came oozing from the teazle stalks when cut.

"The largest heads are called kings," Bertram told her, "and a pack of nine thousand of them will fetch about forty shillings."

"Yea," agreed the workman, "but the family can't wait for 'en to grow to kings. I be cuttin' 'en a'ready at middlin' size, and it takes twenty thousand middlin' heads to make a pack."

Ursula and Bertram dismounted and joined the men when they took their midday break for cider and Cheddar cheese. Bertram was unfailingly courteous to the tenant farmers and to Ursula and was an unending source of information about life on the moors. In all respects he had become a perfect and irreproachable companion. Ursula saw him now as Lady Amabel had described him: a good and intelligent man who could prove to be a true friend once his rakish ambitions had been thwarted. He never repeated his importunities and seemed to respect her decision. Together they walked, laughed, and rode across the moors.

There was a stretch of sunny weather at the end of November, and Ursula imagined this was the West Country at its best: cold and brisk and with all the drama of autumn, but also bright, clear, and bracing.

They packed a hamper with cold foods and headed for the banks of the river Parrett, where Bertram assured her that ancient Roman and pre-Roman artifacts could be found in the river silt.

The ride was delightful, but the riverbank unutterably slimy, and the pottery shards that Bertram drew from the muck hardly seemed worth the agony of plunging one's hand into the icy water. Bertram was not knowledgeable enough about the past to infuse the fragments with any sense of grace or mystery.

As they sat on the bank and partook of their luncheon, Bertram waxed eloquent on a subject in which he was well versed: royal gossip.

"Can you imagine," he demanded, "the state of society when a royal princess, the Prince Regent's own daughter, cannot be presented at court?"

He was referring to Princess Charlotte. Although she was now grown to young womanhood, she was being kept from court owing to her attachment to her mother. Caroline of Brunswick had not been the wife of Prinny's dreams, and the unfortunate daughter of this mismatched alliance suffered the consequences. Neither the Prince Regent nor his wife allowed their unsuited marriage to stand in the way of pleasurable connections with the opposite sex. But the child, straining to be loyal to each parent, could find comfort from neither father nor mother.

"And she's a wild one," added Bertram with a smile.

Much as she enjoyed his company, Ursula could not forget how different his values were from her own.

181

While he was frankly amused by the royal predicament, Ursula's tender heart was filled with pity for the seventeen-year-old princess.

"Surely you have some news of the war . . ." she suggested hesitantly. It was a shame, thought Ursula, that Bertram was in such close communication with London, yet so rarely had information concerning the topic closest to her heart.

"Why, yes. Didn't I tell you about the transparencies at Ackermann's? he asked.

This, too, was very much in character for Bertram Moorhead. He had never told Ursula—probably he had not known about—the allied victory at Leipzig. But when the victory was commemorated in London with a large-scale transparency, which featured Death staring Bonaparte in the face, Bertram knew all the details.

"Oh, I do hope it's true," Ursula mused, "that old Boney won't hold Death at bay much longer. The Dutch have lately thrown off the French yoke," she persisted. "It must be true, don't you think, that Napoleon's time draws near its end?"

When the war is over, she told herself, Richard will be home.

Bertram patted her hand indulgently. "Do not be seduced by too much optimism," he counseled, "unless, that is, you choose the path of King George."

"Which is?"

"Madness, my dear."

"Is it mad to hope? To believe?"

"No, I didn't mean that," he hastened to assure her. "But you know the King is very happy these days. He fancies himself to be conversing with angels day and night. He is at last free of suffering, but at what price? Be hopeful, my dear, and true, but don't cling to unrealistic expectations. When the angels whisper to you in golden voices that the war is coming to an end, you must resist hearing their music. . . ."

How very good he was and wise! How different from the dreadful man who had sat beside her at supper not so very long ago!

That night she was awakened by the scraping of a branch against her window. She stretched, imagining herself a child back in Hampshire. She remembered the way the trees had cast shadows against the wall, like bony arms reaching out to frighten her.

Ursula smiled to herself and settled comfortably beneath the bedclothes. I'm safe at Collingwood, she thought.

Then the sudden realization intruded into her sleepy consciousness: There was no tree outside her window.

She distinctly heard another sound, like scratching or scuffling on the casement ledge.

It's not my imagination, she thought. She sat up in bed, uncertain what to do. At that moment the clouds that had obscured the full moon passed. The moon cast its light through the curtains, rendering them almost transparent, so that the silhouette of a man showed plainly as he clambered to the ledge.

Bertram!

"That's a good girl," he said as she ran to the window. "Open up, and help me in. I've had quite enough exertion. Wretched ladder your gardener keeps."

"Help you in?" she exclaimed, outraged at the fantastical thought that she should not only allow but abet such a liberty. "I am making certain all the latches are secure. I had no intention of even addressing you, but since you have spoken, I must in all courtesy reply. I shall limit my words to these: Leave this place at once, sir, and never let me see you again."

Her cold fury gave her the strength to speak calmly, but all the while Ursula was hurt more deeply than she wished to admit even to herself. She would have been angered at such audacity on the part of any man. Coming from Bertram, the action was all the more reprehensible because he had deceived her so thoroughly as to his intentions. Her horror was mixed with shame at her own naïveté.

"Ursula," he began again in a softer voice, "this ladder is deucedly shaky. Do let me in, and I shan't bother you. But see me out of here, won't you, via a more regular route." He had taken on the tone of an errant schoolboy. "I shall break my neck should I attempt to climb down backwards."

"Do you think to fool me with such a half-witted ruse?" she asked.

"It's really deucedly shaky," he repeated, and she divined from the look on his face that the young gentleman was in all truth much concerned for his health and safety.

So he is not quite the adventurer he fancies himself to be, she remarked to herself.

"I shall count to ten," she warned him, "and if you are not gone by then, I shall open the window and push your precious ladder with all the force I have. Equilibrium is all on my side, and I trust it shall outweigh what advantage you may have in strength."

"You wouldn't!" he protested, decidedly uncomfortable.

"If you wish to lay money on the outcome, I shall oblige you," she said with as grim a look as she could muster. "You have ten seconds before I push your ladder and send you flying to the ground. One . . . two . . . three . . ."

"I'm on my way," he assured her, "but if I haven't

quite touched the earth by the time you've reached ten . . ."

"Four . . . five . . ."

He stood frozen a moment, uncertain what to do, caught between his fear of falling and his fear of looking like a fool. Before Ursula had reached "seven," he had found a compromise solution to save his masculine pride. "I shall be back tomorrow night," he hissed, "with a better ladder." Having said his piece, he climbed backwards to the ground as quickly as his trembling legs would carry him.

Ursula's triumphant flush was soon superseded by an attack of nerves. It had all happened so quickly that she had had no time to be afraid. Now that the incident was over, she shook with fright. No doubt there would be more attempts and the very thought was more than she could endure.

What am I to do? she asked herself in despair.

Even if Bertram did not return as promised, she knew it would be impossible to avoid everyday intercourse with him. As a close friend of the family he was constantly at Collingwood. It was only a matter of time before he would contrive to be alone with her. Speaking to Lydia would be of no use, for Lydia continued to believe that an illicit liaison between her friend and sister-in-law would be a romantic and harmless diversion. Though Lydia would not force the issue, Ursula could not expect any protection from her.

I cannot stay here! she sobbed as she paced back and forth.

I must go to Aunt Mary and Uncle Alfred, she decided at last. I shall write Richard from there, so he will know where to find me. I needn't tell him why I chose to wait for him there. . . .

185

The more rational part of Ursula's mind told her to wait until morning and to discuss the matter calmly with Lydia. But she feared that her own affection for Lydia would make it impossible for her to carry out her intention of quitting Collingwood if her sister-in-law asked her to stay.

No, she thought, at all costs I must avoid a confrontation with Lydia. We should end up saying hurtful things, and I care for her entirely too much for that.

If Ursula had contrived to sleep at all that night, matters might have looked less threatening by the light of a new day. But she was too overset and agitated to sleep. Hours passed, and she continued to pace. Her mind, clouded and befogged by nervous fever and fatigue, was not capable of making a reasoned decision.

In this frenzied state she penned a quick note to Lydia, assuring her that she was well and would be in communication again shortly. Then she dressed quickly in her riding habit, packed one hundred guineas into her purse, hugged Gueevie close to her one last time, and slipped down the stairs.

Of course, she knew it was most improper for her to be riding out alone, but Ursula felt that her case was so urgent and her danger so imminent that ordinary considerations could not apply.

No one stirred as she tiptoed to the stables and, with shaking hands, saddled her pony.

All I have to do is find my way to the Parrett, she thought. Then I follow the course downriver a short distance to Langport, and I board the stage for London. Remaining at Collingwood would be so difficult, she told herself, that by comparison running away was no effort at all.

With this thought she mounted and rode off into the night

Unfortunately the pony did not wish to follow Ursula's route. She was afraid to fight the animal's instinct because when the pony balked, she knew it was because she was urging it on to quicksand or the perilous terrain of a bog. So she gave the pony its head and could only hope it would eventually carry her to the desired destination.

It was wonderful to be free with only the vast sky above her, sprinkled with stars that shone brittle and bright in the winter night. But another hour passed, and Ursula had completely lost her bearings. The sky would soon begin to turn light, she thought, and so she resolved to stop awhile and wait for sunrise. Then she would be able to determine which direction was east.

This plan was revolving in her tired head when the pony took off at a sudden trot for a clump of scraggly birch. Ursula's spirits revived at the sight of a grove of trees. It meant firm ground. It meant, perhaps, human habitation not far away.

Beyond the trees she saw a wall of dark shadows rising up into the night. Were they clouds or hills? She had grown so accustomed to flat stretches of ground that the promise of hills was like a spur to her hopes. But which hills? Had she traveled west to the Quantocks? Or east to the Poldens? Where was she?

"Halt, or it's dead 'ee be!" cried a voice, ringing through the silence of the night.

These threatening words were soon backed up by the appearance of a man on horseback pointing a musket at Ursula's breast.

She felt herself flushing as her assailant rode up closer. She could not read his face, which was covered with a mask, but his surprise was evident.

" 'Ee be a wooman!" he declared with delight.

Without another word the highwayman tied her pony behind his own, grabbed Ursula, and set her at the front of his saddle.

She struggled in his arms, but it was useless. Her spirit was ready for a fierce fight, but her body was exhausted. The contest would have been unequal in any event, and in a matter of moments she had utterly collapsed. She lay on the horse's neck, capable of nothing but tears.

A chill rain began to fall, obscuring the wintry sunrise, as the highwayman set his horse trotting. The moor pony followed along behind, and Ursula resisted no further as the stranger carried her off toward the dark hills.

CHAPTER SIXTEEN

When Ursula regained consciousness, she was lying beneath soft, warm animal skins. The scene about her was the strangest, most dreamlike in which she had ever found herself.

She was in a dark chamber—no, not like the chamber of a proper house, but rather beneath the low, damp, and vaulted ceiling of a cave. There was no sound but the howling winds and the crackling of the fire. By the flickering glow of the flames she could see a strange man crouching and stirring the embers. Memory rushed over her, and an involuntary gasp escaped her lips.

He turned, and the firelight flashed through his dark eyes. Squatting, he looked like a wild beast, but when he stood and approached her, for some reason she was not afraid. The expression on his dark countenance was inquisitive and benign.

He handed her a mug. " 'Tis brandy," he said. When she resisted, he added sternly, "I'll abide no argument. 'Ee've been chilled and shocked, and 'tis brandy will restore 'ee best."

She took a tentative sip and felt the strong warmth coursing through her blood. She breathed deeply and knew that, in spite of her situation, the brandy was relaxing her.

He watched her carefully, keeping his distance.

"Are you Pocock?" asked Ursula. Her curiosity gave her courage.

The man smiled but still kept his distance. "That's what I be called," he said.

"But is it your name?" she persisted.

"An' wot's the diff'rence in that?" he asked.

"Pocock is a hero to many people," she replied, "so if I were going to dedicate myself to your line of work, I daresay I'd let them call me Pocock, too. Then, in my troubles, I expect I'd find friends willing to hold their tongues for me or even hide me in their barns."

" 'Ee're a clever un," he answered, but conceded nothing. He watched in silence as she slowly drank down the contents of her mug. "Well, miss," he said at length, " 'ee've the look of a lady to me eyes, an' I hain't ne'er zeed but one reason fer a fine miss to leave her comforts o' home. Wot brute do yer people plan to wed 'ee to?"

This question started the tears streaming hot and free down Ursula's fair cheeks.

"Don' 'ee be cryin'," said the outlaw in a gentle voice. "I hain't got no aim to harm 'ee. An' as fer this man 'ee're to marry—"

"I *am* married," she managed to exclaim.

"Ah, so it's too late," he said, in a voice that surprised her with its sympathy.

"No," she corrected him, still crying. "That's not it at all. I love my husband with all my heart."

"A wooman wot loves her husband ain't to be found wanderin' the heath of a night when she could be home lyin' by his side," he suggested.

"But if only I *could* be! If Richard were home, none of this would have happened!"

How badly Ursula needed someone to talk to! This man, though an outlaw, had not harmed her so far, and it seemed he intended her no wrong. Without further prompting she brought her shaking voice under control and proceeded to tell Pocock her story.

The highwayman sat with his back against the wall of his cave, his knees drawn up, and a mug in his hand. He refilled it again and again as Ursula spoke.

190

When she finished, to her surprise he threw his head back and laughed.

"Do you find my situation so amusing then?" she asked, daring to take offense at his mirth.

"No, milady, that I don't," he replied seriously, and she was surprised by the respectful term of address which he used without the slightest hint of sarcasm. " 'Tis but that it tickled me fancy to think that a lady wot threatens ter break her lover's neck and then rides off alone across the moors in the dark of night"—here he was overcome again by laughter—"beggin' yer pardon, I'm sure, but it makes me laugh to think a female o' sech sperrit as yers could be afeard of *anything*. I just cain't avoid the thought in my head, ma'am, that 'ee'd be perfectly safe at Collin'wood or anywhere else. 'Ee can certain take care o' yerself!"

This speech served to revive both Ursula's spirits and her self-confidence. "Do you really think so?" she asked.

They continued to discuss the situation at some length, deciding on the most politic approach to take with Lydia and settling upon various precautionary measures, such as having Lucy Tuckey move into Ursula's chamber with her at night.

"It really is not all as bad as I thought," concluded Ursula with a sigh. "I suppose I was a terrible goosecap to run away."

"Well, no harm done," he soothed her, " 'cept that 'ee've managed to break Pocock's heart."

"Oh, dear!" she exclaimed in some alarm, causing him to laugh heartily again.

" 'Tis at meself I'm laughing, milady," he gasped between attacks of hilarity. " 'Tis just that I've long thought meself to be the best-loved man in England, 'ceptin' of course His Majesty. And now I'm led to realize that fer all me woomen, not one 'as ever loved me as 'ee do yer Richard."

Ursula was moved by this frank avowal, which also stirred her curiosity. "How much love can a woman show you when you live in a cave and lead the kind of life you do?" she asked.

Pocock laughed again. " 'Tis not I they love, milady," he said without hesitation. " 'Tis only me repute, and now I zee the difference. . . . When first I took to the roads," he explained, "I said farewell to me mother and me sisters at home. But I zeed to it they never wanted for naught, milady."

"I've heard tell," agreed Ursula cautiously, "that you are most generous to the poor."

"I hain't got no special love for the poor, milady," he confessed, "but I'd never let one o' me own go hungry, zee? And everyone knows it, that I'd never let none of me kin go hungry or cold. So the result is, every village girl for leagues around wants a bundle wrapped in swaddlin' clothes off'n me. I obliges best I can."

Ursula wanted to be shocked, and yet wasn't, unless it was at her own failure to express proper moral outrage. /

"But, milady," he said, "I mean to oblige 'ee in another way. Bide where 'ee be for now, but when 'ee've taken yer rest, back on yer pony 'ee go, and I'll lead 'ee to Langport if it's still yer mind to make fer London. But I'd much counsel 'ee to choose home, instead, an' I'll gladly lead 'ee that way, to the very approach to Collin'wood, as near as I dares to go."

Now the tears that filled her eyes were luminous with gratitude and trust.

"Yes, I shall go home," she decided. "And I shall remember you in my prayers, Mr. Pocock," she whispered, "though I fear that is not the kind of recompense you value."

"I doubt it'll help me, but it can't harm me," was his prompt reply. Then, softening, he added, "Milady, it is a recompense that's got value fer such as yerself. A lady such as yerself don't pray for the likes of Pocock without there bein' true feelin', if I daresay so. . . . And knowin' that, milady, I am moved and grateful fer yer prayers. Now sleep awhile, milady, sleep, and soon thereafter I'll zee 'ee safely home."

The evening was pinking in when the highwayman waved farewell for the last time and left Ursula on the heath within sight of Collingwood.

She smiled and sang softly as she headed toward the estate. When her pony began to whinny, Ursula broke out of her reverie and realized that a storm was coming up. The red sky of sunset was turning dark rapidly, not with the onset of night, but with the gathering of an army of black clouds.

"Home!" she cried, kicking the pony, "or we shall be caught!"

Collingwood was clearly silhouetted against the violent sky but seemed as distant as ever. A pitchfork of lightning split the heavens and illuminated the faraway hills.

I do hope Pocock reaches his cave before the storm breaks, she thought with concern. If I get soaked, at least I have a fine, warm house to welcome me.

No, I needn't worry on his behalf, she reminded herself. If the rain catches him, he'll simply hasten to the side of some poor country maid and share a dry bed of straw with her beneath the roof of some barn. Some fine friends I have, she told herself and had to laugh.

Hurry! thought Ursula frantically, as a crash of thunder sent birds screaming and scurrying for shelter. The skies opened, and a torrential rain began to pour. She was in a fever to be off the moor. The ground could be treacherous when wet, and her pony's hooves were already sinking deep and making sucking sounds in the mud.

Why, we are caught in a real tempest, she thought.

But this idea made her forge ahead with renewed confidence. It made her think of the tempest that had thrown a shipload of survivors onto Bermuda hundreds of years before. It brought to mind the terrible storm that had shaken the *Fortitude* from bow to stern and the tempestuous emotions that had transformed her once placid life since meeting Richard.

Water coursed down her spine, and her hair was plastered against her skull, but Ursula was no longer aware of the elements.

The tempest was the final test. I must pass through the storm before I can reach shelter, she thought. Richard will come home soon, and there will be no more trials to endure, no more days of longing and waiting. If I can but get through the storm!

The pony bolted with fear as lightning tore through the night again, but Ursula kept the beast under control. Finally, through the blinding rain and sleet, her eyes were dazzled by the lights of home.

She pounded on the heavy door. Her heart was thudding until she thought it would burst. At last Ursula saw servants' eyes regarding her through the window, but no one opened to her, and water from the eaves kept running down her back while her knuckles smarted from knocking.

I must look such a sight, she realized in stunned surprise, that they don't even recognize me!

The battering of the rain against the roof drowned

194

out all other sounds, so Ursula did not hear the foot-steps approaching or the creak of the door swinging open.

Although she was already predisposed to offer a most joyful greeting to whatever person should help her escape the wrath of the elements, Ursula was hardly prepared for the wonderful sight that met her eyes.

"Richard!" she cried. She fell into his arms. How she had dreamed of this reunion! How many times she had pictured it and lived it over and over in her fantasy!

She felt his arms held rigidly about her a moment. Then her husband pushed her firmly from him and set her apart on her own feet.

"Welcome home," he said in a cutting voice. "I hope your homecoming proves to be as happy as my own."

His eyes were cold and cloudy as polluted ice. She understood immediately what had happened. Richard had come home and found her gone. He had drawn his own conclusions as to where she had spent the night. What a stupid, stupid thing I have done! she thought.

"Richard," she began again, and her voice, which only moments earlier had expressed absolute love, now reflected fear and confusion. There was an edge of desperation in it. and he seemed to remark upon it silently and bitterly. "Let me explain," she began, but a fit of coughing racked her slender frame.

Lydia joined them and took her brother's arm while avoiding Ursula's eyes. "Richard, have you given this any thought?" she asked.

"We can't leave her out there to die," Richard snapped at his sister. "After all, she is my wife." The last word was pronounced with such disgust that Ursula felt the ground give way beneath her. "Take

195

her in." Without addressing another word to Ursula, he turned on his heels and was gone.

Lydia stepped aside, and Ursula stumbled into the entryway, groping for something against which to steady herself.

"You're very fortunate you married such an honourable man," remarked Lydia.

"But do let me explain," begged Ursula.

The coachman has explained enough," Lydia answered coldly, "about finding Bertram climbing down from your window."

"Ohhh! But that is evidence in my favor, Lydia, don't you see? It was to escape Bertram that I ran away."

She could well understand Richard's shock in arriving home and finding her gone, but Ursula was unsettled by Lydia's attitude. Surely Lydia could not believe such evil of her, and even if it were all true, wasn't a tryst with Bertram just what Lydia had been advocating all along?

But Lydia would not even look directly at her. Lucy!" she called. "Kindly see that your mistress is put to bed and kept warm." Having imparted these instructions, Lydia followed her brother's lead and quitted the room.

Lucy saw to her needs in silence. Ursula could barely stop coughing, but this indisposition was nothing compared to the pain in her heart. If only Richard would come to see her, she was certain she could convince him of her innocence. All she had to do was tell him the truth. She fought against the fever that threatened to cloud her mind. I'll be sick later, she thought, but for now I must stay well long enough to explain to Richard.

"Please, tell him I must speak with him," she begged Lucy.

She would have gone in search of him herself, but she was so weak and dizzy that she could hardly sit up in bed without assistance.

He can't believe this of me, she thought. Now that I'm home, he'll come and see me. I must be delirious, she told herself. Richard is home at last. Everything is going to be all right now. This is a bad dream and nothing more.

It was not until the following morning that Richard composed himself enough to visit Ursula's chamber. He found her delirious and thrashing about beneath the coverlets. At moments she would suffer terrible chills that made her huddle beneath the blankets. Then searing heat would course through her body and cause her to thrust all covering away with whatever weak strength she could muster. When she looked up at him, her eyes rolled in her head. He panicked at the thought that she might be dying.

Curious! he thought to himself. I ought to wish her dead. And yet . . .

Impassioned love battled in his breast against his suspicious rage.

He felt something dart between his feet as a small spaniel lunged toward the bed. Gueevie swung crazily on the hanging coverlet and then scampered up to lick Ursula's face.

The dog is a faithful beast, he reflected, but it was my misfortune to be born a man, subject to a lifetime of betrayals, infidelities, and an infinite series of blunders.

He wanted to cry out in pain. Yet how he longed to take that faithless woman into his arms and comfort her!

"Lucy!" He stood in the doorway and bellowed. The girl came running and bobbed a quick curtsy.

"Milord?"

"Have my sister send for a doctor immediately. Then come back here directly. You are to tend my wife until she is conscious and well enough to see me. She is not to be left alone. Now make haste!"

In her delirium Ursula clutched Gueevie to her.

Look, thought Richard bitterly, how she reaches out to any warm body she finds near.

His mind was overcome, and every beautiful memory associated with Ursula seemed irretrievably tainted. He thought of how delighted he had once been by her ardent response to his caresses. Now he had a new interpretation for her passion; it wasn't usual for an inexperienced girl to take pleasure in physical love so quickly and easily, he told himself. I should have known from the start, he thought, that I was dealing with a brazen wanton.

Through her fever Ursula was vaguely aware of her husband's presence, and she fought against her illness. I must explain to him, she thought. I must tell him what happened. He will believe me; I know he will. But her mind was full of nightmare images, of lightning striking ships while the world turned over and over again, of bodies engulfed in mud, sucked down to a bottomless pit. Lord Charles waved his vinegared handkerchief at her, and it was raining, cold, wet, and raining, and Richard would never come home.

She clenched her fists, and her body was shaken with spasms.

Richard could hold back no longer. No matter what this woman had done, he loved her with all his heart and soul. Much as he had suffered since he had arrived home, filled with eager love, to learn that Ursula had run off with Moorhead—much as he had suffered then, it was nothing compared to the pain that tore through his heart at the sight of Ursula's suffering.

He surrendered and flung himself beside her. "Ursula," he whispered, "it will be all right. You're going to be well." He held her hands, unclenching the fists and gently massaging her fingers to make them relax. "I'm here, darling. You're going to be all right." With these words Richard bent to kiss her forehead.

Ursula knew he was with her, and an immense relief flooded through her. But the trial wasn't over yet. She had to explain. The real world glimmered through to her at moments in between dreaming, and she tried to hold herself and her consciousness there—in the chamber where Richard waited for her explanation. It was there that her fate would be decided. Ursula prepared her words in her mind and tried to speak but lapsed back into the place of nightmare visions. The only sound that escaped from her lips was an eerie moan.

"I'm here, darling," Richard repeated, stroking her face and running his fingers through her damp hair.

Richard! she said or thought she said.

The room was spinning and filled with a lurid red glow. I have to explain, she thought, and began to force out the words.

Richard strained to understand the unintelligible syllables that poured forth from Ursula's cracked lips.

"I'm here, darling," he repeated.

Ursula made a final effort to finish what she had to say, grasping Richard's hand and expelling her words with vehemence as though they were poison.

But in all her garbled feverish speech, the speech of a woman murmuring nonsense syllables in her sleep, Richard understood but one word.

199

"Bertram," she said.

Richard recoiled in horror.

So she really loves him, he thought and ran blindly into the hall.

CHAPTER SEVENTEEN

The doctor was from home, but Lydia, with a stern and unyielding expression on her face, supervised Betsy in boiling up some withy reeds. This yielded a bitter brew that was said to have the virtue of lowering the heat of a fever. From this brew Ursula was given to drink, and compresses soaked in the solution were placed on her brow. By evening she was conscious and lucid, though subject to fits of coughing and still in a weakened state. Her porcelain skin was almost transparent, and the receding fever left only the slightest flush high on her prominent cheeks.

"Leave us," said Richard, appearing suddenly at the door. He stood silently until Lydia and Lucy had made a nervous exit together. Then he pulled a chair up near Ursula's bedside and stared at her thoughtfully while composing his thoughts and emotions. "We must discuss our arrangements," he said at last, and was surprised by the tremor in his own voice.

"Richard, you would not be so unjust as to condemn me without hearing my defense," she said softly. Her eyes were the colour of evening shadows—candid, honest, yet smoky with a mystery all their own. If he could but penetrate those depths!

"What justification can there be . . . ?" he began.

"I do not speak of justification, Richard," she replied passionately, "but of truth. I can only guess what you have been imagining about me, but you must believe I have never been unfaithful. It was only love for you that made me flee from this house. . . ."

"Do you accuse my sister and my servant of lying?" he asked in a slow and menacing voice.

"I accuse no one," she answered, losing some of her innocent assurance. "All I can do is tell you what I know." The blue eyes closed a moment, as though the light, the world, were too much to bear. "If someone has made a mistake," she said softly, "it shall be for you to judge."

Then, because it seemed he might cut her off, Ursula hastened to tell him everything that had happened since her arrival at Collingwood. Her confidence grew as she spoke. Hadn't this very story melted the heart of an outlaw? How could her own beloved husband fail to be moved?

Although she told Richard that Lydia had encouraged her friendship with Bertram, she stopped short of confessing that Lydia had actively promoted an amorous liaison. She hadn't the heart to disillusion Richard about his sister.

"But all I have is your word," he argued. "And to believe it, I must deny my sister and all the servants in the household. I even rode today to confront Bertram Moorhead, only to find him gone. The butler was terrified by the sight of me and hastened to tell me that his master had departed only that morning for parts unknown. That's as clear an admission of guilt as I require."

"Of *his* guilt!" she cried. "Not mine!"

"Everything tells against you, Ursula. You ask me to believe you, but who will second your claims and tell me that you speak the truth?"

"Everyone knows . . ." she began to say, and then swallowed her words as she realized the extent of her predicament. There was no one. Of course, neither was there anyone who had actually witnessed her and Bertram together in any compromising position, but there was no denying that they had been virtually inseparable companions. He had taken most of his meals

202

at Collingwood and had frequently stayed the night. They had often been unchaperoned. In retrospect Ursula had to admit that her conduct, while essentially blameless, had rendered her most vulnerable to suspicions of this sort.

To Richard, her tongue-tied confusion was an admission of guilt. "You've had your say," he said impatiently. "Now I shall have mine. I'll not burden you with recriminations. I'll not tell you what your treachery has done to me. You are my wife, alas, and so I shall provide for you. You are free to remain here at Collingwood, but henceforth our lives shall be separate. This wing is yours. I have my own. Eat your fill at the table, and dress as you please. Your allowance will continue without interruption. I do not care what you do with yourself. However, I shall not allow my family's name to be disgraced. You shall leave the premises only under close supervision. We shall not see each other. There may be formal occasions when I shall require you to make an appearance as my viscountess. You shall do so graciously and mind you keep a proper tongue in your head at such times—"

"Richard," she interrupted, a broken sob rising in her breast, "I love you. . . ."

"That no longer signifies, my dear," he said coldly. "You should have considered that before, when your appetites drove you to the arms of my foppish neighbour."

"Richard, my husband," she tried again, "don't you remember our days and nights in Bermuda? How many times did we promise to love each other forever?"

"And how much value, Ursula, did you place on those vows?" he demanded.

"The value of my life!" she cried.

"And I would give my life, Ursula," he said violently, "if you could only convince me of that."

Ursula's mind raced frantically, trying to devise some means of proof.

"Pocock, if you can find him, will tell you how we met," she suggested.

"And I'm to believe an outlaw's word and deny my own household?" he countered. "Did you share his bed, too, that he will do as you bid him?" he added savagely.

This cruel taunt left her momentarily speechless, as much with grief for her husband as with hurt and insult to herself.

"Richard," she said at last, "you would not speak to me so harshly were you not suffering. I would not see you suffer for anything in the world. Don't you know that? You have been through a terrible war, and I, too, have suffered here without you. Can we not put the past behind us and find some happiness together now?"

Can I simply forgive her? he was wondering. Can we simply start anew? His pride was wounded, and his honour; and yet the thought of a reconciliation made Richard begin to soften.

He was on the verge of speaking when Ursula cried out in despair "You really do believe all those things you said that night to the sailors! You really have no faith in a woman's heart at all!"

So, Richard thought angrily, she'd force me to forgive her misconduct by reminding me of my own. In his agitation he completely misconstrued her motive in calling the regrettable incident to mind.

The memory of his ill-judged words also brought back many other memories—of women whose characters lacked constancy and sincerity. These recollections served but to increase his rage.

I thought she was different, he said to himself bitterly, looking at his wife. Without another word he left the room.

Ursula passed a sleepless night. The events of her life had simply raced out of her own control. At first she wanted to die, so impossible of favourable resolution did her situation appear. But as the night wore on, she tried to take a cold and rational view. She realized that if she allowed herself to be overwhelmed by despair, the intensity of her suffering would in itself preclude the chance of reestablishing her good relations with Richard.

It may take time, she told herself, but the truth will have to come out eventually. I have waited this long for him to come home, and I can go on waiting awhile longer. What other alternative do I have?

There was no way they could live under the same roof, she told herself, in such close proximity without resuming their former intimacy. It was only a matter of time.

Dawn was already streaking the sky when Ursula at last convinced herself that she had reason to go on living. Richard had come out of the war unscathed, and that was the important thing. He was home, and so, no matter what cruel words he spoke to her, nothing could convince her that their love was over or that her cause was lost.

Weeks passed, and Ursula's only companions were Edmund and Gueevie. The boy was aware that his dear aunt had somehow earned everyone's disapproval, but he could not guess what the reason might be and dared not ask.

Ursula took many of her meals in her room. Her husband's silence at table was oppressive to her in a way that pure solitude could never be. Though she endeavoured to remain optimistic, she found that she and Richard increasingly avoided each other.

One afternoon the family was gathered for a dinner of haricot mutton when a note was delivered to the viscount. Richard read it, and his face reflected minor annoyance.

"Amabel has it in her head to give a Christmas ball," he reported, "so I suppose we must go."

Lydia's countenance immediately brightened. "That's wonderful!" she exclaimed. "You needn't act as though it were a tragedy."

"I wonder if it's to be a German Christmas," he said. "Deuced nuisance if it is."

Ursula said nothing and toyed with the food on her plate while she tried to imagine what it would be like to appear in public with Richard, playing the roles of happy man and wife. The strain, no doubt, would be terrible, but at the same time she could not help but look forward to the ball.

"But you are the most generous of men," Lydia was arguing. "I should think you would welcome the opportunity to offer gifts."

"I do," he replied, "but I still wish the custom had never been introduced. I happily give presents to the people I love and just as willingly offer charity to those in need. But what a tedious nuisance it is to have to devise appropriate gifts for all the neighbours Amabel is certain to invite."

"I shall gladly make the selections," said Lydia.

Her eagerness made Richard smile in spite of himself. "Very well, you may have the responsibility—as a Christmas gift from me to you."

The evening of December 24 came at last and found Ursula and Lucy in earnest debate on the topic of petticoats. Ursula's toilette had proceeded no farther than her chemise, and she stood before the fireplace to keep warm while Lucy insisted that most ladies had quite given up the wearing of additional undergarments.

"But, Lucy," Ursula objected, "you know the viscount is most scrupulous about propriety. Besides, Lady Amabel's castle is said to be terribly draughty. I should not wish to catch cold as a result of excessive vanity and inadequate clothing."

"Milady, 'ee'll grow heated enough in the dancin'—"

"Dancing? Lucy, I'm an old married lady and most likely shall not stand up once," she answered.

"His Lordship will dance with 'ee all night," insisted the girl.

This assurance was well meant, but misplaced. It encouraged Ursula to make up her mind at last, rather than continue a conversation on so poisonous a theme.

"Yes, bring me my petticoat," she said firmly, "the flannel one. I shall be not only respectable but comfortable and warm."

"Yes, milady," said the resigned abigail.

Without further ado Lucy fetched the petticoat and helped her mistress into a dove-grey satin robe which provided an elegant background to a gauze confection enlivened with embroidery in shades of violet and blue. Ursula stood before her full-length glass, trying to decide whether her sapphires would look right above the low, square-cut neckline.

"What do you think?" she asked Lucy after the abigail had fastened the catch.

"I think you can do better," said Richard from the doorway. "May I come in?" He stepped behind his wife, removed the necklace, and handed it back to Lucy.

Ursula trembled at his touch and hoped he had not been aware of it. She still stood facing the glass, watching Richard's reflection rather than his person, as he placed a golden tiara amid her curls. It was set with six different cameos, carved in classical style from agate and onyx. A matching necklace, with a seventh cameo, replaced the sapphires.

"It's perfect, milord," said Lucy, unable to restrain her delight.

Lucy's enthusiasm gave Ursula a moment to collect herself and conquer her confusion. Could the jewels be a peace offering? she wondered. Richard's fingers had been stiff and impersonal when he touched her neck, but was it possible his long coldness was coming to an end?

"Thank you," she whispered at last.

"It's nothing," he replied. "Now when you are asked what your husband gave you for Christmas, you will have an answer. Stevenson will be ready with the carriage in no more than ten minutes, and we shall await you downstairs."

"I'm quite ready now," she said, fighting tears. "Thank you, Lucy, and Merry Christmas." She took her husband's arm, knowing he would not draw back from her now. The performance had begun. He had made it quite clear that he was concerned not with emotion, but only with appearances. As they walked down the curving staircase together, she noted bitterly what a fine picture they made.

Indeed, they were the focus of all eyes as they entered Lady Amabel's ballroom thirty minutes later.

The castle was as draughty as anticipated, and Ursula was glad she had insisted on her flannel petticoat. Most of the other ladies seemed oblivious to the cold; the Greco-Roman nymphs that graced the statuary niches were clad no less scantily than some of the guests.

"You mustn't mind all the rude stares," their hostess teased as she greeted them warmly. "It's just that you've been out of society so long."

"Though not out of people's gabble, I collect," commented Richard.

Lady Amabel laughed gaily. "It's all well intentioned, I assure you. Why, no one has dared visit you in the month you've been home, so as not to intrude on the privacy of your reunion with your bride."

Under the best of circumstances Ursula might have taken offense at such frank speech. Considering the true state of her relations with her husband, Lady Amabel's amorous insinuations could not fail to stab her through to the heart. She was thoroughly relieved when the hostess turned her attention to Lydia.

"Lydia, darling, I must impose on you most ungraciously, I'm afraid," she confessed. "The wretched musicians I engaged have not come. They are convinced there's to be a snowstorm, and it's doubtful they will be induced to leave their firesides. You may wonder that I smile when I've invited the entire district to a ball and then am left without music . . . but you know me well enough to understand my disposition. I refuse to let anything vex me. But I do implore you, Lydia, tell me you will play for us."

Lydia, who loved to dance, was understandably displeased.

"What a shame that you don't play," said Richard to Ursula, and she flushed, guessing his meaning at once. If it could have been arranged for her to spend the night on the piano bench, he would have been relieved of the unpleasant chore of standing up with her.

"Don't you play, Amabel?" asked Ursula, turning from her husband.

"No. Shocking, isn't it? I ordered the best instrument Broadwood's could send me and cannot play a note." Concluding her arrangements with Lydia, she added, "You'll find a wide selection of music—

waltzes, country-dances, minuets, even a quadrille to make old Mrs. Ogilvie happy. I have all the music anyone could want," she said with a sigh. "Following my brave resolutions to become an accomplished pianist, I made no effort, but I spared no expense."

The fortunate arrival, at just that moment, of the musicians was a great boon to Lydia's state of mind. To Lady Amabel it seemed a matter of supreme indifference.

It was quickly decided that the Viscount and Viscountess of Uxbridge should lead off the first set. They took their places together in a perfect counterfeit of young, happy love.

How much longer can this go on? Ursula wondered.

"You are doing very well," Richard commented as the musicians struck up the next dance, "concealing the strain."

She was pleased even by this praise and hesitated before answering. "The difficulty," she said slowly, "is somewhat offset by the pleasure of spending some time with you."

They executed a turn, and when they faced each other once more, she tried to read the uncertain expression flickering in his eyes. Was she imagining it, or was he unbending just a trifle?

But when the music stopped, he left her with an abrupt explanation. "I have promised the next set to Amabel."

When she had to dance with another, Ursula was miserable. But to her surprised delight Richard returned to her, again and again, and his initial formality began to give way.

"This is much easier than aboard the *Fortitude*," he said as they whirled together in the waltz. "It was not easy to be graceful when the floor was shifting its position beneath our feet."

Had he really squeezed her hand a little? She returned the pressure very shyly, hoping it would pass unnoticed if she had been deceived. "And these musicians," she answered, "seem able to play the piece to the end, unlike dear Mr. Crandall."

They smiled together at the memory, and he held her a little closer. As she looked into his eyes, Ursula was sure that he would have kissed her had they been alone. She felt as if her feet were no longer touching the floor as they continued to glide.

All the blazing candles, the music, the beauty around them suddenly became a celebration intended for them alone. If he hadn't avoided me so assiduously up until now, she thought, we should have been reconciled weeks ago.

But the past no longer mattered. She did not even care when the music ended because Richard resisted efforts to match him with another lady as table partner. They went in to supper together, and Ursula was convinced that appearance and reality had finally been made to coincide.

The only conflict left in her swelling heart was a pleasant one. On the one hand, she would have liked the wonderful party to continue forever, but at the same time she was anxious to be at home with her husband, alone.

In spite of her usual aversion to calves' brains and oxtails, she brought a hearty appetite to the mock turtle soup. Her appreciation for the baron of beef and green peas was all it should be, and Richard seemed to take considerable pleasure in her unaccustomed animation.

"You are so amiable tonight," he said. "If I hadn't been counting your cups, I should suspect you of taking too much port."

"You've been counting my cups?" she cried, taking feigned offense.

"Out of concern, not distrust," was his gallant reply, and she gladly read a deeper meaning into his disavowal of the latter sentiment.

In short, Ursula was so much in charity with her husband that it was almost inconceivable to her that hours earlier they had been enemies. Her attention was so thoroughly and delightfully captured that Ursula was not at first aware that Lady Amabel was addressing her from the other end of the table.

"You must know where he is, Ursula," that lady was saying insistently.

Ursula apologized, and Lady Amabel repeated herself. "Bertram. Bertram Moorhead. I should have wanted him to be here tonight, but he's gone off no one knows where, and I was just saying surely you know—"

"No, I don't know where he is," she said with a fervent hope that she was not turning scarlet. She sensed Richard stiffen beside her.

"You don't?" cried Amabel in disappointment. "I was just saying to Lord Geoffrey that if anyone knows where he is to be found, it must be Lady Ursula. After all, you are such particular friends."

"If I knew his whereabouts, I should be only too happy to share my knowledge." Ursula dared cast a glance at her husband. He was regarding his fingernails with meticulous interest. Had any woman ever had such wretched luck as hers? "We haven't heard from him at all, have we, Richard?" she ventured to ask.

"I have not," he answered.

The rest of the night was a disaster for Ursula. How could she have guessed that the new bond between her and Richard would prove so fragile? She did not blame Amabel. If Richard's suspicions were truly so far from being allayed, she had to admit that her happiness could never have lasted long, even had no indiscreet remark been made at supper. Such philosophical reflection did not help ease her pain. Her misery was now increased one hundredfold in proportion to her recently increased hope.

When the meal was over, Richard used the threatening weather as an excuse to hurry his wife and sister back to Collingwood. A few snowflakes were falling as they left the castle behind them.

"Now that I've seen my neighbours and enjoyed country society," said Richard in slow, deliberate terms, "it is time I saw to my unfinished business. I shall leave for London in the morning."

"Oh, Richard, no!" protested Lydia, and asked the question Ursula dared not. "How long will you be gone?"

"Indefinitely, I'm afraid."

"Oh, no!" Lydia made no attempt to hide her distress. "You've just come home, and now you are leaving again. I really wish . . ." She continued arguing and coaxing, while in the darkness of the carriage Ursula cried silently all the way home.

CHAPTER EIGHTEEN

The New Year began like a blight over England with a thick and unlifting fog that trapped and stranded travelers. No ship moved on the frozen rivers. No coachman dared, even for the highest sums, attempt to fight a way through the fog, winds, and ice.

Ursula knew all this, and in a strange way it was a comfort. I may be fooling myself, she thought. But it was less painful to believe that Richard was unable to return home rather than unwilling. She was pleased when the Post Office suspended service. Since Richard's letters could not be delivered, she could not be disappointed by his failure to write.

She tried not to think of Richard's life in London without her. At times, though, she pictured him in her imagination, rising to his feet to make a speech in Parliament. But at other times she feared he was spending his time not in the House of Lords, but rather in the house of Harriette Wilson.

For weeks Collingwood was isolated. It seemed to make little difference to Ursula, but Lydia was quite sunk at being confined to the house. She spent hours pacing about, muttering, "It must lift, it must. This can't go on much longer."

When the weather changed at last, a sudden thaw melted the snow and ice and turned even the safest tracks across the heath into treacherous bog. Although the sun shone and the air was fresh and clear, no one dared venture from the house. Edmund in particular felt the restriction more than ever.

"Mother, you know I can find my way," he insisted.

"I'll be ever so careful, but do let me go down to the cottages and see how everyone gets on." Lydia sternly forbade any such plan, and Edmund's thoughts turned to his uncle. "When Uncle Richard finishes his business," he said, "I'll wager he won't care a feather for the mud. Ice, sleet, quicksand—none of it will signify. When he's ready to come home, he will."

These words of praise lowered Ursula's mood, for she wished to give her husband every possible excuse for staying away.

One afternoon, when Edmund was with his governess and the two women sat alone in the parlor, Ursula at last dared ask what was most on her mind.

"Lydia, do you really believe I . . . that anything improper passed between me and Mr. Moorhead?"

Lydia immediately busied herself with the needlework that had been, up until that moment, lying untouched upon her lap.

"Please," Ursula persisted, "you know how I resisted all along any suggestion that I allow any liberties." When Lydia still did not answer, Ursula sighed. "Is it that you think me a hypocrite?" she asked. "Are you angry with me because you think I eschewed virtue in my actions while espousing it in words? Because, if so, believe me, Lydia, that was never the case."

Lydia at last raised her eyes to regard her sister-in-law but found it hard to meet her gaze evenly.

"Even if you don't care for me," beseeched Ursula, "don't you see what this is doing to Richard?"

At these words Lydia began to tremble. "We manage along, you and I," she said, barely able to keep her voice under control. "But I won't talk about this with you. The subject is too . . . much too painful." She rang for tea.

*   *   *

Before another sennight had passed, Edmund's views were proved correct. Although the weather remained problematic, Richard returned.

"You see!" cried the boy. "Uncle Richard, I told them no amount of rain or mud would keep you from home."

Richard chuckled and flattered his champion with a manly handshake rather than an embrace. "There's no reason to boast of recklessness, though, Edmund," he told his nephew. "If I'd had a notion of how bad it was before I started out, I should have stayed longer in London."

But you didn't stay in London, thought Ursula. She tried to catch his eye. Had he hastened home because he had reconsidered? Was he ready to give her another chance?

"By the time I could fully appreciate the dangers of the journey," he was saying, "I was midway 'twixt here and there, and so no purpose would have been served in turning back."

"You weren't in danger?" Ursula asked quickly.

"No," he said to her, and then, speaking to everyone, added, "When I reached Sedgemere, I heard of a shepherd who had just disappeared. He set off with his flock, bound for winter grazing, and was not heard of again."

"What happened to him?" asked Edmund.

"It is generally believed that he and the sheep were swallowed by the mud."

Lydia clasped her son to her. "I hate for him to hear such tales, Richard," she scolded, "but I suppose it's as well. I had a horrid time keeping him home. He *would* go wander the heath, but I didn't let him stir forth."

"I'm glad you're home, Richard," said Ursula quietly.

He regarded her from beneath heavy eyelids, searchingly and uncertain. Then he shook himself abruptly, as if trying to wake from a dream. "It's been a most fatiguing day," he said. "I pray you will all excuse me."

Days passed without Ursula's path crossing that of her husband again, but her spirits refused to flag. She dressed carefully and could hardly keep from smiling. After all, Richard had chosen to return. It was only a matter of time, she told herself.

In the meantime, Ursula once more found that Edmund was the mainstay of her family life. As they spent more time together, Edmund took his aunt more and more into his boyish confidence.

One afternoon he told her that he was slipping out of the house at night to go on an adventure. Ursula pressed him for details, hoping the boy was not involving himself in an escapade unsuited to his youth.

"The elvers are here," he told her with excitement. Then, noting the look of incomprehension on Ursula's face, he explained, "Elvers, that's tiny baby eels. They're delicious, Aunt Ursula, and they're coming upriver right now. You catch them at night, and"—here he lowered his voice—"you know how Mother doesn't like it for me to associate overmuch with the common folk. But it's my last chance because I do expect they'll send me off to school next year. In any event I was out riding today, and I had a word with Toby Hawkins—you remember him, don't you, from the wassail?—and he said if I meet him after dark, he'll take me along for the catch."

Edmund's eyes were gleaming, and his face lit with happiness. Ursula felt a sudden pang.

"I wish I could go too," she said wistfully.

Now Edmund's smile grew broader, and he forgot his new maturity long enough to hop up and down.

"But you can, Aunt Ursula!" he cried. "I'll take you with me. Toby won't mind."

The thought of slipping out and spending the night down by the river was delightful. But the sure knowledge of defeat swept over her. It was impossible, and she hadn't the heart to tell Edmund why.

"No, dear," she said at last. "You go and tell me all about it tomorrow. I shall be waiting to hear . . ."

"No, no!" he insisted. "Wait for me tonight. I'll knock very softly when it's time to go, and——"

"I'm locked in at night," she blurted, and then covered her mouth with her hand. She was ashamed of herself when she saw the dark look cross her nephew's face. For a moment he seemed to pout. She knew he was angry at the people who were mistreating his aunt, at his aunt for having committed some unknown crime, at everyone for keeping him in ignorance. Then the look of childlish hurt was succeeded by one of adult resolution.

"Your windows aren't locked," he announced as though giving an order. "I shall have a ladder, Aunt, and you will come with me, like it or not."

She started with alarm. The very thought of a ladder at her window was enough to make her heart stop with horror.

"And I'll be sure you're safely back in your room before anyone knows you're gone," added Edmund. "After all, remember I'm not supposed to be gone either. It's my own neck as well."

She had to remind herself that Edmund knew nothing about her disgrace. He had made his startling suggestion in complete innocence.

"Oh, do say yes," he urged.

It would be lunacy, she thought. And yet . . . Part of her had quietly submitted to her unhappy fate, but another part of her rebelled angrily against Richard's treatment.

I shall not be kept prisoner another moment, she told herself, suddenly furious at the humiliation of being locked up at night.

"Very well." She laughed at last, and she and Edmund clasped hands like conspirators.

That night Edmund did not have to rap upon the pane, for Ursula was waiting anxiously for him.

The ladder made such a clatter against the outer walls that she was certain the whole household must have been alerted, but moments later she was climbing down backwards, laughing a little with nervous fear and pleased to note that her presence had made the expedition even more exciting to her nephew.

Toby was waiting in the garden with three Shetland colts.

As they set off, she could not help but think back on the last time she had made a secret departure in the dead of night. How unfortunate and ill-timed her flight had been!

"Oh, look, Aunt Ursula!" cried Edmund, breaking into her gloomy train of thought.

She looked where directed. Up in a sky thick with stars, a single light detached itself from the firmament and cut a curving arc across the heavens.

The three of them were hushed by the sight until Edmund asked, "Do you believe in miracles?"

The question cut Ursula to the heart. Somehow it seemed to refer not to the glories of the universe, but rather to her blind faith that something would happen to restore Richard's love.

Is that really what I am patiently awaiting? she asked herself. Will only a miracle repair what has been broken?

Aloud she replied, "I believe in elvers. Shall we go on?"

They saw the gleam of lanterns before they could make out the black river flowing or the men bending over its banks. Toby, Edmund, and Ursula tied up their ponies and quietly joined the other fishermen. Toby unpacked his gear from where he'd tied it to the saddle.

"Sorry, milady, I hain't got a net to spare. There's only fer the young master," he said apologetically.

"Aunt Ursula can try mine," interjected Edmund. He accepted a frame woven of withy reeds and fumbled to attach its cheesecloth net. Then, taking his aunt by the arm, he pulled her over to the river's edge. "But we need a light," he complained in exasperation, which quickly changed back to excitement when Toby joined them with his lantern. "It's the light that attracts them," Edmund whispered to Ursula.

"An' 'tis the whisperin' wot drives 'en away," warned Toby. " 'Ee can put in the net, Master Edmund, and I'll hol' the lamp."

Edmund squealed with delight as the net filled with shining, squirming bodies. Ursula noted the fond smile on Toby's face. The young master dumped his catch into a tightly woven basket and eagerly handed the net to Ursula. "Try it, Aunt."

She took the frame and ventured close to the water, leaning over and ignoring the mud that immediately engulfed the hem of her dress. It was indeed easy. She didn't have to do anything. The net simply filled up with elvers, poor, stupid creatures that swam blindly into the trap and didn't even realize they had been caught. She giggled to feel the net thrashing about as if it had taken on a life of its own.

"Lift it out, milady, or they'll swim free," instructed Toby.

When they had filled all the baskets that Toby had brought, they loaded up the colts and headed for home.

" 'Ee have ter return empty-handed now, so's no one'll know 'ee been out wi' me," Toby warned. "But I'll pass by Collin'wood tomorrer," he promised, "an' I'll give His Lordship a coupler baskets o' elvers. As a token o' me esteem."

"Please be very sure you give him the ones that we caught, Toby," said Edmund in a very serious tone, "and not yours. When Mrs. Jenkins cooks them up, I want to be able to think that I caught them myself."

"I promise 'ee, Master Edmund," said Toby, equally sober, but though it was dark, Ursula fancied she saw the man wink at her over his shoulder.

"Did you touch them at all, Aunt Ursula?" Edmund was asking. "They're frightfully mucky, don't you think? But once they're cooked, they taste quite nice."

"Well, 'ee see," explained Toby, "the way the missus fixes 'en, first she puts 'en in hot water and the slime come right off 'en. Then, wot 'ee ought ter see is when they be cookin'. You fry 'en up with eggs and such, and a thick curdly milk come runnin' out and form on the top of 'en. 'Ee gets rid of that, an' then 'ee've got elvers fit fer a King. Or a Prince Regent if that's the times 'ee live in."

"They sound quite loathsome," ventured Ursula.

"Oh, no, Aunt Ursula!" cried Edmund. "Elvers are a great delicacy. Uncle Richard loves them. He's always said he is eternally grateful to anyone who brings him the first elvers of the season."

So Toby Hawkins would win that gratitude. But as they rode homeward in the dead of night, Ursula's musings turned fanciful. After all, she thought, if I believe in miracles, why shouldn't my miracle revolve around a basket of elvers? Richard will eat them and be seized by an unaccountable feeling of eternal gratitude toward me. She could not keep from laughing aloud.

"I'm so glad you had a good time, Aunt Ursula," said Edmund cheerfully, attributing her laughter to the companionable fun and the successful catch.

"Thank you both for letting me join you," she answered politely, and would have said more, but her words were cut short by a tremendous yawn.

"Don't 'ee sleep too late tomorrer, milady," counseled Toby, "or 'ee'll wake up ter find His Lordship has went and ate 'en all and left none fer 'ee at all."

"Never fear," she answered, smiling. "I shall be there at the table when my husband samples the first elvers of the season. I shouldn't miss that moment for anything."

Ursula awoke with the sun after only a few hours' rest. In the dining hall she lingered on, hour after hour, and drank cup after cup of tea. Mrs. Jenkins was eager to serve up the elvers that Toby Hawkins had brought, but Ursula insisted that she was not hungry and would not take her breakfast until her husband had appeared.

Edmund was not so willing to wait and ran down to the kitchen to watch Mrs. Jenkins at work. He was curious to see the curdly milk come out of the bodies. ("Curdly milk?" exclaimed Mrs. Jenkins. "Whar do 'ee get yer ideas? 'Tis *whey* wot run off.")

"And just look!" cried the boy as he rushed back to the table, brandishing a handful of flowers like a sword. "Toby brought us these, too"—and in a lower voice—"I'll wager they're for you, Aunt Ursula."

"They're irises. Wild irises," she whispered.

Was it another sign? How long ago that day was, she remembered, when she had first met Richard . . . when he had come across her arranging irises much like these in a vase. *They remind me of my West Country home,* he had said.

Ursula took the flowers and found a glass bowl. Very slowly and meticulously she began to arrange the bouquet as a centerpiece. She was not aware of her husband's entrance until she heard her nephew cry out a greeting.

"Uncle Richard!" he called excitedly. "Good morning, Uncle Richard. Toby Hawkins has brought us the first elvers of the season . . ." But even Edmund's high spirits were speedily deflated by Richard's lack of enthusiasm.

The Viscount of Uxbridge cast a cold glance at his wife, who had been patiently waiting for him since early morn. He called to Mrs. Jenkins with a terrible scowl transforming his face. "I'll eat upstairs. Have my breakfast served in the sitting room."

Ursula turned scarlet but still refused to give up hope. After all, the magic wouldn't take effect until Richard had actually consumed the meal . . . oh, but what terrible nonsense, she thought, accepting defeat at last and hating herself for clinging to desperate, superstitious beliefs. "I was just leaving," she said hurriedly, and almost knocked over a chair in her haste to quit the room.

"But, milady, you haven't even been served . . ." Mrs. Jenkins began to protest.

"No appetite, I fear," she murmured.

"Why, but of course," said the woman, smiling broadly. "Now that His Lordship be back, 'tis no wonder you're feeling poorly in the mornings. Wot good news it be!"

223

The wide-eyed, joyous expression on the cook's face shocked Ursula profoundly. The assumption that she was with child was the cruelest possible mockery of her true situation.

CHAPTER NINETEEN

Life was so dreary that it was almost a pleasure, thought Ursula, to be able to lock herself in her room and cry. That was how she spent the remainder of the morning until she dried her eyes in embarrassment at the sound of a knock on the door.

It was Edmund, and he, too, seemed embarrassed to have caught his aunt at an awkward moment.

"Will you come for a ride with me, Aunt Ursula," he asked. "I can show you how much I know about plants."

What a wonderful yet curious nephew, she thought. "Really, Edmund," she said, smiling, "I think a botany lesson would make me feel much better, too." Would Richard consider Edmund an adequate chaperon? she wondered. She knew she was not to be allowed out of the house unsupervised. Well, at worst, Lydia would accompany them.

It was a beautiful and warm spring day, and Ursula's spirits rose just to be out-of-doors beneath the sun.

"The Lapps must be a very gloomy people!" she exclaimed to Edmund. "How can you feel like a human being when you live deprived of the sun?"

"You've been rather gloomy yourself, Aunt Ursula," he answered pointedly, but just as pointedly refrained from asking why.

They carefully approached the nearest bog, and Edmund edged close to the bushes that grew there, disguising the treacherous nature of the terrain. He swung himself over his saddle and dangled there while he reached to pluck off an olive-green branch.

"This is bog myrtle," he explained patiently. "You

can tell it by where it grows and by these waxy berries. They also call it candleberry."

He handed her a sprig and ran his finger over it, pointing.

"If you throw this catkin in water that's at a very fast boil, a scum comes up that the poor people make candles of," he said. "That's the derivation of the common name."

"How do you know so much?" she asked.

"I've read all the botany books in Uncle Richard's library," he answered proudly, and then confessed, "but mostly Toby tells me things." Edmund looked around and lowered his voice. "Toby knows the old man of the heath," he said in an awed and solemn tone.

"Who's that?" asked Ursula.

"The old man of the heath," Edmund repeated. "No one knows his real name or where he lives. At least I don't know. But people see him on the heath, on the other side of the northern mere. They say his mother was a witch, and his father was hanged for some evil doings. The old man knows everything about plants. He can make medicines and poisons. Toby says he cures better than a doctor and kills better than a dagger and—" The boy broke off suddenly. He leaned over the saddle again and tore off another sprig of myrtle. "I think the women get a yellow dye from it for their clothes," he said, dropping the branch into the basket he had ready. "I read about that in one of Uncle Richard's books."

"How wonderful!" said Ursula with enthusiasm. "Do you know," she asked, "in Bermuda, the only dye the ladies had to stain their laces with was coffee?"

"I don't believe you," replied Edmund, laughing.

"Have I that dishonest a face," she asked, trying to make a jest of it, but hurting deep inside, "that no one will ever believe me when I speak the truth?"

Not recognizing the anguish that lay under her light tone, Edmund merely laughed more heartily. "Ladies staining their laces with coffee! Really, Aunt Ursula. You'll have to do better than that. I shall have to tell Uncle Richard that you've been telling me lies."

She grabbed his arm, forgetting all discretion and decorum. "Edmund, please. Don't do that. Not even in fun."

"Very well. Of course, I shan't," he answered, but it was clear her desperation had made him uncomfortable. "Come on, I'll show you something else." And he kicked his pony.

It was another hour until they headed home, loaded with specimens: myrtle catkins and a basket of woad which Edmund explained yielded a dye much like indigo. But for the rest of the outing he kept his pony in the lead. They did not ride side by side, nor did they engage in any conversation that did not relate directly to the botany lesson.

Have I lost him, too? wondered Ursula. What have I done?

But as they approached the house, Edmund slowed until Ursula had overtaken him.

"I don't know why we're quarreling, Aunt Ursula," he said in a chastened tone of voice. "I'm sorry if you are."

She wanted to cover his face with kisses. Was his the only adult sensibility at Collingwood?

"I should hate it unless we're friends again," he added.

"Of course, we're friends," she assured him.

Then, after another pause between them, he said, "If everyone goes to bed early enough tonight, I plan to slip away with Toby again. . . . Shall I bring you the ladder?"

Since the elvers had not worked the miracle that Ursula had dreamed of, she was disinclined to go fishing for them again. But she realized that Edmund was offering her another nighttime outing to seal the peace treaty between them, so she smiled at him warmly. "I would love to go again," she answered. "I'll be waiting by the window."

Her disagreement with her nephew was thus conciliated very simply. Why wasn't it so easy and natural to come to terms with Richard? Hadn't he been away at war long enough? she wondered. Shouldn't he be the first person to seek an end to hostilities?

That night, after Lucy had helped her into her nightclothes, Ursula slipped out of bed. Just as she had done the night before, she dressed herself and waited by her window for the sound of the ladder being raised against the wall.

She opened the window in preparation and breathed deeply of the warm, perfumed air. She tried to discern signs of movement in the garden, but all was shadowy, and she could not distinguish what passed below. What a beautiful night, she thought. What a perfect night to be standing here with Richard by her side. Such beauty went to waste without him. More's the pity, she thought and wondered if such perfect evenings would ever come again, later, when the day came, the day she still believed in, when everything would be as it had been before.

There was a rustling and a crash, and the ladder began to loom into view. Just as suddenly it fell back and disappeared. Then the ladder rose again out of nowhere and rested in place at her sill. Ursula felt experienced now at this procedure and without the slightest fear or trepidation climbed forth and began her descent.

At last she felt the soft earth beneath her feet,

sighed, and turned about. Her eyes widened with astonishment. In front of her Richard stood, glaring. He held Edmund tightly, one hand clapped firmly over the boy's mouth to keep him from calling out.

"Where were you going?" he asked in an ominous voice. "Whom did you intend to meet tonight?"

She shook her head in angry defiance. "Edmund and I were going to catch elvers," she replied. "As we did last night. The breakfast you enjoyed . . ."

Richard ignored her answer. "Get back to your room, Edmund," he said in a peremptory tone. "We shall talk tomorrow." He released the boy and walked a few paces with him around the corner of the house so that he could watch Edmund's form enter the door and disappear from view.

Ursula did not move from where she stood, waiting for her husband to come back.

"Who is he?" Richard demanded when they stood face-to-face again.

"I shall listen to your accusations no longer!" cried Ursula. Now her own eyes were blazing with anger. She had submitted to his will long enough. She had accepted his ill-treatment and forgiven him for believing of her things that made her shudder with horror and shame. "There has been no other man, Richard. You are the only man in my life."

His fierce glance condemned her, and her pride would stand for no more.

"You *were* the only man in my life," she corrected herself. "For now there is none. I am innocent, and you wrong me, sir. There is nothing between us anymore. I have done nothing wrong and shall not go on trying"—she fought to finish the sentence without allowing her voice to break—"trying to win back the love of a man I can no longer forgive."

For an instant she believed he was about to strike

her. Instead, he spoke coldly. "Upstairs," he said. "Get back to your room."

When she started for the path leading to the door, he cursed beneath his breath. "By the ladder, my dear. I don't allow wantons the use of the front door."

An instinct told her not to fight with him. She turned and began to climb the ladder. She realized with an unsettling mixture of fear and pleasure that he was climbing right behind her. By the time she was clambering through the window and into her chamber, his hands were upon her shoulders—rough hands, not the hands she remembered so well.

He's no better than Bertram, she thought in a rage.

He spun her around toward him and pulled her close while his burning lips sought hers. His touch set her on fire, and yet it was a sad, cold flame, a poor and bitter imitation of what they had once known.

"How many men have you lifted your skirts for?" he demanded hoarsely. "Whom were you meeting tonight?"

"You are mad," she replied, trying to break free of his bruising grip.

"But you are my wife, dishonest though you may be, and tonight you'll lift those skirts for your husband."

Love for him and desire raged, but Ursula's pride rebelled. As his face drew near to kiss her again, she hissed like a cat, surprising herself as much as she surprised Richard. He had her hands pinioned tightly. She had no way to defend herself physically. All she had were her words and her blazing eyes. Richard drew back a moment but then crushed her body against his again.

"I am yours, Richard," she said. "I am entirely

yours, and yours alone. But I shall not be yours like this."

He did not even dignify her declaration with a reply but hungrily sought her lips another time. He forced her to the bed and overpowered her, overwhelmed her with the passionate violence of his caresses and long-pent-up feelings. Her dress was quickly reduced to torn shreds as he ripped her clothing from her.

But then he held himself back, restraining himself with an even greater violence than that he had shown his wife. He held her and kissed her and fought against his own desires until the moment when he sensed that her surrender would come willingly, completely, and with heartbreaking abandon.

Ursula woke briefly before dawn, when the birds began to chatter outside the window. Richard was lying beside her, one arm thrown around her waist. As she stirred, he drew her closer.

The night had started with bitterness and anger, she thought, and yet . . . She looked at his face, and her heart flooded with tenderness. However wrong it had been to begin with, surely what had happened between them had gone a long way toward repairing the terrible breach. There would be no turning back now. From this point on they would be man and wife again, and steadily their love and trust would be renewed.

Gueevie whimpered from her place of exile, asleep on a cushioned chair.

Ursula was tempted to stay awake and simply watch Richard, to feast her eyes on the sight of him. But she felt so peaceful and happy that after staring at him fondly for a while, she snuggled closer to him and fell back asleep.

When she woke again, she was alone. Richard was gone without a trace, as though he'd never been there at all. No, not quite. When Ursula closed her eyes and breathed deeply, she found that his scent still lingered in the room around her. It was true. It had really happened. She had not been dreaming, and yet what had it meant?

When I open my eyes, she thought, I'll find him tiptoeing back from the buttery with slices of thick home-baked bread, fresh-churned butter, and cold ham. No, that was Bermuda, she remembered. That's all gone.

When I open my eyes, I'll find him lying by me.

But when she opened her eyes, she was still alone.

Downstairs at breakfast she was informed that His Lordship had been up with the sun and had gone out riding. He was not expected back for luncheon or supper.

If I think about it, it will destroy me, thought Ursula, eating her breakfast mechanically and trying to remain detached from everything around her.

Lydia joined her shortly. It seemed she had some notion of events of the previous night and was subjecting Ursula to her scrutiny in an attempt to discern exactly what had happened.

When Edmund took a seat a few minutes later, he kept his eyes lowered and merely toyed with his oysters and toast while fidgeting in his chair.

No one spoke.

The morning could hardly have been more wretched. Ursula no longer clutched at hope but let herself experience all the pain of her despair. It was better, she told herself, to endure the hurt than to let herself grow resigned to her fate.

* * *

After a sennight of unmitigated wretchedness Ursula began to force herself to come back to life. She sought distraction by going through the books in Richard's library. To her dismay she found shelf after shelf of Greek and Latin classics.

"To be sure, I do love Virgil and Horace," she said to the volumes, "but really a Maria Edgeworth romance would be a tonic."

Up above her head she noted some books in simple bindings. She quickly carried over a library chair and unfolded the stepladder that was fitted into its back.

"Oh, I do hope there's something wonderful up there," she said to herself as she climbed the steps. "Oh, dear," she murmured in disappointment. *"A Treatise on Scientific Stockbreeding, Dissertation on the Origins of the Sedgemere Wild Pony . . .* What else have we got here? It does seem I've already read all the light books this library offers."

When she came across *Some Useful Notes on West Country Flora,* she paused. Edmund's botany lesson had been quite interesting, she recalled.

She ended by taking the *Useful Notes* upstairs to her room.

She read with fascination that the teazles, about which she had begun to consider herself quite the expert, were carnivorous plants. They trapped insects and dissolved their bodies in order to obtain sustenance. She learned how the basketmakers obtained withies of different colours by various methods of stripping and boiling. Stomach troubles of all sorts could be cured, she read, by drinking the "still-liquors" made from the lees at the bottom of a cider cask.

"From woad," she read, "is derived an indigo dye." Edmund had told her that. "The prized indigo colour gives woad its principal value, but the humble plant

233

yields a wide range of other colours, from green to black."

Something in these words stirred a memory within her, but the idea refused to emerge full-blown into her consciousness. Ursula went on reading, learning that the West Country people had their own names for plants: Flowering rushes were "adders' tongues," and the round-leafed pond weeds were "shillings and sixpence." Her concentration wandered. While she read about the difference between "gouty" and "sleat" withies, a deep indigo colour swirled before her eyes. West Country flax was prized for use in making Coker sailcloth. The image of sailing ships passed before her. Then a tiny dot grew larger as it hove into view: a trim Bermuda sloop gliding through an indigo sea. No, not indigo—a colour she had seen once, and never before or since, a blue that contained the sky and sea and all the love that two people had shared one afternoon lying together on the sand. She tried to hold the colour in her mind, to memorize it. It was a colour that Richard had said he would never forget. As she sat entranced by the memory of that day, Ursula knew now with a certainty that had nothing to do with miracles, patience, or magic that the colour that flooded her senses was the key. That colour captured and held the best of their love; if Richard should ever see that shade of blue again, memory would flood over him and wash away everything that had gone awry.

Edmund had said that women derived a yellow dye from the bog myrtle. And from woad, there was indigo, green, black. Ursula turned the pages of the book in mounting excitement. Surely it would tell just how these dyes were extracted from the plants. If she could but produce the colour to match that burning memory . . .

Edmund was at his lessons, and Ursula waited impatiently until he should be done.

"Do let's be scientists together," she suggested eagerly once they were alone. "I've been reading a botany book, and there are many experiments we can try!"

Edmund was more than agreeable. Together they amused and confounded the household staff by commandeering a stove, fuel, and several cauldrons which proved sufficient to transform Ursula's sitting room into a laboratory.

"I'm afraid I feel more like a witch or an old woman of the heath than a scientist," confessed Ursula as she and her nephew set out to fill several baskets with plants. Edmund laughed, but silently Ursula reflected that she was indeed a witch, brewing a love potion to win back her husband.

"Are we going to make poisons?" Edmund asked.

"Poisons! Gracious heavens!"

"It was just an idea," he said with some disappointment. "But you're quite right," he said in a mysterious voice. "Our products could easily fall into the wrong hands." This latter thought satisfied his imagination so that he was willing to devote himself energetically to his aunt's more gentle desire. If Aunt Ursula wished to extract silly blue dyestuffs, he concluded, well, so be it!

In the days that followed, Ursula and Edmund were often in her room, leaning over the stove and stirring the contents of their cauldrons.

Time and again Ursula followed the instructions in the book and extracted the dyestuff, mixing it in combination after combination.

Edmund began to find her single-mindedness rather a bore. "That's a nice colour, Aunt Ursula," he'd say. "Now can we try something else?"

"No, no, it's not quite right. Maybe it should be a little lighter? Maybe it needs a little more yellow. Have we got any more candleberry?"

It was intolerably hot in the sitting room with the steam rising from the cauldrons. The conspirators would stagger to the open window every now and then and breathe deeply, looking out over the spring countryside spreading out mistily in shades of brown and green.

"What colour are you trying to make, Aunt Ursula?"

"A colour I remember. The colour of the Bermuda sea."

Edmund would take the dipper and pour a sample of the latest brew into a glass cup. "Is this it?"

"No." Time after time Ursula would discard the result and say, "Let's try again."

In the meantime, the bolts of fine white silk she had ordered from Langport were delivered and stored away.

"Is this the colour, Aunt Ursula?" asked Edmund, holding up still another sample to the sunlight.

"No." She sighed. "It's all wrong." Ursula began to wonder if the blue she sought was as elusive as a moonbeam. But one day she studied the sample thoughtfully. "It's a trifle dark," she said.

"It will be lighter when it dries," he suggested.

Their eyes met a moment over the blue liquid.

"Let's put it to the test," decided Ursula, much to Edmund's relief.

Laughing together, they tumbled a bolt of silk into a tubful of dye.

The next morning she held it in her hands, a dress-length bolt of silk, dyed in the colour of her dreams. Too deep to be called azure. Too clear and drenched with sunlight to be called indigo. A blue from which a golden glow seemed to shine forth. The color of the sea below the cliffs. The colour, substance, and memory, the thread that led through the maze to her love.

"It's beautiful, Aunt Ursula," said Edmund, breaking the trance that held her spellbound. "I've never seen a colour like that before. What are you going to do with it?"

"I shall sew myself a dress," she answered.

"Well, you won't have my help with that." He laughed. "I have no skill with needle and thread, I'm glad to say."

"You've given me help enough," she said, and stepped forward to kiss him, never letting the blue silk out of her hands.

The dress was a simple confection. She wanted something that would fall about her, flowing, without any formal lines. It was amazing how the texture of the silk made the colour shimmer in different subtle gradations. When she wrapped herself in the dress, she looked as if she were clothed in the sea itself.

"You are ravishing!" cried Edmund. "But I hope you aren't planning to wear it for a while yet."

"What do you mean?" she asked.

"Look at your arms Aunt." He laughed. "You're stained with dye up to the elbows."

He was quite right. Further study of the botany books yielded a host of suggestions. Edmund obligingly went far afield, gathering cucumbers and teazle water, and they concocted, according to the book's receipts, a number of mixtures that were supposed to be beneficial to the complexion.

"This may benefit my complexion," Ursula complained after several experiments, "but nothing seems to clean my hands. I feel like Lady Macbeth."

"Don't worry, Aunt Ursula," Edmund reassured her. "I've never seen such beautiful blue fingers in all my life."

Outrageous as this new predicament was, Ursula had to laugh along with him. After all, she had nothing to complain about. Eventually her skin would be clean again. The dress was completed. Once the stains were gone, she would be ready.

Richard was still in his banian, having a cup of tea and going over some correspondence from London. Fortuitously enough the letter referred to the report he had presented about Bermuda's smugglers and pirates and raised some further questions. The Viscount of Uxbridge found himself unable to repress a sigh as his mind harked back to the golden days of his life, the first months of his marriage in Bermuda.

So engrossed was he in his thoughts that he did not hear the knock on the door. Nor was he aware that his visitor had opened the door and entered without waiting to be invited in. When he turned, he thought the scene before him was his memory's image rendered miraculously in flesh.

It must be the sunlight dazzling my eyes, he thought.

Ursula stood before him, his Ursula, the woman who had never done him any wrong, the woman whose peculiar mixture of shyness and confidence had endeared her to him. Her golden hair was a mass of curls and damp tendrils, as though she had just stepped out of the ocean, and the mysterious robe she wore swirled about her form like the ocean's waves. Blue, not azure, not indigo. The colour of her robe brought back memories of happiness, what it had felt like once, when he had loved being alive, when every day had held a special joy. Ursula had brought him that happiness. She had given it to him as simply and willingly as she had given him herself.

Whatever she had done, he no longer cared. He wanted to know once more what it meant to love life, to love her, to hold a treasure in his hands.

Would she vanish like a dream if he reached out to her?

She lowered her eyes a moment. Then, as he approached, and the blue robe fell to the floor, she raised her face to him again, radiant with love.

CHAPTER TWENTY

Ursula was in love, but that love was bittersweet.

She was happy. Richard loved her. They were husband and wife once more, sharing not only their nights but all the simple incidents of daily life. And yet . . .

She could not forget how Richard had been driven from her at Christmastime by an innocent chance remark. Anything could happen, she thought. Their love was not secure now, not the way it once had been. It might be destroyed all over again for the most trivial reason.

Ursula loved her husband more than ever because he had shown he could forgive her. But because he was not convinced of her innocence, there were doubts between them that kept their love from becoming whole.

"I think it's time for us to take a house in London." Richard brought up the subject as he and Ursula rode back from a land auction outside Bridgwater. They had gone for an afternoon's diversion rather than to bid.

"Do you think we can find ~omething suitable in the space of time of a candle?" she asked, referring to the custom to which she had just been introduced. At rural West Country auctions a candle was lit at the time of the opening bid and the sale was consummated with whoever had the highest bid at the moment that the candle burned out.

"No," he replied, "it won't be quite so easy. That's why I think it best for me to go on alone and send for you later."

His tone of voice indicated that he had given the matter ample reflection and that his mind was made up. Ursula knew she could do naught but accept the plan. At moments like this her fears, usually in abeyance, rose about her like demons. Once she would have been naturally downcast at the thought of a temporary separation from her husband. Now she could not keep from wondering if there were not some deeper motive for his decision to leave. She dared not ask, but might not this circumstantial separation be the first crack in their new solidarity? Might he be seeking an innocuous way to be rid of her?

"You're taking your parliamentary duties seriously," she said.

"Quite."

That *must* be why he wants a London house, she thought. It *cannot* be that he has some woman he plans to install there.

She tried to banish her suspicion and her fear.

What a hobble we're both in, she thought, to have to go blundering along together, never quite knowing when the ground beneath us will turn to bog.

"No vapours or fidgets now," he warned, reading her mind and wishing to avoid debate. He, too, was always aware, in some part of his consciousness, of the smoky uncertainties that still hung like a curtain between them. But Richard believed that to discuss such matters would not dispel their sinister power. Wouldn't the tentative bridge between them become all the more fragile if they put that fragility into words?

But once the terrible topic had been introduced, even though they let the conversation die, each was separately left at the mercy of doubts and fears that made it impossible to think or talk of anything else.

They rode on in silence, victims of a past they could neither speak of nor forget.

"That's Dr. Jameson's carriage," said Richard as they approached Collingwood. They exchanged a worried glance and spurred their horses to a gallop.

No one met them at the door. Richard and Ursula rushed into the house, their anxiety mounting. It was clear that the routine of the household had been interrupted; the doctor's visit must indicate a serious matter.

Hearing the tread of feet overhead, they directed their steps up the stairs. Richard clasped Ursula's hand, and they hurried together.

An involuntary cry escaped Ursula's lips when they found the doctor and Lydia leaving Edmund's room. The stunned expression on Lydia's face left no doubt that her son was in danger.

"What is the matter?" demanded Richard.

At this Lydia began to weep. "I begged him, again and again, to stay away from the cottages. . . ."

"Typhoid," said Dr. Jameson.

"Typhoid? But that's impossible!" insisted Richard.

"It's his friendship with the tenants, going down there in those filthy daub-and-wattle dwellings . . ." repeated the distraught mother.

"Perhaps," temporized the doctor. "But it also seems he's taken to bathing in the rhines. . . . At any event, now the question is not how he fell ill, but rather what we are to do to save him."

He took Lydia by the arm. "I shall give her a sleeping draught, Your Lordship," he reported calmly, and left Richard and Ursula alone outside the child's door.

How selfish I've been, thought Ursula. How could she have panicked over a trivial problem such as

Richard's decision to go to London, while at the very same moment Edmund's life had been hanging by a thread?

She gently opened the door and saw Betsy sitting frightened by the bed, not taking her eyes from the boy, ready to call for help at the slightest change in his condition. Edmund was talking wildly in his delirium, and Ursula shuddered when he opened his yellowed eyes and fixed them upon her blindly for a moment.

"I shall nurse him, Betsy. You may go," she said, dismissing the girl and taking her place by the sickbed. The child had been her one friend and ally. She loved him as though he were her own.

When some time later Dr. Jameson insisted that Ursula go to bed and get some rest, she spent a sleepless night while Richard paced back and forth and paid constant visits to the sickroom.

"Any change?" she would ask each time he returned to their room.

"No change," he would invariably reply, although he knew the boy grew steadily weaker, nearer death.

"What is Dr. Jameson doing for him?"

Richard shrugged. "He bled him once or twice. Compresses, infusions . . . At this point I think he just sits, watches, and waits."

"And Lydia?"

"The doctor leaves Edmund only long enough to insist that she take another sleeping draught. I don't think Lydia is fully conscious of what is happening."

Richard would pace the hall again, and on his return Ursula would still be sitting restlessly in bed and would ask, "Any change?"

On the fourth day the skies were clear and blue at morning light. When Richard appeared in the doorway, Ursula's heart sank into a deep pit. His face was exceptionally haggard, and his shoulders drooped with defeat.

"The doctor is not giving Lydia any more draughts," he said slowly. "He thinks she should be awake now."

Ursula looked at her husband with alarm. Say it, she said to herself, if it's true. Don't leave me here guessing.

"He doesn't expect him to last the night."

When Ursula began to cry, he hurried to her side to hold and comfort her. "Please hush, darling," he whispered. "Don't let Lydia hear you crying."

"Isn't there anything he can do?" she cried violently.

"Don't you think he would if he could? Don't you think the doctor has used all his skill?" Richard replied, and then apologized for raising his voice. "I know how you feel. I want to scream, too, because we are so powerless to do anything else."

"I can't believe that," she insisted. "There's always something one can do. There were so many moments when I could have given up . . ." But she realized she was treading on dangerous ground and did not finish the thought. Instead, she bathed, dressed, and hastened downstairs.

She forced herself to eat and to go about the morning as if nothing were amiss. It was she who received Toby Hawkins when he came hesitantly to the back door to enquire about the young master's health.

"Toby!" she cried, with sudden, blinding certainty. "You know the old man of the heath. The old man will save him."

"Yairs," replied Toby slowly, "if anyone can do't, 'twould be t'old man. But thar's a storm comin' on. We hain't got the time to reach him 'fore it breaks."

"I've been soaked before," she told him.

244

" 'Ee don' unnerstan', milady. Wi' the floodin' we've had o' late, I'd say the seawalls broke down, all the way from Gore Sound. . . . If the rain starts now, likely we couldna reach him alive."

"I'm not afraid," said Ursula, making a sudden and irrevocable decision. "Tell me where to find him, and I shall go myself."

Toby hesitated. "Very well, milady. I'll go," he said.

"And I shall go with you."

Toby hesitated again, torn between a sincere desire to help the young master and a fervent wish not to risk his own life. If he went alone, he would feel compelled to see the journey through to the end. If Ursula came with him, he'd be careful for her safety, and they would turn back at the first sign of danger. "A'right, milady," was his final reply. "I'll wait for 'ee by the stables."

"I'm ready to go as I am," she answered. "Let's have my pony saddled and be gone before some well-intentioned person can stop us."

They set off.

"We shall reach the old man of the heath by hedge or by stile!" she stated defiantly, as if shouting a battle cry.

"Yairs, milady," he answered with a lack of enthusiasm that showed he was skeptical but was not one to argue. "The old man knows the weather," he added thoughtfully. "On this side of the heath there be some high ground, and wi' a storm brewin', 'tis likely there we'll find him."

Both of them knew that the expedition was completely in Toby's hands, yet he waited politely until Ursula had given her assent to the plan. Then Toby led the way carefully to the high road.

After they had been riding close to an hour, he said

245

suddenly, "Can 'ee see the wisp o' smoke risin'? Likely 'tis he."

Her eyes sought his with gratitude and excitement. "Then we've done it. Toby! We've found him!"

"*Likely* 'tis he," repeated Toby, stressing the first word. As if dismayed by her premature jubilation, Toby added, "And *p'raps* he can help," emphasizing his uncertainty.

Minutes later they were at the old man's campsite, and Ursula was looking at his white, disheveled hair, his ragged beard, his broken yellow nails, and his startling blue eyes.

The old man nodded to them noncommitally without speaking. If two strangers had business with him, it was clearly their responsibility to present it. It wasn't his business to offer, without solicitation, so much as a "good morning."

When it became clear that Toby was not going to make any introductions, Ursula spoke.

"Good morning," she began conventionally, and then searched for how to begin. "My nephew," she said at last, "will be most envious of me, being able to meet you." The old man made no response. He was digging at a callus on his little finger and did not look up. "He's very interested in the plants of the moors and their uses, and he has said many times that you know all there is to know about the medicinal virtues. . . ." The old man did not seem to be listening. "My nephew is dying," she said, "of typhoid. We've somehow stayed out of the bogs and flooded ground, taking our chances on the way, hoping to find you. The doctor has no hope. Only you can help us—"

"Doctors!" muttered the old man. He spat copiously and noisily into the fire, where his spittle sizzled as it fell.

Ursula looked at Toby in desperation, but before Toby could say anything, the old man sighed and spoke. "Typhoid, eh?"

"Yes . . ." Her voice cracked.

The old man reached into his filthy and ragged coat and began to pull forth small packets wrapped in the grimiest of handkerchiefs. He undid the knots in one handkerchief after another, and all three regarded the collection spread out before them—lumps of charcoal, piles of dried leaves, seeds, roots. "I don't know," muttered the old man.

"I shall pay whatever you ask," Ursula assured him.

Her words seemed to awake a spark in the old man's eyes, but it was a spark of anger rather than interest.

"Don't signify," he said coldly, fingering a small bundle. "It ain't for me to say 'twill serve, but if 'ee've a mind ter try . . ."

"Yes, whatever you suggest . . ." she insisted.

The old man squatted down by his specimens and tied a lump of charcoal back in its filthy wrapper. " 'Ee can burn this in his room," he said. He handed the packet to Ursula, who tried to hide her disappointment. What good could it possibly do? "And this," he said as he wrapped up another packet, "brew it up as tea and have him drink it all at once."

She put the packets securely into the pocket of her petticoat and from the same pocket withdrew two golden guineas. These she handed silently to the old man.

He seemed satisfied and even wished Ursula and Toby a safe trip home. As they left his campsite, he called something after them.

"What did he say?" asked Ursula.

247

"I collect he was wishin' the young master good health," interpreted Toby.

"Thank you, Toby, for everything," she said before they spurred their beasts to a trot.

They had just come down off the high road when a gust of wind sent black clouds billowing across the sky. Thunder pealed.

"Turn back!" hollered Toby over the thunder as in the same moment a storm broke above them. "Back to the high road, milady." He had already forced his pony to turn around and was putting his instructions into action.

"But we haven't far to go," argued Ursula, thinking of Edmund agonizing in bed and of the many hours that had passed since she had left the house.

She pushed her pony on toward Collingwood, but Toby turned back again and swooped down upon her like an eagle on its prey. He grabbed her reins. "Follow me, milady. Wi' all respect, 'ee'll zee the two o' us drownded if 'ee go that way."

"We must head for home," she insisted again, and was about to say more but froze in horror. "Oh, Toby, I'm so sorry," she cried, knowing full well that no apology could ransom back a life that had been lost, knowing that her stubbornness had doomed them both. She could not believe the scene before her eyes: The floodtides were sweeping across the moor without any obstruction to slow their course. The great rushing waters were already upon them, cutting short even her pathetic and useless apology. The waves lifted her right off the pony's back. Then she was thrown under again, and completely submerged, she was carried off into a wet, cold, and recklessly churning world.

With a terrific crash Ursula's body was flung into a hard and immovable object. The air was black as night. By the illumination of a lightning bolt she realized that she had been thrown into the arm of an apple tree. The entire orchard was inundated, and the wild waters were rushing among the highest branches.

She clung to the tree with all her strength, but the waters were still rising, and her shoulders were already immersed. Water slapped her face, and Ursula feared all was lost.

She had wanted to save Edmund. Instead, the people at Collingwood would now have three deaths to mourn. Her sense of guilt was so great that Ursula forgot to be afraid.

A sudden wave tore her from the tree, carried her forward, and then under.

Then she was rising, surfacing, held by two strong arms and deposited . . . where? Her last conscious memory was the painful but welcome crack of her head against the wooden bench of a rowboat.

"This one, at least, I promise you I can save," said Dr. Jameson when Richard carried Ursula into the house. "Take her to her room."

The first thing Ursula did upon regaining consciousness was to reach wildly for her pockets. "How is Edmund?" she demanded of the doctor, who was still bending over her.

"No change."

An anguished wail rose from her breast.

"What is it?" Richard was beside her, holding her hand.

"They're gone," she moaned. "The packets . . ."

Richard and the doctor exchanged concerned glances. Was she half out of her mind with exposure and shock?

"The medicine!" she cried. "The medicine that I bought from the old man of the heath . . ."

"Why, that charlatan would have poisoned the

child!" barked Dr. Jameson in a professional huff. Though he was curious to hear a more detailed account of Ursula's encounter with the charlatan, he felt it incumbent on his dignity to stalk out of the room and return to his principal patient.

"That's why you went out?" asked Richard, ignoring the doctor.

"Yes," Ursula began. "Oh, Toby! Is Toby drowned?"

At least on this account Richard could reassure her. "He's recovering nicely in a guest room," he said. Then he explained more fully. "I found you were gone when a letter came for us from Amelia. I set off to find you to share the news."

"Oh, what does she say?" demanded Ursula.

"I'll let you read it and find out for yourself, but I'll give you one hint. She signed herself Mrs. George Manning."

"How exceedingly wonderful!" she cried.

"What was more wonderful," he corrected her, "was that if the letter had not been delivered I might not have noticed your absence from home and set off to track you down. It was easy to follow the hoofprints, but when I realized a storm was brewing and we stood a chance of flooding, I went off in the other direction in search of a boat. I was just in time, too. I found Toby on the high road, in water up to his chin. He was in such poor condition when I took him aboard that he wasn't able to tell me much of what had happened—only that he'd been with you and had lost you when the waters swept over."

He kissed her gently. "I ought to give you a good trimming for running such a risk, but I'm too happy to have you safely home."

"It doesn't seem right," she murmured. "We want to rejoice because a tragedy was averted. But I only went out on the heath trying to avert another tragedy, and Edmund . . . it seems nothing can be done for Edmund. I'm not sorry to have survived, darling, but I hardly feel I can rejoice."

Life was too complicated, she thought. Edmund was dying, but she had been saved, and saved by Richard, who had risked his own life for her. The terrible incident had brought them closer together than all the forgiveness in the world could have done. But what good did that do for the dying child?

"May I come in?" Lydia stood swaying in the doorway.

Richard hurried to give her his steadying arm and lead her to a chair, but she refused his assistance, pushing him away as though she dared not touch him.

"Please," she said, "go back and sit by your wife." He did so, while Lydia kept her distance and then began to speak in a slow, careful monotone. "My son is dying," she said.

"Lydia, darling, please . . ." Richard tried to calm her.

"Let me speak!" she snapped. "Edmund is dying. There is nothing that I, his mother, can do to prevent it." She laughed bitterly, then went on. "I love my son, and he is dying, and here I am, helpless. Helpless, when I would have stolen for him and killed for him. There is nothing I wouldn't have done for his sake."

"I know, darling," said Richard in a conciliating tone.

"No, you don't know," she replied angrily, and fell to her knees so suddenly that Richard at first thought she had swooned. He stepped toward her, and she remained supplicant at his feet.

"I was willing to ruin your life, Richard, and your wife's. It wasn't enough for me that my son and I have lived off your charity all these years. I wanted Edmund to inherit Collingwood. I wanted my son's future to be secure. He was to be the next Viscount of Uxbridge, and so it was necessary to prevent you from ever having an heir."

"What are you saying, Lydia?" he whispered.

"I am saying that in spite of everything I have done to her, your wife risked her life trying to save Edmund. Richard, I'm telling you"—and now Lydia stood and faced her brother, her eyes steady, not darting or flinching, her words slow and clear—"I am saying that Ursula has always been faithful to you."

"What do you know of it?" asked Richard slowly.

"Everything," sobbed Lydia. "And how you will hate and despise me now!" She struggled to control herself, then went on. "Richard, I could never have schemed against Ursula. A better friend I've never found, nor could you ever find a better wife. But when it all worked out so conveniently for my own purposes, forgive me, but the temptation was too strong."

"I don't understand," said Richard.

"Listen. While you were away, I felt sorry for Ursula. I urged her to take a lover—"

"You!" he cried.

"—and only succeeded in shocking her no end."

"But Stevenson saw Bertram Moorhead," objected Richard.

"Yes, he did," Lydia agreed. "And there was a small scuffle between them which woke me. I had a private conversation with Bertram after Stevenson had gone back to his quarters. He confessed that he'd tried to enter Ursula's window and almost been killed by her for his pains. I was furious with him. Yes, it's true. I thought a liaison between them would be nice, but I swear to you both, I was appalled to learn that he had tried to force himself . . ." Now she turned to her sister-in-law, who was listening to the confession with combined relief and heartache. "Ursula, believe me, I never intended to do you wrong. It just all happened. I thought Bertram's misconduct so heinous that he deserved a lesson, and so I tried to frighten him. I assured him that I would report everything to Richard upon his return and that I was quite certain Richard would call him out. Bertram can hardly handle a pistol, so the idea was hardly calculated to give him pleasure," she commented. "Then Richard did return home, totally by surprise, in the morning. I sent Mr. Moorhead news of the arrival."

"That explains his sudden flight," muttered Richard. "I jumped to such terrible conclusions," he whispered, "and with precious little evidence it seems." He turned to Ursula, filled with shame and horror at how he had treated her.

"And I could have disabused you of your suspicions if I'd but said a word." Lydia was weeping now with abandon. "If only you knew how many times I made up my mind to speak . . . but the longer I waited, the more impossible it became. How poorly I've repaid both of you for your love and generosity! And now my son is dying, and all my wickedness will be paid for in misery."

Ursula looked at her husband, her eyes pleading for him to be gentle. She was still weak, but with a great effort she forced herself from her bed, moved toward Lydia, and embraced her.

"No, don't!" cried Lydia, shrinking back. "I don't deserve your forgiveness."

"Accept it, please," said Ursula. "You've been through difficult days, with no one to direct you . . ."

"No, no. I confess," moaned the unhappy woman. "I renounce all my ambitions. I throw everything away," she cried. "But now, won't he be allowed to live? That's all I want. Won't my son be well again?"

Richard tried to lift his sister to her feet.

"Go for Dr. Jameson," said Ursula. "Have him bring something to calm her nerves." She began to stroke Lydia's hair. "It will be all right," she assured her. "Edmund will be well. Don't worry about his future. You must know we shall see to it. Everything will be all right."

Before Richard could do as Ursula bade him, Dr. Jameson himself appeared in the doorway. At the sight of him Lydia shrieked in agony as if the devil himself had walked into the room.

"He's dead!" she wailed. "You've come to tell me he's dead!"

"No, no," the doctor hastened to assure her. "Be thankful and calm yourself." Dr. Jameson paused a moment, not knowing how to announce what he could not explain. "The crisis seems to have passed. Suddenly. He is sleeping calmly now and will surely come through it alive."

Lydia ran from the room, with the doctor a few paces behind her, while simultaneously Richard lifted his exhausted wife and placed her gently on the bed.

"Can you ever forgive me?" he asked, afraid to look in her eyes.

"Darling," she said softly, "it's all over now, all the doubts and fears. I hope that we shall never need any forgiveness between us again. Everything is all right now."

Richard was silent a moment and brought her hand to his lips. "Our nephew is going to be all right now, too," he said, smiling. He rose tentatively to his feet.

"He'd be much better if he had a cousin," said Ursula.

"He will. But if you don't rest now, you'll require Dr. Jameson's ministrations, too."

"Not at all," she argued. "Not now when you and I are healed and whole at last."

He lay beside her and held her close against him.

As she drifted into sleep, they shared a single thought—that no further shadows would mar their union. They had come to harbour, with all their love, safely through the storm.

Love—the way you want it!

Candlelight Romances

			TITLE NO.	
☐ A MAN OF HER CHOOSING by Nina Pykare	.....$1.50	#554	(15133-3)
☐ PASSING FANCY by Mary Linn Roby	.....$1.50	#555	(16770-1)
☐ THE DEMON COUNT by Anne Stuart	.....$1.25	#557	(11906-5)
☐ WHERE SHADOWS LINGER by Janis Susan May	....$1.25	#556	(19777-5)
☐ OMEN FOR LOVE by Esther Boyd	.....$1.25	#552	(16108-8)
☐ MAYBE TOMORROW by Marie Pershing	.....$1.25	#553	(14909-6)
☐ LOVE IN DISGUISE by Nina Pykare	.....$1.50	#548	(15229-1)
☐ THE RUNAWAY HEIRESS by Lillian Cheatham	.....$1.50	#549	(18083-X)
☐ HOME TO THE HIGHLANDS by Jessica Eliot	.....$1.25	#550	(13104-9)
☐ DARK LEGACY by Candace Connell	.....$1.25	#551	(11771-2)
☐ LEGACY OF THE HEART by Lorena McCourtney	....$1.25	#546	(15645-9)
☐ THE SLEEPING HEIRESS by Phyllis Taylor Pianka	.....$1.50	#543	(17551-8)
☐ DAISY by Jennie Tremaine	.....$1.50	#542	(11683-X)
☐ RING THE BELL SOFTLY by Margaret James	.....$1.25	#545	(17626-3)
☐ GUARDIAN OF INNOCENCE by Judy Boynton	.....$1.25	#544	(11862-X)
☐ THE LONG ENCHANTMENT by Helen Nuelle	.....$1.25	#540	(15407-3)
☐ SECRET LONGINGS by Nancy Kennedy	.....$1.25	#541	(17609-3)

At your local bookstore or use this handy coupon for ordering:

Dell | **DELL BOOKS**
P.O. BOX 1000, PINEBROOK, N.J. 07058

Please send me the books I have checked above. I am enclosing $ _____
(please add 75¢ per copy to cover postage and handling). Send check or money order—no cash or C.O.D.'s. Please allow up to 8 weeks for shipment.

Mr/Mrs/Miss _____

Address _____

City _____ State/Zip _____